# THE USBORNE COMPLETE RIDING SCHOOL

Gill Harvey, Rosie Heywood,
Kate Needham and Lucy Smith

Designed by Ian McNee
Illustrated by Mikki Rain
Photographs by Kit Houghton
Consultant: Juliet Mander BHSII

Series editors: Felicity Brooks and Cheryl Evans
Managing designer: Mary Cartwright

## Contents

Additional designs by Maria Wheatley, Mary Cartwright,
Martin Aggett and Susannah Owen
Additional photographs by Bob Langrish

# FIRST PONY

## Contents

# A PONY OF YOUR OWN

All riders dream of a pony of their own, but having a pony is a big commitment. As the owner, you are responsible for looking after your pony, so it's not enough to know how to ride. You need to learn how to care for him too. Here are some questions to ask yourself before you take on that commitment.

*Can you really afford to look after him?*

It's not just what he costs to buy, you will be paying for everything he needs: food, training, new shoes, vet's fees, tack, blankets, bandages and so on.

*Is there an expert who can help out?*

If your parents don't know about ponies, you'll need the support and help of someone who does, such as your instructor or staff at the local stables.

*Do you have somewhere to keep him?*

A backyard is not big enough. A pony needs at least an acre (½ hectare) of land to graze. You must consider where you might be able to ride him too.

*Here are just some of the things you will need to care for your pony.*

*Do you have enough time for him?*

You can't just take him out for a ride when you feel like it. He needs regular exercise to stay fit, and don't forget about all the chores, such as feeding, grooming or tack cleaning.

*Looking after a pony can be great fun but it is hard work and will take up a lot of time. Make sure you know what you are letting yourself in for.*

# GETTING EXPERIENCE

The best way to get experience of looking after a pony is to help out at the local stables. By working with several different ponies, you'll learn a lot about how they behave and find out the best ways of dealing with them. When it comes to getting your own pony you'll have a clearer idea of what suits you best. Spending time at the stables is also a good way to meet other horsy people.

Be prepared for hard work and an early start. Pay attention to the daily routine so that you know when to help.

Learn how all the various chores are carried out, such as feeding, mucking out, grooming and tack cleaning.

Watch how the ponies are loaded into a trailer or prepared for the vet or farrier, and pick up tips for when you have to do it.

## THE RIGHT PONY FOR YOU

*Choose a pony that enjoys the same activities that you do.*

*A calm pony helps give a nervous rider confidence.*

*A pony that has already done well will cost more.*

Not every pony suits every rider, which is why it's important to assess your own riding ability and confidence before you choose. Think carefully about what you plan to do together, too.

If you are nervous, a pony will sense your fear so look for one with a quiet temperament and gentle manner. An older pony, that has had several young riders, is often calmer than a young one.

If you are confident, you may be able to handle a more fiery pony which will be a greater challenge for your riding. If you are competitive, you might decide to look for a pony that has already done well.

# CHOOSING A PONY

Before you choose a pony, think carefully about what you want him for, where you will be able to keep him and how much time you will have to look after him. An experienced person can help you choose what type of pony would suit you best. Here are some of the things you will need to consider.

## WHAT TYPE OR BREED?

Many breeds of horses and ponies have been developed over the years. Some of the pony breeds are Welsh, Shetland, POA (Pony of the Americas) Exmoor and Connemara, among others. They vary in temperament, size, looks, strength, and speed. Many ponies are crossbreeds. This means they are a mixture of several breeds.

The boarding arrangement and climate should be taken into account when considering breeds. For example, the Welsh and Shetland breeds are designed to live in the wild and are very hardy.

Your riding interests are an important consideration too. Different breeds excel in different events. For example, Thoroughbreds are known to be fast.

One of the oldest and prettiest breeds is the Arab. But beware of judging a pony by its looks alone! Its temperament and previous training are far more important.

A good first pony will have a quiet, gentle temperament and plenty of experience. A younger, more spirited pony is better for experienced riders.

*Thoroughbred*

*Arab*

*Exmoor*

## WHAT HEIGHT?

Choose a pony that is big enough to last you a few years, but not so big that it's too strong for you. Ponies are measured in hands, from the ground to the withers (see page 6). A hand is about 4in (10cm), so a 12.2hh pony is 50in (125cm) tall. If you want to compete, check the height limit of classes you want to take part in.

*Goldie is an 11.2hh, Welsh type palomino, with a stripe.*

*Legend is a 14hh Connemara dun, with a star.*

*William is a 13hh, Welsh roan, with a star, a snip and three socks.*

# HOW OLD?

If you don't have much experience it is helpful to have a pony that does. Eight or nine is an ideal age for a first pony. It will have some experience but still have plenty of years ahead of it. You can tell a pony's age by looking at its teeth. A young pony has small straight teeth; an old one has long sloping ones.

At 4 years    At 7 years

*A hook appears here.*

At 10 years   At 20-25 years

*The hook has gone. This groove has started.*

# COLORS AND MARKINGS

A pony's color and markings are not the most important features, but it is useful to know how they are described.

### Grey
*white or any shade of grey*

### Palomino
*gold with white mane and tail*

### Bay
*brown with black mane and tail*

### Chestnut
*light brown all over*

### Skewbald
*white and any other color*

### Brown
*dark brown all over*

### Piebald
*patches of white and black*

### Dun
*beige with black mane and tail*

Snip

Blaze

Star

Stripe

Sock

Stocking

# USEFUL TERMS

* A horse is usually bigger than 14.2hh.
* A pony is usually 14.2hh or smaller.
* A mare is a female.
* A gelding is a male that has been gelded. This means its testicles have been removed. It can be any age.
* A colt is a young male, that hasn't yet been gelded.
* A filly is a young female.
* A stallion is a male that hasn't been gelded.
* A yearling is one year old.
* A foal is from birth to one year old.

*Weeney is a 12.2hh New Forest, light grey.*

*Poem is a 13.2hh, black Welsh pony, with a star.*

*Habibi is a 14hh chestnut Arab, with a blaze and four stockings.*

# CONFORMATION

Conformation refers to the shape of a pony and the way it is made. Although looks are not the most important thing in an all-around pony, there are some features that affect its performance, health or temperament. The picture below shows the names used for different parts of a pony's body. These are called the "points".

## POINTS OF A PONY

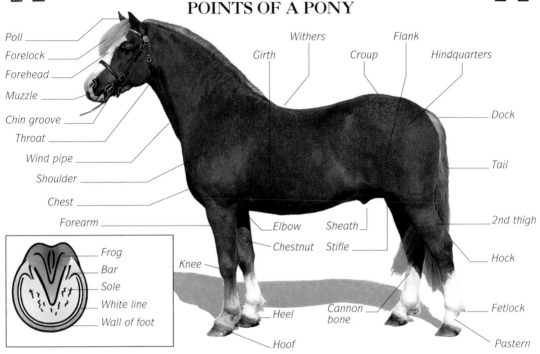

Poll
Forelock
Forehead
Muzzle
Chin groove
Throat
Wind pipe
Shoulder
Chest
Forearm
Knee
Heel
Hoof

Frog
Bar
Sole
White line
Wall of foot

Elbow
Chestnut

Sheath
Stifle

Cannon bone

Withers
Girth

Croup

Flank
Hindquarters

Dock

Tail

2nd thigh
Hock

Fetlock
Pastern

## FIRST IMPRESSIONS

Take a good overall look at the pony first, from the front, the back and both sides. See if any part of its body seems too large or small. It should fit roughly into a square like this:

*Checklist for body*
* Back - strong, to carry your weight. A long back is likely to be weak; a short back can be uncomfortable.
* Hindquarters - strong and muscular as this is where all the power comes from.
* Withers - neither too high, as this makes the saddle hard to fit, nor too low, as the saddle may slip. Ideally, about the same height as the croup.
* Chest - wide to allow plenty of room for the heart and lungs.

* Girth - deep to allow space for heart and lungs.
* Neck - slightly arched from the poll to the withers. A "ewe" neck is arched the other way. It may mean a pony is less balanced and therefore harder to control.

*Good neck*    *Ewe neck*

# THE HEAD

You can tell a lot about a pony's temperament and breeding by its head, in particular its eyes and ears.

The length of neck and size of head are important, as these are what the pony uses to balance with.

*A pony with a "Roman nose" may be related to a heavy carthorse.*

*A pony with a dish face may have Arab blood in it.*

*A pony showing the whites of his eyes may be nervous or moody. Ears laid back show bad temper.*

*Large clear eyes are a sign of a kind pony. Ears pricked forward show attentiveness and intelligence.*

*Loppy ears often indicate an easy-going nature. They might also mean he's not feeling well.*

## LEGS AND FEET

The legs and feet are extremely important as they take all the shock of a pony's movement. When looked at from in front or behind, both pairs of legs should be straight with the feet pointing forward. If too close, the pony may kick himself. Watch him walk and trot. The movement should be as straight as possible. "Winding" is when a pony puts one foot right in front of the other. "Paddling" is when he swings his legs outward. Both can lead to injuries.

*Winding*

*Paddling*

*Checklist for legs*
* Shoulder - long and sloping back toward the withers for a good stride.
* Elbow - check to see that there is plenty of room between the body for free movement. Try fitting your fist inside.
* Forearm - long and well-muscled for strength.
* Knees - broad and flat.
* Hocks - a clear shape, free of swelling, as these are the hardest working joints.
* Cannon bones - short and straight for strength.
* Fetlocks - free from swelling and heat.
* Pasterns - medium length, ideally sloping at the same angle as the shoulder, as they absorb all the shocks.
* Feet - in good condition with a smooth wall and large frog. Front and back should be matching pairs.

# BUYING AND TRYING OUT

It's very easy to fall in love with the first pony you see, but always try out several before you decide on the right one for you. It is also essential to get advice from a knowledgeable person, such as your riding instructor. Talk through what type of pony would best suit your level of experience and, if possible, visit the ponies together.

## WHERE TO LOOK

The best pony to buy is one you know already. You may have an older friend who has outgrown hers. Ask the instructors at your local stable or pony club whether they know of a suitable pony for sale.

If they don't, ask if they can recommend a breeder. Some breeders have lots of experience matching ponies to children and are very helpful. They may even offer a trial period. Do get a recommendation though, as not all breeders are good.

A horse sale is the worst place to buy from. You can't find out about the pony or ride it, before you buy.

Pony magazines have advertisements of ponies for sale. Look for ponies described as "good first pony", "family pony" or "pony club all-arounder". (See right for some of the abbreviations used.)

Telephone to find out all you can about the pony before you go and visit. Most owners want their ponies to go to a good home, so don't be surprised if they ask you lots of questions too.

Any pony you buy should be "vetted". This is when a vet does a thorough examination of his body and checks for signs of past illnesses or accidents. This vet is checking the flexibility of the pony's hind leg.

### Questions to ask
* How old is he?
* What experience has he?
* How long have you had him?
* Why is he being sold on?
* Does he have any vices (bad habits)? (See opposite).

### Questions to answer
* How much experience do you have?
* Where will he be kept?
* What are you hoping to do with him?

### Abbreviations
* TB Thoroughbred
* PC Pony Club
* RC Riding Club
* XC Cross country
* SJ Show jumper
* SP Show pony
* HT Hunter trials
* WHP Working hunter pony
* ODE One day event
* PB Part bred
* X Cross bred
* DR Dressage
* LR Leading rein

8

# PLANNING YOUR FIRST VISIT

If possible, visit the pony in the field first to check that he is easy to catch. If he is already in the stable, ask to see him turned out later.

See how relaxed he is in the stable. Is he happy or pacing around? Does he like his neighbors? Help groom him to see how he reacts.

Ask to see him led out. Watch from in front, behind and both sides, checking to see that he moves evenly on all four legs. (See page 7.)

Help tack him up. Ask someone else to ride him first, so you can see how he behaves. Ask the rider to take him over a small jump.

Try him out yourself in a confined space, such as an indoor arena. If he seems calm, take him outside to see if he is easily controlled.

See him ridden on the road to make sure he is safe in traffic and to check that he doesn't try to run toward home. (See below.)

Find out if he is good to shoe and load in a trailer. If he is a local pony you could ask the farrier about him yourself.

If you do decide to buy the pony, you must arrange for a vet to examine him. He will check his age, health, and conformation.

## VICES TO ASK ABOUT AND AVOID

⁕ Biting equipment or people is a nuisance, and indicates bad temperament.
⁕ Kicking will cause problems with other ponies in a field.
⁕ Bucking may just be high spirits but it can be scary.
⁕ Barn sour describes a pony who always tries to return home. It can become a serious problem.

*Never buy a pony that rears. It can be very dangerous and is hard to cure.*

⁕ Rearing is a dangerous vice which can be difficult to cure.
⁕ Weaving is when a stabled pony rocks from side to side. It is bad for his legs, and other ponies may copy.
⁕ Cribbing is when a pony grabs the stable door and sucks in air. It can damage his teeth and lungs as well as the stable door.

# WHERE WILL HE LIVE?

Most ponies can live out at pasture year-round but ideally you need a stable, too, in case he is ill or gets too fat in the spring. If you don't have a field at home, you will need to lease one nearby or find a boarding stable to keep him at.

## KEEPING A PONY AT HOME

It is great to have your own pony at home. It's more convenient, it's easier to keep an eye on him and he will quickly become part of the family. But do make sure that the paddock and stable are suitable (see the checklists below and opposite), and if possible that your pony has a friend. Ponies live naturally in herds and without the company of others they do get lonely.

The main disadvantage for you is that you will have to care for your pony on your own, with little help and advice from experienced people. If you are ill or go away, it may be hard to find someone to look after him for you.

*The best companion for him is another pony but a donkey, or even a sheep will do.*

### Stable checklist
* At least 3x3½m (10x12ft).
* Built of brick or wood.
* It should have wooden boards halfway up the inside walls.
* The doorway should be about 1½ m (4½ft) wide by 2½m (8ft) tall.
* There must be a top and bottom door which open outward.
* The bottom door should be 1½m (4½ft) high.
* There must be two bolts on the bottom door.

### Paddock checklist
* At least an acre (½ hectare) of good grass per pony.
* Shelter from bad weather in winter and sun in summer.
* Constant supply of fresh clean water.
* Safe fencing and gates - hedges or post-and-rail are the best type.
* Free from any trash, machinery and poisonous plants, like ragwort or yew.
* Close to home so you can keep an eye on your pony and prevent people feeding dangerous tidbits.

*This picture shows you some of the facilities that a good boarding stable might have.*

*The arena - an enclosed area to exercise in*

*Nearby bridle paths*

Bridle path

*A neat muck heap that's easy to get to*

# KEEPING A PONY BOARDED

A boarding stable is a place where you pay to keep your pony. There are usually several experienced people on hand to help you out, and there is plenty of company for your pony and for you. You can use the stable's facilities and land to ride on too, and you are more likely to meet people to ride with.

You can choose between several different types of stables, depending on how much of the work you plan to do yourself.

Do It Yourself boarding is the cheapest because you do everything yourself. You will need to visit the stable twice each day, before and after school.

Partial board is more flexible, as the stable takes some responsibility for your pony. You still organize his

food, muck out his stable and exercise him, but if you go away or can't manage to visit every day, the stable will help out.

Full board is the most expensive, as your pony is completely looked after for you. He will be fed, shod, wormed and even exercised if you want, but find out who will ride him when you are not there.

If you do decide to keep your pony boarded, choose the stable carefully. The checklist below shows a few things to bear in mind when you choose.

*A dry hay barn.*

*Roomy stalls, at least 3x3½m (10x12ft) for each pony*

*A neat tack room*

*Safe area to groom and tack up in*

*A trailer to share or rent for shows*

*Fire extinguisher*

*Feed room free from rats*

*Several grass fields*

*Friendly, helpful people*

## Boarding checklist
* How close is it to your home? If it is easy to get to, you and your pony will spend more time together.
* Are the stables and fields in good condition?
* Do the ponies already there seem well cared for and happy?
* Is it secure?
* Is there an arena that you can use for exercise? An indoor one is useful on rainy days.
* Are there safe places to ride in the area?
* Are there other children and experienced adults around?
* Who is responsible for the overall running of the stables?

# FOOD AND ROUTINE

A pony's natural food is grass. In the wild, ponies wander around eating all the time, so they have small stomachs which are designed to cope with a little food at a time. A pony kept out can survive at pasture alone during the summer, but in winter you need to provide extra food, such as hay.

## HAY

Hay, which is dried grass, is the most suitable type of extra food. It should be brownish green and smell sweet. Avoid dusty or moldy hay and, if you buy in bulk, make sure you have somewhere dry to store it.

With several ponies in a field, it is easiest to feed hay loose on the ground, though it can be wasteful. Put down more piles than there are ponies, spaced well apart, so that the fastest eaters don't steal the others' hay. A less wasteful way to feed hay is in a haynet or a hayfeeder.

*If you feed hay in a haynet make sure you tie it properly so that your pony can't get his feet caught in it. See how to tie it below.*

## HOW TO TIE A HAYNET

*Ask the farmer before you attach a ring to a tree trunk.*

*When empty it must not be lower than the pony's chest.*

*Pull tight before knotting.*

Pick a strong fence or sturdy tree in a sheltered spot to tie it to. It needs to be about the height of your pony. Loop the string around the rail or branch.

Thread the string through the mesh at the bottom of the net and pull it up as tight as possible. This will stop the net from sagging as it empties.

Keeping the string pulled tightly upward, tie it back onto itself near the ring. Use a quick-release knot (you can find out how to tie one on page 23).

# WHAT TO PUT IN AN EXTRA FEEDING

If your pony is working hard, he may need a small feeding for extra energy.

This could be a grain or a rich grass such as alfalfa (opposite), sometimes with an addition of vitamin or mineral supplements. Processed pony food made into pellets (below) is handy, but more expensive.

Most ponies love rich food and gobble it down fast. If you feed a more bulky food, such

as hay, at the same time, it will slow him down and help him to digest.

A carrot or an apple is a good treat, but always cut it into long pieces. If chopped small, it can get stuck in his throat.

It can be dangerous to feed too much, so always get expert advice on quantities.

*Rules of feeding*
* Feed little and often.
* Feed plenty of roughage, such as grass or hay.
* Feed according to size, age, work and temperament.
* Feed at the same time each day.
* Feed good quality food.
* Feed something succulent every day, such as a carrot.
* Don't work for at least one hour after feeding.
* Don't feed when hot and tired, let him cool down first.
* Make no sudden changes to his diet.
* Keep feed bowls clean.

# PLANNING A DAILY ROUTINE

Ponies are creatures of habit and are much happier with a regular routine. It's as if they have a built-in clock. They can get very upset if things don't happen at the usual time.

Try to organize it so that you do each task in the same order and at the same time every day. The list opposite is a good routine to follow if caring for a pony while at school.

*Before school*
* Catch your pony and check that he is warm and well (see page 30).
* Check his water. In winter you may need to break the ice if it has frozen over.
* Feed him his grain. If stabled, turn out to pasture.
* Pick up droppings from field and muck out stable.

*After school*
* Catch your pony and give him a quick grooming.
* Tack him up and take him out for exercise.
* Let him cool down and brush off any dry sweat. Then turn him out.
* If stabled at night, groom him thoroughly, straighten his bedding and give him water, feed and hay.

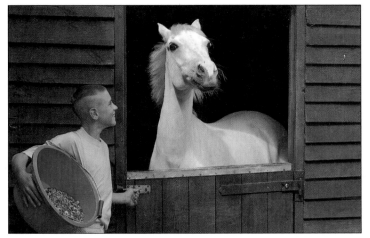

*Ponies get used to things happening at the same time each day and hate to be kept waiting - especially for food.*

# VETS AND FARRIERS

Every pony owner needs a good vet to give vaccinations, advise about worming doses, check teeth and be on hand when a pony is sick. A farrier is the person who looks after a pony's feet and shoes, and is equally important. Ask around to find out who is best locally.

## WHEN TO GET YOUR PONY RESHOD

A pony needs regular visits to (or from) a farrier to have his feet trimmed. If he is ridden on the roads, he will need shoes to protect his feet and the shoes need to be replaced about once every six weeks. Have your pony ready for the farrier with cleanly picked out feet. See below.

*Signs he needs shoeing*
* The clinches are risen. These are the ends of the nails that hold the shoe on.
* A shoe is loose. You will hear it "clank" on the road.
* He's lost a shoe.
* Part of the shoe has worn thin.
* The foot has grown too long.

*Your farrier is an important friend so make your pony behave while he's at work.*

## LIFTING UP AND PICKING OUT THE FEET

*Have the hoofpick ready in the other hand.*

*Frog*

For the front leg, run your hand down the back of the pony's leg. You may need to lean against him to make him lift his foot.

For the back leg, run your hand down the front of the hock. Grasp the toe as he picks up his foot, so your arm is in front of his leg.

Gently pick out any mud from the foot. Always start from the top, by the heel and move down either side of the frog, toward the toe.

## VACCINATIONS

Your pony needs to be vaccinated against equine encephalomyetis and tetanus. Both illnesses are easy to prevent but hard to cure. He will need an initial course of injections and then a booster every year.

* You will also need to produce a Coggins test certificate for most shows and arenas. This states that the horse is free of Equine Infectious Anemia.

* Tetanus is easily caught from cuts. It can be deadly so it's vital to keep the vaccination up to date.

*Vaccinations are injected into the pony's neck or hindquarters.*

## TEETH

Your pony needs to go to the dentist as often as you do, which is once every six months. His teeth are growing all the time and may get sharp edges which make his mouth sore.

A horse dentist or vet smooths these edges down by rasping his teeth.
He will also check for wolf teeth. These are small teeth that often cause pain as they grow and may need to be removed.

*Ponies need to have their teeth inspected twice a year.*

## WORMING DOSES

All ponies get small types of worms living inside them. A few won't harm them but too many can make them very ill. To stop this from happening you must "worm" your pony. This means feeding him a special worming powder which you can buy from your vet. Ask for advice on a worming program. It usually needs to be done once every 6-8 weeks. See below for more tips about preventing worms.

*Keeping worms at bay*
* Remove droppings daily from the field. This is where worms live.
* Swap paddocks for a while.
* If possible, let cows or sheep graze in the field. Worms cannot live in their stomachs.
* Dose all ponies that share a field at the same time.

## IDENTIFICATION

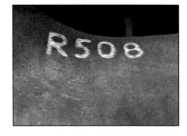

Unfortunately, ponies do get stolen and it can be hard to get them back. A good prevention is by an identifying number on the pony. Until recently this was done by branding. Now microchips that can be read by a scanner are inserted under a pony's skin . Don't worry - it shouldn't hurt him.

# CHOOSING TACK

When you buy a pony you may well get his saddle and bridle thrown in, especially if his old rider has outgrown them. This is often useful, as second-hand tack is usually more comfortable than new, as long as it is in good condition. The leather should be supple and the stitching secure. Even if your tack is passed on, you must make sure that it fits well.

## THE SADDLE

The saddle distributes your weight evenly over your pony's back. It can also help you to sit correctly. Saddles are expensive but if taken care of properly they last a lifetime, so buy the best you can afford.

Never buy a cheap one. Poor quality leather can make your pony sore and, if it breaks, puts you in danger. A good quality second-hand one is a much better buy.

There are different types of saddles for jumping or dressage, but for all-around use, choose a general-purpose saddle. It must be the right length and width, so have your pony's back measured by an expert.

Cantle

Seat

The tree, which is made of wood, is the framework of the saddle.

Pommel

Stirrup guard

Knee roll adds comfort for the rider.

Panel

Buckle guards stop girth buckles from wearing away the saddle flap.

The gullet keeps any weight off the spine.

Girth straps

*Checklist for saddle fit*
* It should lie flat on the pony's back, with the weight evenly distributed.
* It must not be too long, or it will press on the loins.
* You should be able to see daylight when you look down the spine from the pommel or the cantle.

* The pommel must not press on the withers - make sure that you can fit four fingers comfortably between them.
* It should not slip when the pony moves.
* The panels should be evenly stuffed - check by looking from behind.

* If buying second-hand, check that the tree is not broken. With the pommel in one hand and the cantle against your side, pull toward you. All saddles will give a little but if the tree is broken it will start to fold. Ask for an expert's opinion.

## WHICH GIRTH?

The girth is the only thing holding the saddle on, so make sure you get a safe and comfortable one. They come in different lengths so measure your pony before you buy.

*Padded nylon girths are soft and comfortable.*

*String girths are not ideal. They can pinch the pony's skin.*

*Leather is strong and long-lasting but it must be kept clean and supple.*

## WHAT SIZE STIRRUP?

The wrong size stirrup can be dangerous. If you fall you want your foot to slip out of the stirrup easily. If too small, your foot may get wedged into it; if too big, it may slide all the way through.

Wear your riding boots when you go to fit your stirrup. There should be about 1cm (½in) on either side of your boot.

You will need to buy stirrup leathers separately. Buy them long enough to allow for adjustment, but not so long that they trail off the saddle.

New ones are likely to stretch as you use them and the one you use to mount may end up longer. To stop this from happening, switch them around from time to time.

— 1cm (½in) —

*You can add rubber treads which help to stop your foot from slipping through.*

*Rubber stirrup tread*

*Safety stirrups have a rubber band at the side which flicks open if your foot is pulled out of the stirrup.*

## PUTTING ON A SADDLE

With the stirrups run up and the girth over the seat, lift the saddle over the withers. Slide it back into position. Never move it forward against the grain of the pony's coat.

Ducking underneath the pony's neck, go around to the other side. Lift the girth down gently. Check underneath the saddle flap to see that the girth straps and guards are lying flat.

Go back around. Check under the flap on this side, then reach underneath for the girth. Fasten it so that it is firm but not tight. You will need to tighten it once you are ready to set off.

17

# THE BRIDLE

Bridles are sold in three different sizes, pony, cob and full, and they come in various widths. Choose one that suits your pony's head.

Most come with a cavesson noseband, which is the mildest. A drop noseband or flash can be useful on a strong pony (see page 26).

Plain leather reins are the most common. If you find them slippery in wet weather, try rubber or braided ones which have a better grip.

*Rubber*

*Plain leather*

*Braided*

*Headpiece*

*Browband*

*Throat latch*

*Cheek-piece*

*Cavesson noseband*

*Eggbutt jointed snaffle*

The bit is always sold separately. There are hundreds to choose from but the best type for a first pony is a snaffle, which is the mildest. An eggbut jointed snaffle is a good choice. It has smooth rings that prevent the bit pinching the corners of the pony's mouth. Stronger bits can be helpful but they can also do lots of harm, so ask your instructor for advice before trying one out.

If buying a secondhand bridle, undo all the buckles and check for cracks in the leather.

*Loose ring snaffle*

*Hollow-mouth snaffle*

*Double-jointed snaffle*

## PUTTING ON A SNAFFLE BRIDLE

First make sure that the throat latch and noseband are undone. Untie the lead rope in case he pulls back, and slip the reins over his head. Undo the halter and refasten it around the pony's neck.

Hold the top of the bridle in your right hand. Have the bit on your left hand with your fingers flat. Place your thumb on the bar of his mouth (near the corner where there are no teeth) and squeeze it gently.

As he opens his mouth, slip the bit inside. Then pull the headpiece gently over his ears. Pull his forelock from under the browband. Buckle the throat latch and noseband and check the fit of the bridle. (See opposite.)

*Checklist for bridle fit*
* The throat latch must be loose enough to allow the pony to breath easily. When it is fastened, you should be able to fit your fist inside it.

* The cavesson noseband should sit four fingers below the cheekbones, and be loose enough for you to get two fingers between it and the pony's nose.

* The bit reaches the corners of the pony's lips so that they are just wrinkled and it looks as though he's smiling. It should stick out about 5mm (¼in) on each side.

* The browband sits just below the ears, but not touching them. It should fit closely, but not so tightly that it pulls the bridle forward over the pony's head.

## THE HALTER

A halter is what you use for catching and leading your pony. It can be either leather or nylon. You need a lead rope with a snap to fasten onto the back of it.

Like bridles, halters are sold in three sizes. Once fitted, it must be loose enough for the pony to chew easily but tight enough to stop him from putting a foot through it.

*Spring clip*

*Lead rope*

*You should be able to get three fingers between the noseband and his nose, and the noseband should be about three fingers below his cheekbone.*

## OTHER THINGS YOU WILL NEED

| For grooming and tack cleaning | For feeding | For mucking out |
| --- | --- | --- |
| Dandy brush<br>Body brush<br>Hoof pick<br>Metal and rubber curry combs<br>Sponges<br>Hoof oil and brush<br><br>Saddle soap<br>Oil for tack | Mouse-proof<br>feed cans<br>Buckets<br>Feed bowls | Fork<br>Broom<br>Shovel<br>Wheelbarrow |

# SETTLING IN

It will take a little while for a new pony to fit in and feel comfortable with his surroundings. Don't be tempted to show him off to all your friends on the first day. He will be much happier left alone to get used to his new home quietly. Handle him gently so as not to frighten him, but firmly so that he knows who is boss.

## THE FIRST DAY AT HOME

Plan your pony's first day at his new home carefully. If he is to live outside, bring him home early so that he has plenty of daylight hours to get used to his new field and companions.

In all herds of ponies there is a pecking order, where one pony is boss, another number two, and so on. If your pony is to live with a lot of others, see if it is possible to turn him out with just a couple of the quieter ones to start with. Avoid turning a new pony out at feeding time, as this is when the others will be most aggressive.

Don't worry if your pony is left on his own at first. After a few weeks, his position in the pecking order will be established and he will have his own special friends.

If you do bring your pony home at night, settle him in a clean stable, and turn him out the next day.

*When two ponies first meet they usually sniff noses, stomp and squeal.*

# TURNING YOUR PONY OUT

Wait until the other ponies are far away from the gate, then open it wide so that it doesn't swing and catch your pony's legs. Lead your pony through it.

Turn your pony to face the gate and close it. Remove his halter and step out of the way. Push him away from you as you turn, so he doesn't step on your toes.

When turning several ponies out together, let them all loose at the same time. Otherwise one person will be left struggling as the others gallop off.

# APPROACHING AND CATCHING YOUR PONY

Walk quietly toward him talking calmly as you go. Never come up from behind as your pony will not see you and may be surprised and frightened.

Keeping the halter behind you so he can't see it, approach his shoulder. Pat him as soon as you are near. You could take a few pellets as a reward.

*Poll*

Place the lead rope over his neck and slip the noseband over his nose. Lift the headpiece over his poll and fasten. For tips on catching difficult ponies see page 25.

# LEADING YOUR PONY

*Wear a hard hat and gloves.*

Always lead from the left, unless on the road when you lead from the right. Have one hand near the halter and the other near the end of the rope.

Stand by his shoulder and say "walk on". He should move forward with you. Never pull him. Push gently forward if he is reluctant to move.

When turning, push him away from you. He will stay better balanced and avoid treading on your toes. For longer distances, use a chain on for better control.

# BECOMING FRIENDS

A pony soon recognizes the person who visits each day and feeds him, but the more time you spend together, out riding or in the stable yard, the better you will grow to understand each other.

## YOUR PONY'S SENSES

*Large eyes are a sign of a kind pony. If frightened, they may look white.*

The five senses are sight, taste, hearing, touch and smell. With eyes on each side of his head, your pony's sight is good. The only place he can't see is behind and immediately in front. He sees things farther in front well, using both eyes.

*Stroking and patting are soothing gestures that tell your pony he's done well.*

You communicate with your pony by touch too. Out riding, your legs tell him what to do. Your pony uses his soft muzzle and long whiskers to touch and investigate things. He greets a friend by touching noses.

*If you talk to your pony all the time, he will soon recognize your voice.*

His hearing is good too. By moving his ears around, he can sense where a noise is coming from. Although he doesn't really understand what you say, he does understand the tone of your voice. So, if you are mad, sound it. If pleased, pat him as you talk.

*Ponies recognize each other and their home territory by smell.*

This also allows him to smell his friends which is how ponies recognize each other. They use their strong sense of smell to check their food too. A crafty pony can gobble up a mixed feed and leave behind the part he dislikes, such as worming powder.

## RECOGNIZING BODY LANGUAGE

As you get to know your pony you will sense his moods. He will soon get to sense yours too. You can tell a lot by looking at his eyes and his ears (see page 7). Here are a few more signs that you could look for.

*Signs of mood*
● Swishing tail or stomping feet mean he's irritated (or maybe it's the flies!)
● Snorting shows he is frightened or spooked.
● Tail clamped down hard can be a sign that he is about to kick. He could also be cold.
● Tail held high shows he is excited about something.

## GROOMING

Grooming is essential to keep your pony clean, but it is also one of the best ways to form a bond with your pony. Choose a nice shady place where you can both be comfortable as you work. Tie up with a quick-release knot (see below).

Don't groom a pony that lives outside too much, especially in winter. He needs the natural oils in his coat to keep warm. Just use the dandy brush to get off the mud and give him a good scratch. In the summer you can use the body brush to get a shine on his coat.

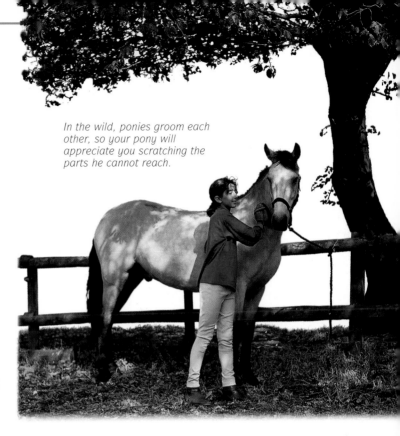

*In the wild, ponies groom each other, so your pony will appreciate you scratching the parts he cannot reach.*

## TYING SAFELY WITH A QUICK-RELEASE KNOT

Always tie your pony in an enclosed place, so that if he does pull free he can't escape. Never tie him directly to the ring. Attach a small loop of string to the ring, and fasten the lead rope to this. If he panics and pulls back, the string will break. Make sure that the wall or rail is sturdy and won't give way before the string does. Use a quick-release knot when tying your pony, so that you can untie your pony fast in an emergency. Here's how to tie one:

Pull the lead rope through the safety string and make a loop with the end of it across the rest, as shown above.

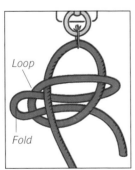

Fold the remaining rope, take it behind the part that is attached to the pony and pull it through the loop.

Pull down on the folded part, making sure the end doesn't pull through. To undo quickly, pull on the loose end.

If your pony can free himself, thread the end through the loop. Unthread it before pulling for a quick release.

# NAUGHTY PONIES

A pony that misbehaves could be frightened or in pain, or he may just be testing you to see what he can get away with. Any bad habit needs to be cured as soon as possible. Never be embarrassed to ask for help. You need to check that you are not doing something wrong before you blame your pony.

## WHY PROBLEMS HAPPEN

| Cause | Reason | Action |
|---|---|---|
| Is he in pain? | Sore back or sharp teeth. | Get the vet to examine him. |
| | Saddle or bridle do not fit properly. | Ask a professional saddler to check his tack. |
| | You may be hurting him. | Ask your instructor for advice. |
| Is he frightened? | Something has made him panic. | Find out what he is scared of and get him used to it quietly. |
| | You're asking him to face something new. | Let him follow another pony. |
| | He's had a bad experience in the past. | Use patience to calm his fears and win his trust. |
| Is he too full of beans? | Too much rich food. | Cut down on high energy foods such as grain or alfalfa hay. |
| | Not enough exercise. | Ride him more often or turn him out for longer so he gets more exercise. |

## MAKE SURE HE KNOWS WHO IS BOSS

Some ponies misbehave simply because they know they can get away with it. This is why it is vital to show him that you are in charge right from the start. Ponies are used to a pecking order (see page 20) and you become part of it, so make sure you are at the top not the bottom. Always be strict about stable manners. If you are not boss on the ground, you will stand little chance of being boss out riding.

If you once let your pony think he is boss, he may start to make fun of you and misbehave.

# HARD TO CATCH

If a pony is hard to catch, use patience and stealth to teach him to come to you.

*Catching tips*
* You could leave a halter on, but make sure it is a leather one that fits well (see page 19).
* Take a carrot or handful of grain or pellets. Rattling a bucket is effective, but if he shares a field, watch out for a stampede!

* Get as close as he will allow, hold out your hand with his treat, and make him walk the last few steps, even if it takes ages.
* Ponies hate leaving their

friends, so catch him when the others are coming in.
* Bring him in at the same time each day and make him look forward to it by giving him some hay.

## TROUBLE MOUNTING

If your pony starts jumping around as you try to get on, make sure he is not in pain. If he is just acting up, try these solutions.

Ask someone to hold him while you mount or put him near a fence so he can't walk forward.

If he is too tall, use a mounting block or find someone to give you a leg up, as shown here.

If he turns to nip you, keep the reins tight and have the one on the other side slightly shorter.

If the saddle slips when you get on, ask someone to hold the stirrup on the other side.

## ALWAYS EATING

If you let your pony eat with his bridle on, he may pick up the irritating habit of snatching at every blade of juicy grass while out riding. To stop him from doing this, you need to spot the grass first, hold the reins firmly and kick him on. If it becomes a real problem, you might consider using grass reins.

Grass reins go from the bit to the "D" rings. They prevent him from putting his head down to eat.

*Grass reins help teach your pony not to eat with a bridle on, but you can't wear them in shows.*

## BOLTING

A pony's natural reaction to fear is to run. It is very scary when a pony bolts, but you must try to stay calm. Screaming for help will frighten him even more. Sit tight, with plenty of weight in the saddle and talk calmly to him. Turning large circles may help to slow him down. Have him checked by the vet and if the problem continues ask your instructor to help.

## TOO STRONG

Some small ponies are very strong, and if they start to pull against you, can be hard to control. If yours does this, first make sure that he is not in pain from sharp teeth or mouth ulcers. Check his food. Is it too rich? Does he get enough exercise? If he is just playing up, there are various pieces of tack that make a strong pony easier to control (see below), but always ask an expert for advice.

## SADDLE SLIPS

If the saddle slips forward check that it fits properly (see page 16). It may be the shape of your pony that is a problem, particularly if he is fat. Try fitting a crupper - a leather strap with a loop that goes around the tail. It fastens to a ring on the back of the saddle (see below).

*Some ponies blow out their tummies as you fasten the girth, so check it before you get on and after a few minutes' riding.*

*Flash*

*Drop*

*Kimblewick*

*Curb chain*

*Dr Bristol*

*Crupper*

*Stronger tack*

⚫ A flash or drop noseband fastens beneath the bit. It stops the pony from opening his mouth wide and pulling against you.

⚫ A change of bit can help, but the wrong one may make things worse so get advice. The strongest have curb chains that fasten under the chin.

⚫ A running martingale stops the pony from bringing his head up high, where it is difficult to control. It must be fitted carefully.

If your pony pulls you around while you are leading him, put on a bridle. It will give you more control.

# BUCKING

The infrequent buck is not a serious problem. It often just shows that a pony is in high spirits. Check on his routine. You may need to cut back his feed or ride him more frequently.

If he bucks persistently, there may be something wrong that is causing him pain. Ask the vet to look at his back and teeth, and get an expert to check that his tack fits correctly.

If he is simply taking advantage of you, you need patience and forceful riding to straighten him out. Don't stop when he does it. Sit up, keep your leg on him and ride him through it.

# SHYING

Shying is when your pony is spooked by something and won't go past it calmly. It can be dangerous when riding on the road. A pony in high spirits is more likely to shy at things so check on his food.

*Tips to calm him*
◉ Ride him in an enclosed area before taking him outside.
◉ Find out what spooks him and try to get him used to it.
◉ When passing a spooky object, look at it yourself but turn your pony's head away.
◉ Use your outside leg to stop him from swinging out and ride strongly forward.
◉ Ride out with a quiet pony to give him confidence.
◉ Get his eyesight and hearing checked.

# BARN SOUR

A pony is barn sour when he refuses to leave his friends. He may stop dead, or he may turn and dash for home. Keep him moving forward. Use a whip if necessary, and carry it on the side he usually turns to. When out riding, try to take a circular route as returning home along the same road can encourage him to turn for home when he feels like it. If he is strong and willful ask an older person to help you.

*Acting barn sour leads to rearing, so never let him get away with it.*

# WHERE TO RIDE

Once you have your own pony, it's up to you to make sure that he gets enough exercise. Otherwise, he may become too lively and hard to handle. It is safest at first, to ride him in an enclosed area such as an indoor or outdoor arena, but once you are used to each other it is fun to explore your local area.

## BRIDLE PATHS AND TRAIL RIDING

Trail riding can be a lot of fun for you and your pony but you must make sure that you have permission to cross someone else's land.

Many state and federal parks have trails for riding, but you might need to get permission to ride there as well. Ask at your local stable or park.

Go with someone who knows the area and can show you the route the first few times.

### Trail etiquette
* Always keep to the trail, especially when crossing a field planted with crops.
* Be considerate to other users, for example, walk past them, never canter.

* Never ride through the middle of livestock, such as cows or sheep. Go around.
* If the land is very wet, keep off. Riding through will cut it up and make it worse when it dries out.
* Close any gate you open to pass through.
* Be extra careful during harvest time when there is "spooky" machinery.

Riding with friends is nicer for you and for your pony. It's also a lot safer.

Until you get used to your pony, ride out with an experienced person.

# SAFETY ON THE ROAD

Riding on the road is not ideal but it is often the only way to reach safer riding areas. Here are some points to remember.

## Safety checklist

- Make sure your pony is familiar with traffic before taking him out on the road.
- Have a safe horse on your outside the first time.
- Always keep to the right.
- Where possible, keep to the grass shoulder.
- Try to avoid the busiest periods.
- Thank motorists who slow down. Nod and smile if you can't take your hands from the reins.
- Make sure you know your Highway Code.
- Wear reflective clothing so that you are easily seen.
- Wait for a clear road before passing scary objects.
- If leading a pony on the road, put yourself between the pony and the traffic.
- Your local pony club or 4-H club will have more safety tips.

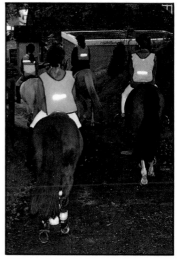
*Make sure you can be seen at dusk.*

# WHAT TO WEAR

You will probably have your own riding gear from the first day you began to ride, but here's a reminder of what you should wear.

Hard hat
Silk

*A hard hat that fits well with a chin strap. Make sure it meets current safety standards.*

*Body protectors are a good safety measure for all types of riding.*

*Jodhpurs protect your legs from rubbing against the saddle.*

*Gloves with a good grip protect your hands and keep them warm in cold weather.*

*Riding boots with a small heel. Tennis shoes or rubber boots can get stuck in the stirrups.*

# GOING FURTHER

With your own pony there is no limit to how much riding you can do.

One of the best ways to get involved in lots of different events is to join a local pony club or 4-H club. (You can get the address from the organizations listed on page 128).

Joining a local club is a good way to meet fellow riders too.

## Pony Club events

- Picnic rides
- Gymkhanas
- Summer camps
- Shows
- Hunter trials
- Stable management courses
- Riding and road safety exams
- Mounted games

# CHECKING HIS HEALTH

Your pony can't tell you when he is feeling ill, so it is important to recognize the signs. The main thing is to get to know him well, including all his favorite habits, so that you notice any unusual behavior. Make sure you check him over carefully at least once each day.

## SIGNS OF GOOD AND BAD HEALTH

|  | Head | Ears | Eyes | Nostrils | Coat |
|---|---|---|---|---|---|
| Good sign | Looking up<br>Watching your approach | Pricked up<br>Feel warm | Bright and shiny<br>Salmon pink membrane | Pink and clean | Lying flat<br>Looking glossy |
| Bad sign | Hung low<br>Barely notices your approach | Drooping or laid back<br>Feel cold | Dull<br>Sad-looking | Full of discharge | Dull and patchy<br>Standing on end |

|  | Skin | Ribs | Appetite | Droppings | Legs |
|---|---|---|---|---|---|
| Good sign | Loose and supple | Can't be seen<br>Can be felt | Eating up<br>Chewing well | Soft balls that break as they hit the ground<br>Passed about 8 times a day | Check that he is standing square (Resting a back leg is usual but a front one is odd) |
| Bad sign | Tight and dry<br>Sore or rubbed patches | If you can see them he's too thin<br>If you can't feel them he's too fat | Refusing food<br>Having trouble chewing | Sloppy like a cow's<br>Not passing any at all | Lame or limping<br>Cuts and grazes<br>Heat or swellings |

## PULSE

*Feel for the pulse under the jaw, or just above his eye, here.*

A pony's pulse rate should be 36 to 42 beats a minute, at rest. Use two fingers to feel it under his jaw or just above his eye. You may need help finding it at first.

## RESPIRATION

*Flank*

Respiration is his breathing rate. At rest, it should be 8-12 regular breaths a minute. To count them, watch his flanks go in and out or put your hand near his nose.

## TEMPERATURE

A pony's temperature should be 38°C (100.5°F). It is taken by putting the thermometer in his bottom and should only be done by an experienced person.

# WHEN TO CALL THE VET

If in doubt, call the vet out, but try not to do it outside business hours unless it's an emergency. Consult an experienced person first if there is one around, but if not, call the vet right away. An early visit could stop a serious problem from developing.

## Signs to worry about
* Sudden lameness that has no obvious cause. Check for stones in his foot first and consult the farrier if he is around.
* A deep wound that won't stop bleeding and may need stitches.
* Any hot, painful swelling on the legs.
* Continual coughing.

* A pony who won't eat for more than a day.
* Hot feet and a reluctance to move are signs of laminitis which must be dealt with immediately.
* A pony looking at his flanks and kicking his belly may have colic (tummy ache) which is serious, so call the vet immediately.
* Soft or sloppy droppings, or none at all, can also be a sign of colic.

*Ponies love to roll for fun and to scratch their own coat. But a pony that keeps rolling, breaks into a sweat and starts kicking his stomach, may be very ill, so call the vet.*

# KEEPING RECORDS

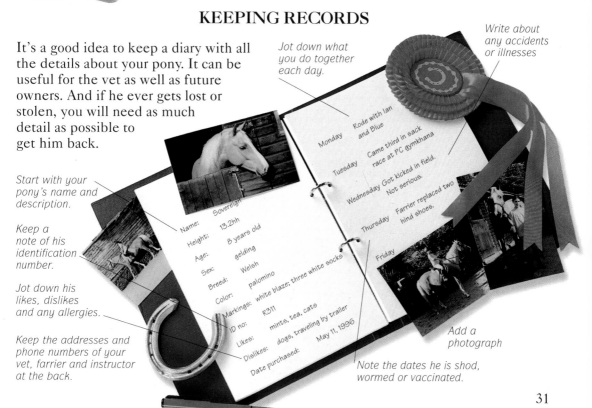

It's a good idea to keep a diary with all the details about your pony. It can be useful for the vet as well as future owners. And if he ever gets lost or stolen, you will need as much detail as possible to get him back.

*Jot down what you do together each day.*

*Write about any accidents or illnesses*

*Start with your pony's name and description.*

*Keep a note of his identification number.*

*Jot down his likes, dislikes and any allergies.*

*Keep the addresses and phone numbers of your vet, farrier and instructor at the back.*

Monday    Rode with Ian and Blue
Tuesday   Came third in sack race at PC gymkhana
Wednesday Got kicked in field. Not serious.
Thursday  Farrier replaced two hind shoes.
Friday

Name:      Sovereign
Height:    13.2hh
Age:       8 years old
Sex:       gelding
Breed:     Welsh
Color:     palomino
Markings:  white blaze; three white socks
ID no:     R311
Likes:     mints, tea, cats
Dislikes:  dogs, traveling by trailer
Date purchased:  May 11, 1996

*Add a photograph*

*Note the dates he is shod, wormed or vaccinated.*

# GROOMING AND STABLE MANAGEMENT

## Contents

# THE PADDOCK

Keeping a pony is rewarding, but as you will find out in this part of the book, it is also hard work. If you are at school a lot, the cheapest and most practical way for your pony to live, as long as he is hardy, is at pasture. This means he lives in a field or paddock most of the time, where he can roam and graze naturally as he would in the wild.

## CARING FOR THE GRASS

Your pony will mainly eat grass while he lives outside. It is a good food, but it needs some care to grow well. Ponies are fussy grazers. They tend to eat all the short, rich grass and leave any that is long, or has manure or urine in it. If they graze a field for too long it gets "horse-sick", with bald patches which they have cropped bare, and other areas full of long, worm-infested grass, where no new shoots can grow.

For one pony, to prevent over-grazing, you need a field of about one hectare (two acres) which you can split into two or three parts. You can then rest two parts while the other is being grazed. Make sure the part the pony grazes has shelter, water and a gate (see opposite). It is also important to clear manure from the field each day. This prevents worms which live in the manure from being eaten by the pony.

## DEADLY PLANTS

*Remember to check any hedges around the paddock for poisonous plants that the pony might eat.*

Before using the paddock, check to see if any poisonous plants are growing there. The types will vary depending on where you live. Ask someone who works with ponies, such as a riding instructor or your vet, for advice about which ones to look for.

Pull up all poisonous plants by the roots and burn them. This will help to stop them from growing again. Get rid of any which the pony could reach over the fence, too.

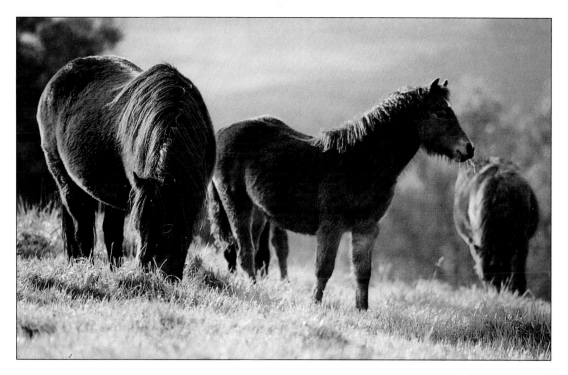

## TYPES OF FENCING

The paddock must be surrounded by a strong, safe fence. This should be at least 1.2m (4ft) high so ponies don't jump out. It needs to be solid enough to take the weight of ponies leaning or rubbing against it. Make sure there are no sharp edges where a pony could cut himself, or gaps where he could escape.

*Thick wooden posts and rails are best, but the most expensive.*

*Dense, trimmed hedges with no deadly plants are good and also give some natural shelter.*

*Three strands of thick, rust-proof wire strung taut between posts are cheap and effective.*

*The bottom strand must be at least 30cm (1ft) from the ground, so the pony can't hook his leg in it.*

## GETTING THE RIGHT GATE

The gate must be hung so that it swings smoothly and shuts firmly. Fit a chain with a padlock as well as the gate fastening, and keep a spare padlock key.

The gateway must be wide enough to let you and your pony through easily side-by-side. Put sand on the ground around the gateway to stop it from getting too muddy.

*Ponies are wily and can lift or undo even good gate fastenings like these. You will need a chain and padlock too.*

*A strong, five-barred wooden or steel gate is best.*

# PASTURE-KEPT PONIES

Keeping a pony at pasture is a very natural way for him to live, but he won't be able to fend entirely for himself. You will have to supply shelter and fresh water and visit him every morning and evening to make sure he is all right.

## THE ADVANTAGES OF A FIELD SHELTER

A field shelter protects your pony from bad weather and is shady in summer. If your pony lives mostly outside, it is also a dry, covered place where you can do a lot of your pony care. On the right is a checklist of the most important features for an ideal shelter.

*Shelter checklist*
* Three sides.
* Weatherproof roof.
* Back to the windiest part of the paddock.
* Wide opening (so all ponies can get in and out).
* Enough room inside for ponies to lie down or turn around in.
* Dirt floor covered with straw, so ponies can stand or lie down in comfort.
* Nothing sharp or sticking out from the walls, on which a pony could hurt himself.
* A portable manger for any extra food.

## FRESH WATER SUPPLY

All ponies need a constant supply of fresh, clean water. In the paddock it is easiest to keep it in a trough which should be long, solid and not too deep. If possible, water should be piped straight to it. Otherwise, empty and refill it each day with buckets of fresh water.

*Raise the trough off the ground slightly and put sand down so the grass isn't churned up by hooves.*

*There should be no sharp edges on the trough. A plug in the bottom means you can drain and clean it.*

Put the trough on well-drained land, away from gates or corners where ponies may crowd each other. If the water gets cloudy, empty the trough and scrub it out with a hard brush. Don't use soap or detergents. On frosty winter mornings you may need to break the ice.

## DAILY PONY AND PADDOCK CHECK

Feel his ears to check that he is warm. Tie him up. Examine him all over, especially his feet and legs. Deal with wounds at once to stop infections.

Take his blanket off. Check that he is not getting thin on poor pasture in winter, or fat on rich summer grass. Put his blanket back on and untie him afterward.

Check the paddock. Remove rusty wire, tin cans, broken glass, or plastic bags that could choke the pony. Fill in any holes where he might catch his foot.

Clear manure away to keep worms out of the grass. Fork through muck you can't pick up, to let sunlight in. This kills some of the worm eggs.

## KEEPING PONIES TOGETHER ON PASTURE

Ponies are much happier in a group. When in a "herd" they quickly work out a pecking order. They may bully a new pony by pushing it around and nipping it with their teeth,

as in the photograph above. Introduce "newcomers" gradually and watch them closely to start with. Be especially careful with very young or old ponies living out in a herd.

Ponies get excited when they smell food, so don't use tidbits to catch a pony on your own if he is out with others. You could be pushed or stepped on as they crowd around.

# THE STABLE

Your pony will probably live out most of the time, but you will need a safe, comfortable stable where you can keep him warm if he is not feeling well, or if you need him in tiptop condition to be ready for a show or competition.

## THE STABLE BUILDING

A stall in a stable is where the pony can be left untied as long as the door is shut. This means he can move around easily. The stable should have proper drainage, electricity and water, with a faucet nearby for filling buckets. There should be a road so trucks and horse trailers can get to the stable, and you should be able to walk easily from there to the field with the pony.

*The roof must be water- and weather-proof, give good insulation and allow air to circulate. Shingles are best. (Corrugated iron is cheap but can get noisy in bad weather.)*

*A stall should be at least 4x4m (12x12ft), with ceiling not lower than 4m (12ft).*

*A vent in the back wall or roof lets stale air flow out.*

*Light must be safely wired and out of pony's reach.*

*Wooden kickboards up to 1.5m (4ft 6in).*

*Strong, smooth, brick or stone walls: must stand up to pony kicking and leaning on them. 4m (12ft) high to the eaves and 2.5m (8ft) at the sides.*

*Half-doors that open outward at 180° and hook back securely.*

*The doorway must be at least 2m (7ft) high, and 1.5m (4ft 6in) wide. It must be high enough so he doesn't bang his head.*

*Proper ventilation is essential. Hopper-style windows, hinged along the lower edge and open at the top, let fresh air go up, avoiding drafts.*

# FIXTURES YOU MIGHT NEED

Have as few fixtures in the stall as you can, so they don't take up much room and the pony won't bump into or chew them. Make sure they have no sharp edges and are firmly attached. If possible, put them on the front wall so you don't have to go past the pony each time you feed him.

You need a tethering ring inside, and one outside for tying up the pony. They should be level with the pony's chest.

Put a ring on the outside wall in case you ever want to hang up a haynet for your pony while he waits to be cared for.

The manger should be in one corner, about 1m (3ft 6in) from the floor. Removable ones are easy to fill, empty, and clean.

# HOW TO PREVENT A STABLE FIRE

A fire in a stable is one of the worst things that can happen if you keep a pony. Ponies are terrified of fire, so make sure you know exactly what to do if a fire does break out, and take the precautions in the checklist on the right.

*Checklist*
* Make sure you know how to get your pony out quickly and safely. Have an actual drill, learn it by heart and practice it.
* Keep all supplies of straw and hay away from the stable as these burn very fast.
* Keep fire extinguishers and fire buckets somewhere out of the pony's reach but close at hand.
* Install smoke and fire alarms.
* Don't let anyone smoke around the stable. Put up "No Smoking" signs for visitors.
* Display a fire notice showing the drill, where the alarms and fire extinguishers are, where to meet, and any emergency telephone numbers.
* Practice taking your pony out of his stable safely.

## MAINTAINING THE STABLE

| Every day | Every week | Every few months |
|---|---|---|
| Clean out food and water containers. | Clean windows. | Check gutters, roof, wiring, drains. |
| Sweep stable area. | Check light bulbs. | Check woodwork for rot or woodworm. |
| Muck out (see pages 42-43). | Check first aid kit (see page 63) and fire equipment. | Oil hinges, check doors. |
| Neaten muck heap. | Clean and mend tools. | Ask an adult to put pest killer down in the feed shed, but keep it away from pets and small children. |
| | Clean out the feed shed (see page 49). | |
| | Check supplies. | |
| | Disinfect stable floor. | |

# BEDDING DOWN

Your pony needs a warm, comfortable bed in the stable so he can lie down and rest. A deep bed also helps the pony feel safe and stops him from hurting himself on the hard floor. The pony's bed must be changed every day to keep it clean. Making the bed is called bedding down.

## CHOOSING THE BEDDING

There are several kinds of suitable bedding for ponies. Before you choose a particular type, find out how dusty it is. Dust is very bad for ponies as it can make them cough, which keeps them from breathing properly. You also need to know the cost of the bedding and how much you will need. Make sure it is easy to get fresh supplies, and that you have somewhere to store them (see opposite).

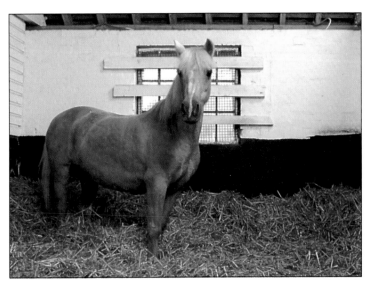

*A deep straw bed like this one will help your pony to feel relaxed and happy in his stable.*

## SOME TYPES OF BEDDING YOU CAN USE

| Bedding | Advantages | Disadvantages | Ways to get rid of it |
|---------|-----------|---------------|----------------------|
| **Straw** <br> *Use wheat straw only as ponies eat other kinds.* | *Comfortable* <br> *Dry* <br> *Easy to get* <br> *Cheap* <br> *Easy to spread* | *Dusty - don't use if your pony tends to cough.* | *Burn it (but see below)* <br> *Rots quickly* <br> *Sell used straw and manure to mushroom growers.* |
| Wood shavings | *Not too dusty* <br> *Absorbent* <br> *Easy to use* <br> *Pony can't eat them* | *Expensive* <br> *Take a long time to rot* | *Might be used as compost for fields and gardens, so check first with friends and neighbors. May need to be burned.* |
| Shredded newspaper | *Dust free* <br> *Absorbent* <br> *Light and easy to lift* | *Hard to get* <br> *Very light, so tends to blow around when you are mucking out.* | |

40

# HOW TO MAKE A BED FOR YOUR PONY

*Take the pony out before you start.*

*Keep the door ajar to air the bed, and so you don't breathe in dust.*

*Put the fresh bedding ready in a wheelbarrow in the doorway.*

*Have the wheelbarrow handles pointing into the stable so you can wheel it out easily.*

After mucking out, spread any leftover clean bedding across the stable floor. Shake it out well as you work, to get rid of any hard lumps that would make the bed uncomfortable for the pony to lie on.

Add fresh bedding with a fork. Undo the bale or bag inside the stable so it can't blow away. If you use straw, toss it first, to air it before spreading. Keep laying down bedding until the bed is ankle-deep.

Build the bed up higher around the walls. This keeps drafts out and encourages the pony to lie in the middle, where he won't get stuck in a corner if he rolls. If using shavings, make the top layer smooth.

## USING A FORK

For laying a straw bed you need a four-pronged fork. The prongs are very sharp, so use it with care like this.

*Keep the prongs down, away from your face.*

Put your strongest hand in the lower position for a firmer grip. Have the other one near the top. Move the fork in a low arc, pushing the prongs away from you.

## WHERE TO STORE BEDDING

It is cheaper to buy bedding in large amounts, so you need a big, dry storage space with room for a truck or tractor and trailer to park outside. A barn is ideal, but you could use an empty stable, shed or garage, as long as it has the features shown in the checklist (see right).

Put wooden pallets on the floor to stop the bedding from getting damp, and keep it neatly stacked. Check it often to make sure it is not rotting. To stop rats and mice from eating it, ask an adult to put poison under the pallets. Keep the storeroom shut so that young children and pets can't get in.

*Storeroom checklist*
* A roof and three walls to keep out rain and wind.
* It must be airy, with proper ventilation.
* Large entrance to let you in and out easily with bales or sacks.
* Set away from the stable as bedding is a big fire risk.
* If possible, it should have a lockable door for security.

# MUCKING OUT

If your pony lives in for part or all of the time, you need to muck the stable out once a day. This means clearing all the droppings and dirty bedding out. You will also need to pick out once or twice a day. This is when you take away just the manure, so that the pony doesn't trample it into the bed.

## TOOLS YOU NEED

A wheelbarrow to carry manure to the muck heap

A shavings fork for mucking out shavings

A four-pronged fork for mucking out straw

A broom with plastic or fiber bristles for sweeping the floor clear

A rubber or plastic tub (a laundry basket will do) for picking out

A large, aluminum shovel for scooping up piles of manure

A hose for spraying muck off the floor now and then

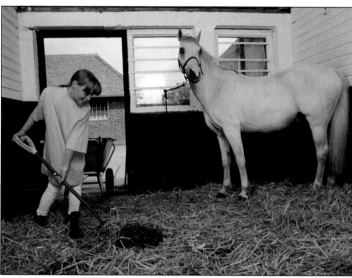

*Ideally, you should take your pony out of the stable when mucking out. If you can't, make sure he is securely tied out of your way.*

## DIFFERENT WAYS OF PICKING OUT

Your pony will produce a lot of droppings in a day, so it is very important to pick out regularly. This only takes about five minutes and you can leave the pony in the stable while you do it. Just move him over to one side.

To pick out a straw bed, use a fork to lift up any piles of droppings. Shake the fork over the tub so that the muck falls in with as little of the clean straw as possible.

To pick out shavings, it is quicker and easier to pick up the manure with your hands and drop it in the tub. Wear rubber gloves for this to protect your skin from germs.

# HOW TO MUCK OUT THE STABLE

*Clear the manure from the cleanest corner first so you can pile clean bedding there.*

*To stop the wind from blowing the dirty bedding away, put the wheelbarrow in the doorway.*

Put the tools you need just outside the stable. Turn the pony loose in the field or tie him in the yard. Pick up dirty bedding and manure with the fork and put them in the wheelbarrow.

Fork all the clean bedding over to one side in a neat pile. You will reuse it when you make the pony's bed. Turn the bedding over as you work, making sure there is no manure underneath.

With the broom, sweep the floor. Let any wet patches dry. If the pony has to be inside while the floor is damp, put down a thin layer of bedding so he does not slip on the hard floor.

## TOOL TIPS

* Store all tools in a safe, handy place out of the pony's reach but where you can get them easily.
* Never leave any tools lying around if the pony is anywhere near.
* Keep tools in good condition. Check them every week. Mend any broken parts at once.
* Use a four-pronged fork for straw. The prongs pick up bedding easily and break up any lumps.
* For shavings or newspaper, use a shavings fork to sort clean stuff from the rest. Its prongs work like a sieve.
* Sweep piles of dirty shavings onto the shovel with the broom. Ask a friend to hold the shovel while you sweep.

## WHERE TO PUT THE MUCK

Horse manure doesn't smell too bad, but it is full of germs which are a health risk. It also attracts flies and pests like rats. You need a neat, safe muck heap where you can dump the droppings. It should be near enough so you don't have far to carry the muck, but far enough away so the smell and pests don't get into your home. If possible, have it near a track, so there is room for a tractor to get in and take the muck away.

*Brick walls around three sides stop the muck from blowing away or falling down.*

43

# STABLE MANNERS AND VICES

Your pony may find living in a stable a little difficult at times. It's a small enclosed space, with little room for him to move around in. If he gets bored or bad-tempered he could be awkward or even dangerous to handle, so teach him good manners from the start and try to stop him from getting bored.

## TEACHING STABLE MANNERS

Always be firm, quiet and confident when you handle a pony in the stable. Make sure you let him know you are coming by speaking, and shut the door after you as soon as you come in. Then approach him from the side, going to his shoulder so he can see you.

If you have work to do in the stable, always tie him up or take him out first to avoid accidents.

*Always insist on good behavior when you enter the stable. To move your pony back from the door, gently push his chest with the flat of your hand. Say, "Back".*

If he tries to push past and get out when you go in, put a bar across the doorway. This will stop him and help to break the habit.

To get him to move over in the stall, stand by his shoulder. Put your hand flat on his side and gently push, saying, "Over".

To make him stand still, tie him up. If he fidgets, say, "Stand". If he crowds you at feed time, say, "Back," then, "Stand". Make him wait until you fill the manger.

If he barges ahead when you bring him in, see if he has bashed himself on the gate. If he is just being pushy, put him in a bridle so that the bit gives you more control.

# STABLE VICES

A pony that spends a lot of time in the stable is likely to get bored. Boredom leads to vices (bad habits) which can be impossible to cure once started, so it's important to keep a stabled pony happy.

*Tips on preventing boredom*
* Give him some time at pasture.
* Try to give him company, but don't stable him next to a pony he dislikes, as this will upset him.
* Keep the top half-door open so he can look out.
* Visit him often.
* Feed him regularly and always have some hay in his feeder.
* Even if you cannot ride him, take him out for a walk at least once a day.
* Give him a few toys, such as a plastic apple hung up so he can push it with his nose.
* Stick to a routine.

*Kicking is a vice which must be stopped early on.*

| SOME COMMON VICES | | |
|---|---|---|
| Vice | What to look for | What you can do about it |
| Weaving | The pony swings his head from side to side in a continuous rhythm.<br><br>He may lift each of his forelegs in turn from the ground as well.<br><br>He may also stall walk, going around and around the stall. | Give him more exercise and try to turn him out more.<br><br>You could fit a special anti-weave grill. This lets him look out, but stops him from rocking. |
| Biting | The pony flattens his ears, wrinkles his nose and bites you or others who try to handle him. Even nipping at your pockets for tidbits can develop into real biting, so watch out. | Never let a pony get away with biting. Tell him off at once by saying, "No" very firmly.<br><br>If you must, give him one hard slap on the chest or shoulder, but never hit him on the head or he will become head-shy and even harder to handle.<br><br>Don't give tidbits which only make him greedy and more likely to bite. |
| Cribbing and wind-sucking | He grips something like the edge of the stable door with his teeth. This can damage them and stop him from eating.<br><br>Cribbing can develop into wind-sucking, where he also sucks in air. | Take out anything he might get hold of and paint the edge of the door with anti-chew fluid, or cover it with a metal chew strip. |

# FEEDING

Feeding is the most important part of how you look after your pony. It affects his health, behavior and looks. A well-fed pony is usually happy, relaxed and much easier to manage than one which is hungry or overfed.

## HOW PONIES FEED AND WHAT THEY NEED

It is best to feed your pony in a similar way to how he would eat in the wild. Ponies have small stomachs in relation to their size, so they can only manage a little food at a time. At pasture, they graze for about 16 hours a day, eating small mouthfuls more or less continuously. This is called "trickle-feeding".

Ponies need bulk food, such as hay or grass, to fill them up and keep their digestion slow and steady. This makes them feel satisfied. They also need concentrated food, such as grain or oats, to give them energy for work.

How you combine the two types depends on how

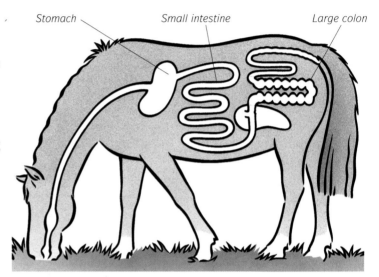

*Small amounts of food move easily through your pony's complicated digestive system.*

much work your pony does. The chart below shows how to get the right balance in his diet.

### GETTING THE BALANCE RIGHT

| What the pony is doing | Ratio of bulk to energy food |
|---|---|
| *No work* | *100% bulk: 0% concentrates* |
| *Light work: (short rides)* | *75% bulk: 25% concentrates* |
| *Medium work: (long rides, jumping, shows, eventing)* | *60% bulk: 40% concentrates* |
| *Hard work: (hunting)* | *50% bulk: 50% concentrates* |

*If you step up the amount of work your pony does, gradually increase the energy ration and reduce the bulk. Don't let the energizing food become more than half of the total food ration. This puts a strain on his digestion and makes the pony overexcited and difficult.*

*Feeding rules*
* Feed according to pony's size, weight, age, work and temperament (see page 48).
* Feed little and often.
* Feed good quality food.
* Feed a succulent (grass, apples, carrots) every day.
* Feed at set times.
* Give the largest feeding at night so the pony has plenty to eat overnight.
* Avoid changes to diet. Make any changes slowly, over a few weeks.
* Keep feed buckets and mangers clean.
* Feed at least one-and-a-half hours before exercise.
* Let pony cool down after work before feeding him.

# THE BEST FOOD FOR YOUR PONY

Hay is an excellent food. It is chewed and digested slowly and contains protein, fiber, calcium and vitamins. Good quality hay is the only food ponies need if they are not working. Choose meadow hay that is fresh and sweet-smelling. It should be four to eighteen months old.

The easiest way to make sure a working pony gets a balanced diet is to feed him compounds prepared by a specialist horse food manufacturer. If you feed hay or grass with them, compounds give the pony all the nourishment he needs. There are lots of different types, so you can choose one that suits him.

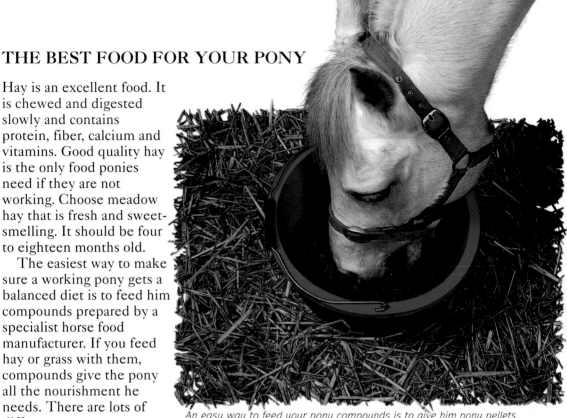

An easy way to feed your pony compounds is to give him pony pellets. These are made of various ingredients ground up, dried and then made into pellets.

## TYPES OF FOOD

| Energy foods | Bulk foods | Other |
|---|---|---|
| Several types of grain can be fed as part of the diet. | Dried sugar-beet pulp: has to be soaked for 24 hours before use so does not choke pony. Full of energy but non-heating. Tasty, useful for dampening feed. | Carrots and apples: feed raw, washed and sliced. Help digestion and appetite. |
| Oats: very nourishing but can make ponies fat and overexcited (called "heating" effect). | | |
| Barley: not widely used but good for putting weight on a pony in poor shape. | Hay: very healthy food. Fills pony up and keeps him chewing slowly. | Linseed and linseed cake: full of protein and oil. Makes coat shine. Linseed must be soaked and cooked or it is poisonous. |
| Corn: very heating. Fattening, so only use as a small part of diet. | Grass: fresh grass added to the feeding is a nourishing treat. Never feed grass clippings, which are poisonous. | |

# HOW MUCH TO FEED YOUR PONY

The amount of food your pony needs depends on how big he is, how much work he does, his age and character. If he is mainly at pasture, he will sometimes need extra food, depending on the weather and how much grass there is. Each pony is an individual, so it's impossible to say exactly how much to give all ponies. The chart below gives you an idea of the quantities involved and how to split up the feedings each day.

*Grazing freely stops ponies from getting bored. Moving about, or foraging for food like this, is also very good for their digestion.*

## SAMPLE FEEDING CHART AND TIMETABLE

| Size of pony, work he does, where he lives | Approx. weight of pony | Total feed per day | A.M. | Lunch | P.M. |
|---|---|---|---|---|---|
| 13.2 hh light work; mainly stabled | 350 kg (770lbs) | 8kg (17.5lbs) | 3.5kg (7.75lbs) hay; 0.5kg (1lb) grain | If possible, turn out for a few hours | 3.5kg. (7.75lbs) hay; 0.5kg (1lb) grain |
| 13.2hh; light work; mainly on pasture | 350 kg | 8kg | Summer: grass; 0.5kg (1lb) grain  Winter: 3.5kg (7.75lbs) hay; 0.5kg (1lb) grain | | Summer: grass; 0.5kg (1lb) grain  Winter: 3.5kg (7.75lbs) 0.5kg (1lb) grain |
| 14.2hh; medium work; mainly stabled | 420kg (925lbs) | 9kg (20lbs) | 3.2kg (7lbs) hay; 1.3kg (3lbs) grain | If possible, turn out for a few hours | 3.2kg (7lbs) hay; 1.3kg (3lbs) grain |
| 14.2hh; medium work; mainly on pasture | 420kg | 9kg | Summer: grass; 1.3kg (3lbs) grain  Winter: 3.2kg (7lbs) hay; 1.3kg (3lbs) grain | | Summer: grass; 1.3kg (3lbs) grain  Winter: 3.2kg (7lbs) hay; 1.3kg (3lbs) grain |

# STORING AND SERVING FOOD

Ponies are fussy feeders and won't eat food that tastes bad or stale, so only buy about one week's supply and store it in air-tight feed bins that keep it dry and safe from mice and rats. Don't put fresh food on top of stale or old batches. Always empty the bin first.

Keep all feeding equipment clean with regular scrubbing and rinsing (the photograph on the right shows you what you need).

If you can, store the food in a separate shed. It is especially important to keep it out of the tack room, as mice that are drawn to the food will also eat leather. It's best to store hay in a high, airy barn. Make sure it's bone-dry when stored.

*Weighing scales are essential as you need to know exactly how much you give at each feeding.*

*A haynet could be handy for weighing hay and is used for traveling and at shows.*

*Feed bins should be tough plastic or metal, with tight-fitting lids, so they are completely rodent-proof.*

*Mangers are useful for keeping food tidy and preventing waste.*

*Metal or plastic scoops are best for measuring out the dry food.*

# GIVING YOUR PONY WATER

Make sure your pony can drink as and when he needs to. This keeps him from drinking a lot at one time, which can cause colic. In the stable, use an automatic water bowl, or give a fresh bucketful at least four times a day, and two for the night.

*An automatic water bowl refills as soon as the pony drinks out of it.*

*Rules of watering*
* Keep water always available.
* Make sure the water and containers are fresh and clean.
* Don't let ponies drink from ponds or unused troughs where the water is stagnant and dirty.
* Don't let ponies drink from streams with sandy beds. Sand causes colic (see page 63).
* Always offer water before a feeding.
* During a long ride, give

him small amounts often, rather than one big drink.
* Don't give large amounts of cold water straight after exercise. Instead, as long as he isn't puffing, give him a small drink while he cools off. This will stop him from getting dehydrated.
* Pour away any water that has manure or urine in it at once.
* Match the amount of water to your pony's needs. These will vary depending on how much work he is doing and how hot it is.

# GROOMING

It is essential to groom your pony regularly, not just to make him look good, but to help him stay healthy. A stabled pony needs a full grooming every day, as he can't roll around to groom himself.

## WHAT GROOMING IS FOR

Grooming keeps your pony's skin and coat in good condition. In the wild, his coat would naturally suit his needs and the season of the year (see page 56), but a pony who lives in and is ridden needs extra help.

By brushing his coat, you get the dirt and oil out of the pores (tiny holes) in his skin, which means he can sweat freely. Grooming also helps the blood under his skin to flow well, which is another way of keeping him fit. Lastly, brushing and rubbing his coat makes it stay smooth and glossy.

## THE GROOMING KIT

Dandy brush for brushing off mud. Has long stiff bristles.

Body brush removes oil and dirt. Has shorter, softer bristles.

Stable cloth polishes coat to make it glossy.

Stiff brush for brushing hooves (see page 54).

Mane comb for thinning or "pulling" mane and tail.

Rubber curry comb for brushing off mud and shedding hair.

Metal curry comb for cleaning body brush. Never use it on the pony!

Three sponges, one each for wiping:
- eyes
- lips and nostrils
- dock (bottom).
Make sure each looks different.

Hoof pick for cleaning dirt and stones out of the feet.

Hoof oil for sealing and protecting the feet.

Sweat scraper for scraping off sweat and water.

# GIVING YOUR PONY A FULL GROOMING

*Tie the pony in a warm sheltered place.*

*Brush along the natural lie of the coat.*

*Scrape brush with curry comb to get oil off.*

Tie the pony up. If you are in the stable, pick it out so the pony won't tread in any manure. Then pick out the feet, being careful not to hurt the frog (see page 54). Check for any wounds.

Take off or fold back any blankets. Stand sideways to the pony, facing his tail and beside his neck. Brush lightly all over the neck and body with the dandy brush. Don't brush the head.

Then take the body brush in one hand and the metal curry comb in the other. Brush the pony firmly all over, leaning on the brush so it pushes through the coat to the skin.

To do the head, put the curry comb down and untie the pony so he doesn't pull back. Hold him by the nose as you gently body brush his head. Tie him up again.

Push the mane over to the "wrong" side of the neck. Body brush the exposed skin. Using a damp sponge, bring the mane back over in small sections.

Standing to one side, lift the tail and hold it out from the hindquarters. Brush it through, bit by bit, starting with the undermost layer. Brush down to the ends.

Carefully sponge the eyes with a little warm water. Change the water, then sponge the nose and lips. Wipe the dock with the dock sponge.

Polish the coat with the stable cloth to bring out its natural shine. Finish by painting each hoof inside and out with hoof oil (see pages 54-55).

## Grooming tips
* Groom soon after riding, once pony is dry. Skin is warm with open pores, so dirt comes off easily.
* Store grooming kit in a waterproof box.
* Don't use kit on more than one pony, as this spreads germs.
* Clean brushes weekly in a solution of dish soap and water. Rinse and dry.

51

## DEALING WITH WET OR MUDDY PONIES

Your pony's coat needs to be completely dry before you groom him, otherwise dirt and oil won't come out. If he lives at pasture, you should also dry him thoroughly before turning him out, or he may get a chill. After riding, always walk him for a while to cool down. Then dry him off like this.

Rub him dry with an old, clean towel before putting his blanket on. Make sure no moisture is trapped under there, or it could make him cold.

If he is very wet, get water off with the sweat scraper. Then cover his back and quarters with fresh straw and fasten a blanket on. This is called "thatching".

Hose muddy legs clean with warm water, then dry them. This stops the risk of scratches (see page 63). Let mud on the body dry, then brush it off.

## GROOMING PASTURE-KEPT PONIES

A pony at pasture should not be groomed very much, as the oil in his coat keeps him warm and dry. Most of the time, you only need to dandy brush him lightly before you ride. Get any mud off the saddle area and where the girth goes to stop it from rubbing and causing sores. Make sure these parts are dry.

Don't use a body brush, except on the head, mane and tail, as it takes oil out of the coat. Pick out and check the feet carefully, then sponge the face and dock. If your pony has a thick coat, feel through it to make sure he is not too thin underneath.

*Ponies at pasture groom themselves naturally by rolling, or by rubbing against a fence. They also groom each other, using their lips and teeth like this.*

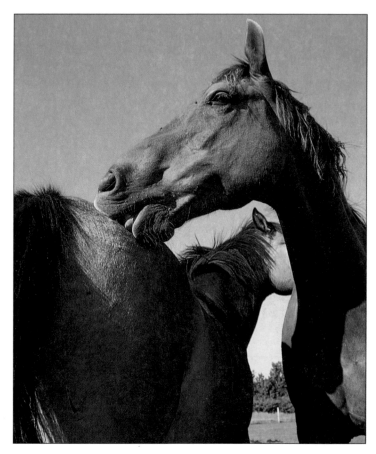

# EXTRA GROOMING

You can help to keep your pony in good shape by giving his biggest muscles an extra rubdown now and then. These are the ones that he works the most. The picture on the right shows you which ones to rub. It's best to give the pony his usual grooming first (see page 51). Then use the stable cloth to rub him down. He will probably enjoy it, but stop if he fidgets.

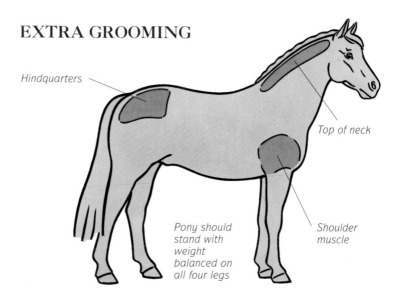

Hindquarters

Top of neck

Shoulder muscle

Pony should stand with weight balanced on all four legs

## PULLING THE MANE AND TAIL

You need to thin out, or "pull", the mane and tail every six weeks so they don't grow too bushy. It doesn't hurt the pony - his hair is much less sensitive than yours. Mane pulling is easier after exercise, when the pores of the skin are open.

To work on the mane, split it into small sections. Comb down the hairs in each section.

Hold the longest hairs and push the rest back with the comb. Tweak out the long hairs.

Only pull the top of the tail. Drape it over the stable door so you are safe if the pony kicks.

## QUARTERING: A QUICK GROOMING

If your pony lives inside, he may get dirty from lying in a mucky bed. Before riding out, you can clean him up quickly without taking his blanket off. This is called "quartering". Tie the pony up, fold the front half of his blanket back, and body brush his front. Fold the blanket back down. Do the same for his hindquarters. Use a damp dock sponge to get muck stains off, and dry wet patches with a stable cloth. Body brush and clean the face as usual. Pick stray bedding from the mane and tail and brush them. Wipe the dock, then carefully pick out the feet (see page 54), checking for loose nails.

Just undo the blanket and fold part of it back. Keep it on so that the pony stays warm.

53

# HOOFCARE AND SHOEING

Your pony's hooves are very important. They support his weight and take the shock of his movements. You need to look after them very carefully and be able to tell if they are healthy or not. You also need a good farrier to trim them and fit horseshoes.

## THE STRUCTURE OF THE HOOF

Hooves, like fingernails and hair, grow all the time, so they need regular trimming. The outer wall is hard and doesn't feel things, which is why shoeing doesn't hurt the pony. The sole is made of hard horn, but has a tender area beneath.

*The frog acts as a gripper and absorbs the shock of movement.*

*The white line is a layer of soft horn between the wall and sole. Farrier uses it to judge how far nails can go so they don't pierce sole.*

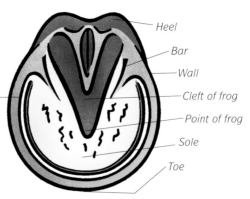

Heel
Bar
Wall
Cleft of frog
Point of frog
Sole
Toe

## LOOKING AFTER YOUR PONY'S FEET

You should pick out and check your pony's feet at least once a day, and two or three times if he is stabled and standing in a bed that may be damp and dirty. Always pick the feet out before and after a ride. Each time, check the feet inside and out as well. Tie the pony up to handle his feet, and then follow the steps on the right.

Fetlock

Run your hand down his leg to the fetlock. Grasp it and lift up, saying "Up." Lean on him so he shifts his weight off the foot.

Work from heel to toe, with the hoofpick pointing away from you. Scrape out all the dirt. Brush the frog gently with a hoof brush.

Nail
Sole
Wall

Check the sole for bruises or wounds, and the wall for cracks. See if the shoes are worn out. Check no nails are loose or sticking out.

*Brush should be wet but not dripping.*

Hooves need moisture to grow and stop them from cracking. Brush them inside and out sometimes with a stiff, wet brush.

Hoof oil

*Use a paintbrush.*

Oiling the feet seals in the moisture and makes them look good. Put plenty on the sole, so it soaks in. Then do the outside.

54

## WHEN DOES MY PONY NEED SHOES?

In the wild, ponies wear their feet down naturally as they roam. When ridden on hard surfaces, they need iron shoes to stop the hoof walls from wearing out too fast, and making their feet sore and damaged. With shoes on, the feet don't wear down naturally, so they need to be trimmed every four to six weeks.

The shoes may also need to be replaced. Make sure you get a qualified farrier for this work.

Try to get the same one each time as he will get to know exactly what your pony needs. Make sure your pony is ready when he comes. Bring him in, wash and dry his feet and legs and pick out his hooves. Prepare a hard, clean surface for him to stand on, preferably outside, where there is plenty of light.

## WHAT WILL THE FARRIER DO?

When you call the farrier, tell him whether your pony needs a set of brand-new shoes, or just the existing ones taken off, his feet trimmed, and the old shoes put back on.

When the farrier arrives, have your pony ready in a halter so you can hold him while the farrier works. The farrier may also ask you to lead your pony up and down so that he can see how he moves.

First, the farrier loosens the nails in the shoes. He can then take them off with pincers like this without tearing the pony's feet.

*Good fit checklist*
Before the farrier leaves, check that your pony's shoes fit properly. This list will help.

* Shoe must fit hoof, not hoof over-rasped to fit shoe.
* Shoe is the right weight and type for the pony.
* Hoof walls trimmed neatly.
* Clenches (nail tips) evenly spaced and level on hoof wall.
* Nailheads fit tightly in holes on shoe.
* No gaps between hoof and shoe.
* Heels of shoes cover heels of feet.
* Six to eight nails per shoe, depending on the pony and the farrier.

Next, he trims each foot, and lightly rasps the soles so that they are even. He looks closely at the shape and condition of the feet.

Then he either puts the old shoes back on, or fits new ones. The shoes are nailed into the hard, nerveless rim of the hoof.

# CLIPPING

For winter, your pony grows a thick, waterproof coat to keep him warm. If you are going to work him hard, it might be a good idea to have him clipped, but only if you have a heavy blanket and a stable. Clipping will prevent him from getting too hot and sweaty when he works, which could make him tired and ill. Never clip a pony yourself: it's a skilled job, so get an expert to do it.

## WHEN AND WHAT TYPE OF CLIP

Your pony's winter coat starts to grow from about September, so his first clip should be in October once most of this has grown in. After clipping, the coat goes on growing for a while, so he may need a second clip in December if he does a lot of work. Make sure you don't clip him after January, because that is when he grows his light coat for the summer, which doesn't need clipping. He should always have the right amount of coat to suit his work and the season.

The more work he does, the less coat he should have (but he will have to wear a blanket when he's resting). Below are three common types of clip.

*If your pony lives outside he needs plenty of coat left on. He may just need a trace clip. Ideally, you should wear a hard hat when helping.*

*Bib clip*

*The chest and throat are clipped.*

This type is ideal if the pony lives outside and does light work. He can winter out and may not need to be blanketed.

*Trace clip*

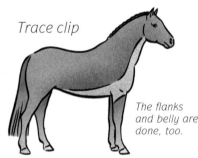

*The flanks and belly are done, too.*

This is fine for a hardy pony who winters out but is being competed. He will need a full, heavy blanket when resting.

*Blanket clip*

*Hair is left on the loins, back and legs.*

This type allows a hard-working pony to keep cool. He must be stabled at night, and fully blanketed when not being ridden.

# GETTING READY FOR CLIPPING

Two to three weeks before clipping, start working your pony so he sweats lightly, which keeps his coat clean. Keep him well groomed. Make sure you have the blankets he needs and that they fit (see pages 58-59). They should be clean and ready to use. You will need one to keep the pony warm during clipping.

*On the day checklist*
● Tie the pony's mane in rubber bands. Groom him so he is clean and dry.
● Put up his bed and sweep the floor. Let it dry. Put straw down, or rubber matting if you have it.
● Make sure stall is well-lit and free from drafts.
● Remove water from stall to avoid electric shocks.

● If you are helping, wear close-fitting clothes, and tie long hair back so nothing gets caught in the clippers.
● Wear rubber-soled shoes to reduce the risk of shocks, and a hard hat for safety.

## HOW A PONY IS TRACE CLIPPED

*Clipping starts at shoulder.*

So the pony doesn't startle at the sudden noise and feel of the clippers, they are first turned on away from him, then turned off and lain on his shoulder. They are then taken off, switched on again, and part of his neck is clipped.

Once the pony settles down, the flanks and belly are done. The clippers are always worked against the lie of the coat. You can help by holding each of the front legs forward in turn, so the skin doesn't get caught in the clippers.

The top half of the neck and the hairs under his head are done last, when he is really settled, so he is less likely to act up about clippers near his head. You can help to soothe him by putting your hand on his nose and speaking to him.

## CARING FOR A CLIPPED PONY

Once your pony is clipped, body brush him to massage his skin and get oil and loose hair off. Check that he hasn't been nicked by the clippers. Shake his blanket out and put it back on.

Brush out his mane and tail and wipe his face and dock to get hairs off. If he lives outside, put him in a blanket (see page 58). Make sure he has shelter (see page 38).

*If his head is clipped, a hood will keep him snug and warm.*

# BLANKETS

Blankets are used to keep ponies warm if they have had their coats clipped, or live outside all through the winter. A blanket is also useful if a pony is very wet, as it helps him get warm and dry off more quickly. Blankets also protect a pony's coat and keep it looking good.

## NEW ZEALAND BLANKETS

As long as they have shelter, ponies that live outside most of the year only need a New Zealand blanket. This is a very hard-wearing, waterproof canvas or nylon blanket which fastens with straps across the pony's chest and between his hindlegs, so that it doesn't come off or stop him from moving freely. If you can, have two so that you can keep a clean, spare one for when the other gets wet and dirty in bad weather.

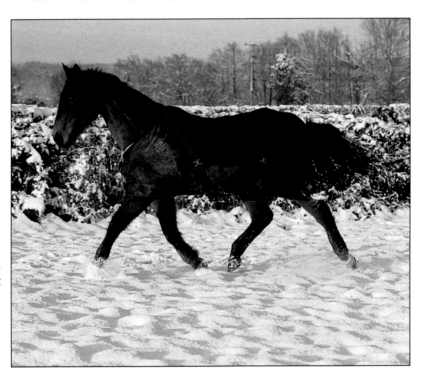

## OTHER TYPES OF BLANKETS

A stable blanket is warm and quilted. It is easy to wash and can be worn day and night. It is suitable for a pony who lives in most of the time and is clipped in winter. You can buy these blankets in different weights and thicknesses.

A sweat sheet is made of mesh so that the air or sweat can evaporate through the holes. You can put it under a summer sheet (see right) to let a hot, sweaty pony cool off gradually, without catching a chill.

A summer sheet is a lightweight cotton or linen sheet. It's good for keeping flies and dust off a stabled, groomed pony, or for protecting a pasture-kept pony from insects in hot weather. It's handy for traveling to shows, too.

# HOW TO PUT ON A NEW ZEALAND BLANKET

Tie the pony up. Fold the blanket into quarters and stand with it at the pony's left shoulder. Stroke him so he knows you are there. Gently put the blanket on his back and unfold it.

*Blanket should lie straight and flat.*

The blanket should cover the withers at the front, and the quarters at the back. Stand behind the pony, slightly to one side. Check that the middle seam lies along the spine.

If the blanket is too far forward, pull it toward the tail. If it is too far back, lift it rather than pulling it, so that you don't rub the pony's hair in the wrong direction under the blanket.

When the blanket is in place, fasten the surcingles (the straps around his belly) so the blanket will stay on if he moves. Buckle the chest straps, making sure they are not too tight.

Next, buckle the leg straps. Fasten the left one around the left leg, then thread the right strap through the left before fastening it around the right leg. This stops the blanket from slipping.

*Blanketing tips*
* Before buying, measure pony from middle of chest to under tail. Give details to saddler who will tell you the size you need.
* Choose the best quality blanket you can afford.
* Check blanket twice a day to see straps are fastened, it has not slipped or torn, and isn't rubbing.
* At night, take off blanket, shake it out, then reblanket so pony is comfortable.

## A WELL-FITTING BLANKET

*Reaches in front of the withers.*

*Fits snugly around the shoulders so it doesn't slip back and cut into the withers.*

*Is not too tight around the neck. It must not press on the throat even when the pony puts his neck down to graze.*

*Wraps under the girth without wrinkling the skin at the elbows.*

*Is not too long. It mustn't drag backward or it presses on the throat and spine.*

*Is long enough at the sides to cover the pony's flanks.*

*Reaches the top of the tail.*

# CLEANING TACK

It's important to clean your tack regularly; if possible, after every ride. It must be washed, dried and rubbed with saddle soap to keep it supple. Never use ordinary soap, which makes leather dry and stiff. If you are pushed for time, you can just wipe it over with a damp cloth, as long as you clean the bit properly, and clean everything thoroughly once a week.

## WHAT YOU NEED

Two sponges, one for washing and one for soaping the leather

A bar of saddle soap

A bucket for water

A chamois leather for drying the leather

Metal polish and a cloth for applying polish

A cloth for buffing (rubbing the metal until it shines)

A stable cloth or dish towel for holding the metal parts so you don't smudge them

A blunt knife for getting off blobs of oil or caked dirt

A matchstick for getting soap out of buckle holes

## WASHING TACK

To wash the saddle, put it on a saddle rack and take off the girth, stirrup leathers and irons, and buckleguards. Never put it in water: this makes the stuffing all lumpy. Wipe it all over with a damp sponge dipped in warm water. Dry it with a chamois. Scrub fabric girths with mild soap and water. Rinse well.

Take the bridle apart. Wash each piece with a damp sponge, and dry it.

## CLEANING METAL

You need to wash and then polish the metal parts, except for the bit, which should only be washed. Take the stirrup irons off their leathers, pull the treads out and wash the dirt off with warm soapy water. Dry them, then put the polish on. Buff them with the clean cloth to make them shine. Put the treads back in and fasten the irons on to the leathers. Take the bit off the bridle and wash it thoroughly in very hot water. Don't use soap, or your pony will get upset by the taste when you put the bit in his mouth. Dry it carefully.

*Cleaning your tack is a good chance to check it for wear and tear, too.*

# SOAPING THE SADDLE AND BRIDLE

Put the dry saddle on the saddle rack. Dip the soap in warm water, then rub it on the soaping sponge. This should be just damp so you don't get too much foam on the sponge.

*Don't dip the sponge in the water.*

Moving the sponge in small circles, rub soap into the whole saddle. Resoap the sponge as you go. Make sure saddle parts that touch the pony, such as the flaps, are well soaped.

*Do the underside of the flaps too.*

Cover the saddle with a clean dish towel and hang it on a saddle bracket on the wall. Then soap the stirrup leathers and the girth if it is leather. Hang all these up to dry.

Lay all the pieces of the bridle out neatly on a clean table and put the bit to one side (remember not to soap this). Put some saddle soap on your damp sponge as you did before.

Starting with the headpiece, wrap the sponge around each strap. Grip it firmly, and pull the sponge down the strap several times in a strong, stroking movement.

When each piece is done, put the bridle back together (see right). Check that hooks face in and buckles face out, and that the noseband is inside the cheekpieces.

*Hang bridle up once it is cleaned.*

# PUTTING THE BRIDLE BACK TOGETHER

Headpiece
Browband
Cheekpieces
Throat latch
Hook

Take the headpiece so the throat latch is on your left. Thread it through the browband.

Fasten the buckles of the cheekpieces to the headpiece. The hooks should be at the bottom.

Noseband
Bit
Reins

Attach the bit to the cheekpieces using the hooks. Make sure the bit is curving upward.

Thread the noseband through the browband, underneath the headpiece. Fasten the reins to the bit.

# HEALTH AND FIRST AID

To keep your pony healthy, visit him twice a day, and make sure you check him over at least once daily. As you get to know him, you will soon be able to tell if he is not well. It's always worth calling the vet if you're worried, but it helps if you already know how to recognize signs of illness (some common ones are shown opposite). Make sure you also have a good first aid kit.

## IN GOOD HEALTH

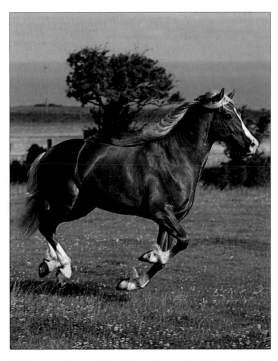

*This pony shows all the signs of good health: gleaming eyes, ears pricked forward, a glossy coat and lots of bounding energy.*

A healthy pony looks alert and at ease with himself. He has bright, clear eyes, and he pricks and moves his ears whenever he hears a sound. He should look neither too lean or "ribby", nor so fat that he can't get around without puffing. His coat should look sleek and shiny when groomed.

*Signs of illness*
* Head droops.
* Body held awkwardly, or "tucked up".
* Ears lying flat and still.
* Dull eyes with bright red rims.
* Discharge from nostrils or eyes.
* Dull coat with no shine or "bloom".
* Sweating or shivering when he hasn't been worked.
* Tail tucked into body.
* Lack of interest in surroundings.
* Doesn't eat properly.
* Hot or swollen limbs.
* No droppings passed, or sloppy droppings.

## FIRST AID KIT

Gauze bandage for dressing wounds

Cotton for cleaning wounds

Antiseptic solution, cream or powder, for putting on wounds

Petroleum jelly for when you use the thermometer, and for bald patches on skin

Several bandages for wounds

Sterile gauze for placing on wounds
Poultice for soothing wounds

Round-ended surgical scissors

Thermometer

Fly repellent

Small clean bucket for washing wounds

Clean, clearly marked container (a box, cupboard or drawer)

Tape for fastening bandages

List of items in the kit, so you can check that you have them

62

# COLIC

| Illness | Causes | Signs | What to do |
|---------|--------|-------|------------|
| This is very bad tummy ache. Colic can usually be cured very quickly with medication, but you should call the vet at once if you think your pony has it. If the pony tries to roll to stop the pain, he can twist his gut and die. | It can come from overfeeding, or from having worms, or from exercising the pony right after feeding him. | Sweating<br><br>Swishing tail<br><br>Biting or kicking at belly with hind foot<br><br>Pawing the ground<br><br>Rolling or trying to roll a lot<br><br>Unsettled, shifting from foot to foot, groaning | Call the vet at once<br><br>If pony is lying still, don't move him<br><br>If he is restless or thrashes around, keep him moving gently and keep him warm.<br><br>Don't let him roll |

# LAMINITIS

| Illness | Causes | Signs | What to do |
|---------|--------|-------|------------|
| This is a very painful fever in the feet caused by inflammation in the tender parts just behind the hoof wall.<br><br>Laminitis needs to be treated by a vet, especially as it may keep coming back if it goes untreated for too long. | It happens if the pony eats too much rich grass or concentrates, which can release poisons into the blood which stop it from circulating properly in the feet.<br><br>Cross-section view of hoof<br><br>This part becomes inflamed | Very hot, painful hooves<br><br>Pony moves unevenly, becoming very lame as illness worsens<br><br>Pony stands with his front legs stuck stiffly out, taking his weight on his heels<br><br>May run a temperature<br><br>Seems upset and very restless | Call the vet<br><br>Only give hay and water<br><br>Soak feet in cold water<br><br>Make a deep shavings bed which is soft on the feet but pony can't eat |

# SCRATCHES

| Illness | Causes | Signs | What to do |
|---------|--------|-------|------------|
| This is a nasty illness where the skin on the heels cracks, gets infected and the cracking spreads up the legs. These become hot, swollen and covered in scabs. In bad cases, scratches can cause lameness.<br><br>You can prevent it if you make sure your pony is on well-drained land if he lives outside. Cover his legs with barrier cream. | Standing on muddy, damp ground for long periods chaps the skin. It then gets sore and scabby, the hair falls out and germs get in through the wounds, causing scratches. | Skin on heels gets red, tender and cracked<br><br>Hot, swollen legs<br><br>Scabs on legs | Wash affected skin with warm, medicated water<br><br>Dry very thoroughly<br><br>May need to clip hair off the affected area<br><br>Ask vet about which ointment to apply<br><br>If bad, get vet to see pony |

# SHOWING

## Contents

# WHAT IS SHOWING?

In a showing competition, ponies are judged mainly on how they look, behave, and move. The competition is divided into different types of classes, organized according to type, breed, size and age of pony. Showing your pony to look his best is great fun and an excellent way of improving his condition and manners.

*In a showing class the judge looks for the pony which most closely matches the standard for that type of class.*

## WHAT IS SHOWING FOR?

Showing classes are a way of improving pony types. By encouraging people to breed ponies that match a set standard, they keep the breeds at their peak.

These classes are also a way for pony breeders to show off their ponies and to keep in touch with other people who breed, buy and sell quality ponies.

It's a good way to see the different types of ponies you can buy. Watching how a class is judged also helps you to see what to look for in a good quality pony.

# DIFFERENT TYPES OF SHOWING CLASSES

There are many types of showing classes. This book concentrates on ridden ones, where you ride your pony, then dismount and unsaddle so that the judge can look closely at him. These are the most popular for children. There are also model classes, where ponies are just shown "in-hand".

Top-level showing is a big business, but the huge range of classes means that there is something for everyone to enter. The ones below are popular in the US and Great Britain.

*Leading-rein classes are for young children who can ride but still need a little help. The ponies are usually under 12.2hh.*

## Show and Riding ponies
These are finely bred ponies who are usually part-Thoroughbred. They are judged on their conformation (see pages 68-69), gaits and manners. They are very beautiful, but not as strong as other types.

## Show Hunter ponies
These are heavier, sturdier ponies than the riding ones, which should be strong enough to be ridden out hunting. You are expected to show them at a walk, trot, canter and gallop.

## Working/Working Hunter pony
These ponies are slightly heavier and have less refined features than Show Hunters. In working classes you ride over a short course of about eight jumps and the pony is also judged on his conformation.

## Mountain and Moorland
These are for pure- or part-bred ponies of the nine British Native pony breeds. Native ponies are not braided (see page 84) and the judge looks for a pony who is beautiful, as well as strong and well-built.

# A SHOW-QUALITY PONY

An important quality for a pony in a showing class is his conformation, or how he is made. In most classes, the judge takes this into account, because the pony's physical characteristics play such an important part in how he moves and what he will be able to do when you ride him. Other vital qualities are described opposite.

## KEY POINTS OF CONFORMATION

This is a Working Hunter pony with excellent conformation. The labels around the picture tell you more about what a judge would look for.

*The head must be a good size so that the pony can balance well when he moves, and looks in proportion.*

*The neck should be nicely arched and strong, but not too thick. You can improve its outline by braiding (see pages 84-85).*

*The quarters should be strong and well-muscled.*

*Large, dark, liquid eyes make the face more expressive.*

*Large, wide nostrils.*

*The withers should not be too high or low.*

*The back should be a good length, with a slight dip.*

*The tail should be fairly full, and properly presented (see pages 77 and 86).*

*The shoulder should slope back well into the body.*

*The pony's front should be broad, with plenty of room for the heart and lungs.*

*The forelegs should be straight and clean, with good, strong bones. Ideally, the pony should stand so that he does not lean forward as much as this.*

*The girth should be deep.*

*The hocks must neither turn out ("bow" hocks), nor in ("cow" hocks).*

*The knees should be flat and in line with the rest of the leg (not bending forward or sloping back).*

*The hindlegs should be made in such a way that the buttock, hock and back of the lower leg form a straight line down to the ground.*

*The feet should be neat, even, well-shaped and, of course, sound.*

# WHAT THE JUDGE LOOKS FOR

The judge looks at the pony both to get an overall impression of his "outline", or shape, and then again in detail to examine specific parts of his body. She looks for the pony to be well-proportioned and symmetrical, with both sides of the body even and matching. Show ponies should be in fine condition with a good "top line", that is, lots of muscle on the top of the neck and hindquarters, but not fat. Few ponies, if any, have perfect conformation, but every pony, no matter what

*The judge looks for a pony in perfect health, with gleaming eyes, sound feet, and well-presented mane and tail (see pages 84-86).*

his type of background and breeding, has a certain amount of potential. With good care and training, you can greatly improve his condition and appearance. The fitness program and exercises on pages 72-75 will help to develop movement and muscles.

## OTHER IMPORTANT QUALITIES

*Temperament*
All show ponies must behave with perfect manners in the pressurized atmosphere of the show ring and in company. No matter how beautiful a pony is, he will not win if he misbehaves or shows a mean temper. Make sure your pony is ready for the experiences he will have in the ring, and train him well (see pages 72-75).

*Movement*
In ridden classes, the judge asks you both to ride and to "show your pony in-hand" (lead him), so that she can see how he moves. Any faults in his action mean that he will be marked down. Your pony must have a nice, straight action in his legs. Special exercises and training (see pages 72-75) can help to improve his suppleness, too.

*Presence*
This is the "star" quality that makes a pony show himself off and draw every eye to him. Presence can't be taught, but as much of it comes from confidence, you can improve it with lots of practice. With time and experience, you may find that your pony is placed higher, because you both know what you are doing and it shows.

# CAN I SHOW MY PONY?

It may be daunting at first to think about showing your own pony, but he does not have to be really glamorous-looking to be worth entering for a class. There are plenty of classes where what counts most is how good a ride your pony is, rather than what he looks like. Getting ready for one of these gives you lots of riding practice and spurs you on to get him into tip-top condition.

## HOW TO FIND OUT ABOUT SHOWS

First, visit a few shows to see what goes on. You will learn a lot about what the judges are looking for, what you have to do, and which would be the best class for you to try. If you belong to a riding or pony club, it will probably hold shows during the year, and you can get newsletters, prize lists or premium books giving you details. You can often get showing schedules from pony magazines or from tack shops, too. Once you have visited a few shows yourself, it's worth taking your pony along just to watch, to get some experience of the crowded, noisy and colorful world of the show, without the nerves and tension of having to perform himself. Start at a local show, where there will be fewer classes and lots of other people who are just starting out.

## WHICH CLASS TO GO IN FOR

The class you choose depends entirely on what type of pony you have and how experienced you both are. The categories vary from show to show, and from country to country. When you visit a show, see which ponies look most like yours and whether what they do is something you think you could manage. To find out the exact requirements for the class, ask your riding instructor, write to the pony or breed societies or contact the American Horse Show Assoc., 220 E. 42nd St., Ste. 409, New York, NY 10017. Opposite is what you have to do in some popular classes.

*If you and a friend have ponies that look similar and work well together, you could enter a Pairs class, where you ride in unison.*

# WHAT YOU WILL HAVE TO DO

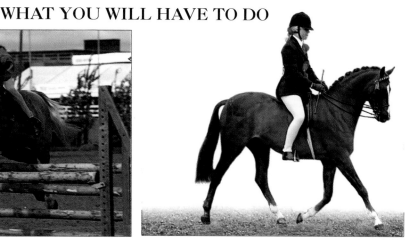

*Working Hunter pony classes*
You ride a short course of about eight jumps. The pony is judged on whether he clears the fences and on his style: he should jump boldly and eagerly, rather than being "sticky" (trying to stop). If you go clear, you put him through his gaits in a group, and then show him in-hand (see page 95).

*Show and Riding pony classes*
You ride your pony at a walk, trot and canter, and at a slightly lengthened canter (see page 74). Then you line up and do an individual show, followed by showing the pony in-hand, as in a Working pony class. Show Hunter ponies have to do the same things, but you also have to ride them at a controlled gallop.

*Pony Club or Family pony classes*
If you are just starting out and have a good all-around pony who is not particularly beautiful, it is worth trying these classes. Your pony is judged on how he performs when ridden rather than on his looks. He may have to jump a small jump, and a Family pony should be suitable for someone else in your family as well as you.

*Tack and turnout classes*
You are judged on how well you have "turned out", or presented, your pony. Your tack must be in excellent condition, correct for the show ring (see pages 80-83), and perfectly clean, and you and your pony must also look polished. He should be turned out with neatly braided mane and pulled or braided tail (see pages 84-86).

# SCHOOLING AND FITNESS

To enter for any class your pony must be glowing with health, which includes being moderately fit. You should build up his fitness gradually, over about eight weeks, and you can combine this with exercises to improve his manners and action. It's a good idea to practice a routine which includes riding transitions and cantering on each lead (see page 74).

## WHAT THE JUDGE LOOKS FOR

It is vital that your pony is obedient and completely under your control. He must also have excellent self-carriage. This means that he carries most of his weight on his hocks, instead of leaning on his forelegs, and that he has good balance, rhythm and impulsion (see below). Some other important points are shown on the right. Your pony will also do well if he looks alert and confident, and moves with a supple, fluent action.

*The pony is taking lots of weight on his hindquarters. His hocks are engaged, that is, well under him, instead of trailing behind.*

*His neck is curved from the withers to the poll.*

*He has plenty of impulsion, pushing forward from his hindlegs.*

*He is "on the bit" (see showing terms below).*

*He moves with a straight action, not crooked.*

*Showing terms*
* Balance: pony's ability to keep his weight and his rider's equally on all four legs, throughout transitions (changing from one gait to another), turns and circles.
* Rhythm: pony moves with regular, even steps.
* Impulsion: energy from the hindquarters that passes through the pony.
* Light on forehand: carrying most of the weight on the hindquarters rather than the forelegs.
* Extension: lengthening stride and using lots of impulsion.
* On the bit: pony accepts the rider's contact well.

### FITNESS PROGRAM

| | |
|---|---|
| Weeks one and two: | *Start with half-hour sessions of riding at a walk. Build up to two-hour stints as stamina improves.* |
| Weeks three and four: | *Introduce short periods of trotting work. Then increase the distance you go. Start "hill work" - trotting up hills.* |
| Weeks five and six: | *Work on obedience (see opposite). Introduce transitions and working in circles covering half the arena. Start with 20-minute sessions, and gradually increase the time. Combine this with hacking. Start canter work (see opposite).* |
| Weeks seven and eight: | *Continue hacking and schooling at the walk, trot and canter. Try lengthening strides at the trot and canter. Start work on your individual show (see page 74) and jumping, if needed.* |

*Pasture-kept ponies can be fit enough for weekend shows if ridden four times a week for one to one-and-a-half hours. Stabled ponies need one-and-a-half-hour sessions six days a week.*

# IMPROVING OBEDIENCE

Your first goal should be to get your pony going forward smoothly by using your legs, and stopping him from your seat. Practice plenty of transitions, as shown on the right, all around the ring or field. To keep the pony flexible, vary the direction and make sure you don't go on the outside track all the time.

*Walk* *Halt* *Trot* Start by going from a walk to halt to trot.

*Trot* *Walk* *Trot* Then try trot to walk to trot.

Then trot to walk to halt and straight into a trot again.

*Trot* *Walk* *Halt* *Trot*

## RHYTHM

Next, work on establishing a good rhythm for your pony's movement. Find his natural stride (called "working him in his own pace"). Don't rush him or let him get lazy, and make sure he is using his hindquarters. Try riding to music as you school. Choose music that has a steady beat that suits his natural action.

## IMPROVING YOUR PONY'S BEND

This means that the pony curves his body around your inside leg and looks in the direction he is moving. Start by riding in circles around half the arena at a walk or trot. Circle to both left and right. Then move on to serpentines (see right). Keep his pace smooth and rhythmic. Make sure he always bends to the inside.

*This pony is bending well.*

*A serpentine is three loops of equal size.*

## WORKING AT A CANTER

The key to a balanced canter is to make sure your pony always leads with his inside foreleg. You change direction as you move around the ring, so you must be able to make him change leads. To canter, start from a sitting trot. Keeping your rein contact, put your inside leg on the girth and your outside leg behind it. To change leads, practice the exercise shown on the right.

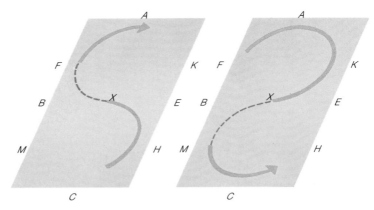

*Canter to the left, with left foreleg leading, from H to X. Trot, then re-establish right lead canter at F.*

*Canter past A, then turn from K to X. Change leads by trotting at X, and re-establishing left lead canter at M.*

# A SUGGESTED PRACTICE ROUTINE

In under saddle classes in Britain, riders have to line up and do an individual show. This is not done in the US, but it's a good practice routine for your pony. It should include putting the pony through all his gaits, riding transitions and cantering on each lead. These pictures show a typical UK individual show.

1. Rides out of the line at a walk and halts next to the judge.

2. Walks on, to the edge of the ring, then turns left and goes into a rising trot.

3. Trots the pony in a figure-eight in front of the line-up.

4. Finishes the figure-eight, and establishes a left-lead canter, making sure the pony leads with the correct inside leg.

Throughout your pattern, keep your pony going forward in his natural rhythm and in a balanced way. Make sure that he bends correctly (see page 73). Once he is going well, you should find that he automatically accepts your contact and is on the bit.

5. Completes half the figure, then changes leads by trotting for a few strides, before re-establishing the canter on the right lead as he turns back.

6. Canters another half of the figure, then trots in order to change leads again into a left canter.

7. Rides behind the line to use as much of the arena as possible. Makes the pony lengthen his stride but doesn't go into a flat-out gallop.

To ride an extended canter, maintain the rhythm, and close your legs on his sides to encourage him to take longer, lower steps. Don't let his action become too long and fast though, or he will go too much on his forehand, which will unbalance him.

8. Slows smoothly back to a collected (shorter strides) canter, then to a trot, and then a walk.

9. Turns in next to the judge, facing the line-up, and halts. Salutes by touching the brim of the hat.

10. Gives the pony a long rein and walks him behind the other ponies back to his place in the line-up.

# SCHOOLING OVER JUMPS FOR WORKING CLASSES

When practicing, try to jump very actively, but with an even rhythm, rather than making your pony collect or lengthen his stride a lot as he does in show jumping. Jump logs and other natural obstacles when out riding. Practice clearing courses smoothly, as marks are given for the pony's jumping style as well as for going clear. You will only have to jump one round, over about eight rustic, fairly solid jumps, laid out in a flowing course with no sharp turns.

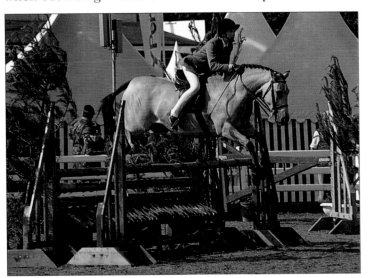

*The jumps in a Working Hunter class are made to look rustic, so that they are fairly similar to obstacles you might jump when out hunting.*

## General schooling tips

* Ideally, build up fitness during the summer break by riding every day.
* Keep schooling sessions short - about 30 minutes - and don't let your pony get bored or overtired.
* Keep to a plan of what you hope to achieve, but vary the activity. Try riding new routes or changing the direction you ride in, so he doesn't get set in his ways.
* Ride in different places, so he won't be spooked at the show.
* Ride with friends and their ponies so that he gets used to concentrating in company. Friends can advise you on how you perform.
* Pay attention to the details of what your pony does and to your position.
* Finish on a success not a failure (ponies have long memories).

# YOUR PONY'S DIET AND HEALTH

Feeding is a very important part of getting your pony into peak condition for showing. You need to feed him in the usual way, and increase the amount of energy food he has as you ask him to do more work. Exactly what you give him depends on his temperament and tastes, but try to find a balance that improves his condition and gives him a shiny coat without making him too

frisky. You can buy ready mixed feeds or mix your own. Good foods for a showing diet include linseed, barley, sugar beet and oil supplements.

## Checklist for health

* Get your pony clipped if he needs it.
* Have his shoes checked every six weeks.
* Make sure he has had his vaccinations and is wormed.
* Start to increase the amount of grooming you do to improve his skin, coat and muscle tone.
* Try not to wash him more than once a week for a grey, or monthly if he is dark.

# GROOMING FOR A SHOW

Regular grooming is a vital part of getting your pony ready to show. Make sure your daily routine includes the tasks shown below, and do all of these really thoroughly the day before the show. Washing and trimming are best done about three days before, to keep his coat from looking too fluffy on the day. Turn to page 79 for tips on last-minute finishing touches.

*Use your fingers to tease out knots in the mane and tail, and remove any bedding or grass. Practice braiding the mane well in advance.*

*Body brush firmly all over.*

*Get mud and loose hair off with the dandy brush.*

*Pick out the hooves.*

*Sponge the eyes, nose and bottom with separate sponges.*

*Polish up the coat with a rub rag, to make it really glossy.*

*Paint hooves with hoof oil.*

## WASHING YOUR PONY

Hose his mane, body and legs, and sponge his head. Dilute some shampoo in water in the bucket and rub it all over the coat until you get a good lather. Don't get any in his eyes.

Rinse thoroughly, using the hose for his body and a sponge for his head. Scrape off water from his body with a sweatscraper, and comb excess water from his mane.

Put on a sweat sheet and walk him around until dry. If it's windy, add a blanket so that he doesn't get a chill. Put on blankets and bandages (see pages 87-89) when you bed him down.

# WASHING THE TAIL

Stand slightly to one side. Plunge his tail into a bucket full of warm water mixed with pony shampoo. Rub some shampoo into the top of the tail.

Put the bucket down and run both hands down the length of the tail. Squeeze it little by little to get extra water out. Don't twist it as this is bad for the hair.

Rub the tail together between your hands to get the dirt out, or use a sponge. Dip the tail in the soapy water now and then to keep loosening the dirt.

*Washing tips*
* Wash as little as possible. Pasture-kept ponies need the oil in their coats.
* Only wash on a warm day.
* Choose a sheltered spot.
* Have blankets handy to keep him warm.
* Use special pony shampoo from a saddler's or tack shop.
* Don't get shampoo or water in his eyes and nose.
* Add coat gloss for shine but avoid the saddle area.

When the tail feels clean, rinse it thoroughly with a hose. Separate the strands carefully with your fingers to check that there is no soap left.

To dry the tail, stand to one side. Take hold of the hair below the tail bone. Make sure you don't hold the bone. Whirl the hair like a propeller until it is dry.

# DAY-TO-DAY TAIL CARE AND TRIMMING

Thick tails look much nicer than thin ones, and pasture-kept ponies need full tails to give them some protection from flies and bad weather. You also need plenty of hair in the tail if you are going to braid it (see page 86). To keep a tail thick, don't comb it except for shows. Instead, just run your fingers through it to get any tangles or stray bedding out, or use a very soft body brush.

To trim it, get a friend to trot the pony out to see how high he naturally carries it. Try to trim so it hangs 8-10cm (3-4in) above his fetlocks when carried.

*Bunch hair tightly together.*

Lift the tail to the right length by putting your arm under the dock. Run your other hand down to just above where you will cut, and snip straight across.

# TRIMMING HAIRY PONIES

Many ponies are quite hairy and look much better if you trim the extra hairs that grow on the ears, face (the jaw and throat), and legs. Before trimming any part of your pony, check the details of the breed or class standard. Welsh ponies, for example, should never be trimmed as they are always shown in their natural state with long, flowing manes and tails.

*Shetland ponies are not trimmed.*

*Checklist*
* Use round-ended scissors.
* Tie the pony up with a quick-release knot so you can manage him if he gets fed-up and fidgety.
* When working on his head, fasten the halter around his neck. Tie the lead rope loosely to string attached to a wall ring. Use a slip knot that can be undone quickly if he panics and pulls back.

## The face

To trim this, use the scissors at an upward slant. Be very careful not to catch any of his skin in the scissors. It may help to put one hand on his nose (see above). Snip off long hairs under his chin, too.

## The ears

Never trim a lot of hair from here - ears are very sensitive. Hold the sides of each ear together with one hand to stop loose hair from falling in. With the other, snip off the hairs that stick out. You could use ear clippers.

## The mane

Never try to shorten the mane with scissors, but you may want to cut a small notch immediately behind the ears for the headpiece to sit in snugly. This shouldn't be more than about 3cm (1in) wide.

## The legs

If your pony has very hairy legs, it's best to trim them so that you get a smooth, clean look. It shows you how to do this on the right. It can be hard to get an even finish, so you may need to ask an adult for help.

To remove hair from the fetlocks and the backs of the legs, draw the hair up

*Fetlock*

and away from the leg with a mane comb. Snip off any that comes through the comb at a slight slant, so it isn't jagged.

*Coronet*

Trim stray hairs growing over the front of his hooves (the coronets), to make a smooth, neat line where the hoof joins the leg.

# QUARTER MARKINGS AND SHARK'S TEETH

These patterns are brushed onto the hindquarters and flanks to make them look prettier and better-shaped. You make them by brushing the hair at different angles, to create contrasting patches of light and dark on the coat. Quarter markings are squares or diamonds which you can put on with a special stencil. Shark's teeth are a zigzag effect, brushed on by hand.

*These patterns will only show up on a pony with a sparkling clean coat.*

For quarter marking, dampen the coat with a sponge and lay the stencil over it. If you can, ask a friend to hold the stencil still while you work.

With a body brush, brush the hair downward. Then slowly peel away the stencil. Be careful not to smudge the pattern. Spray with hairspray.

For shark's teeth, brush the coat as usual, with a damp body brush. Then make several even strokes at a sharper angle upward, as shown, to create dark zigzags.

## WHITE COATS AND MARKINGS

Grey ponies and those with white tails need to look really clean: a yellow tail, or grubby patches, spoil the whole appearance. Wash a grey the day before the show and blanket him well to stop his coat from getting fluffy and soiled. Wash his tail too, and put it in an old stocking to keep it clean overnight.

*Rub chalk or baby powder into a white tail to make it look dazzling white.*

# TACK AND TURNOUT

There are important rules about the tack and clothes you are allowed to use in showing classes. Show tack helps to get the pony to move as he should for his class, and to improve his appearance in lots of ways without being too fussy or impractical. When you are starting out, you can probably manage with your usual tack, but as you advance you may need a double bridle.

## THE SADDLE

An ordinary general-purpose saddle is fine for most beginners' classes, but for other ridden classes it's best to use a straight-cut saddle. These have flaps which slope back slightly and show off the pony's shoulder better. They also have a flat seat which fits snugly to the pony's back so that it doesn't spoil his top line (see page 69). They are cut so that you ride with a longer leg. Working Hunter saddles have knee rolls to grip when jumping. Leather saddles are preferred.

*In Working Hunter classes, tack and turnout should be as plain and workman-like as possible. This rider and pony are correctly dressed for a Working Hunter pony class.*

### Girths

*A girth which doesn't match stands out and spoils the flow of a pony's outline.*

*A matching girth blends in and creates an uninterrupted outline.*

*White girth for greys.*

*Brown girth for chestnuts and light bays.*

*Black girth for dark bays, browns and blacks.*

As well as fitting correctly, your girth should ideally match your pony's coat closely (see right) so that it doesn't look as if it divides the pony in half (see above). But if your pony has a long body use a lighter-colored girth to make him look shorter.

# THE DOUBLE BRIDLE

Although snaffle bridles are most common in US showing classes, double bridles are also sometimes worn. Here's how to put one together and use it.

*Bridoon crownpiece*

*Bridoon*

*Curb bit*

*Lipstrap*

*Put your bridle together as usual but with a curb bit and chain. Attach the thinner set of reins to the lower rings of the curb.*

*Fasten the bridoon bit to its own crownpiece. Thread this through the browband so it fastens on the pony's right.*

*Attach the thicker reins to the rings of the bridoon. The lipstrap should thread through the small ring in the middle of the curb chain.*

*In the US colored browbands are discouraged.*

A double bridle has two bits: a bridoon, which makes the pony raise his head, and a curb which encourages him to flex more from the poll and bring his nose down and in. When used together, the two bits give you more control over his action. The key to using a double bridle well is to make sure it is fitted by an expert and that you ride mainly on the gentler bridoon. You can do this by holding the reins correctly (see right). Only use the curb when you need more control.

*The bridoon is a small type of snaffle bit which has a gentle action.*

*The bridoon should fit just behind the curb. Hold the reins crossed as shown with your little finger between the two.*

*To ride on the bridoon, keep your hands at the same angle all the time, so that the curb stays straight.*

*The curb has a chain which fastens around the chin groove, making a pony flex his neck.*

*To use the curb, apply pressure to the thinner rein by tilting your hands as shown. The curb action starts once the bit is at 45° to the pony's mouth.*

*The chain tightens and presses on the chin groove; the cheekpieces stretch, putting pressure on the poll; so the pony flexes his neck bringing his head in.*

# CHOOSING THE RIGHT NOSEBAND

The best choice of noseband is the cavesson. These come in many different widths and designs which can greatly improve your pony's looks, so choose one that suits your pony's face. In the U.S., a judge will penalize ponies ridden in other types of nosebands. Some countries, however, do allow the use of a flash or grakle with a snaffle bridle, in Working Hunter classes.

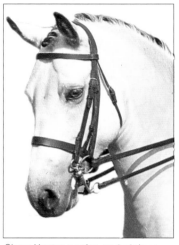

*Show, Riding and Arab ponies look best in narrow nosebands with detailed stitching.*

*Show Hunter ponies and plainer heads need broad, unfussy nosebands.*

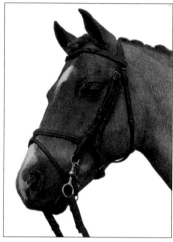

*A flash noseband gives more control and can occasionally be used in Working classes.*

## REINS AND OTHER TACK

Choose reins that you can grasp comfortably, so you are free to think about the way you are riding.

Reins that are too narrow mean that you won't feel in control. Ones that are too wide make it difficult for you to feel the contact sensitively.

Laced leather reins have a good grip and are preferred, but plain ones can also be used.

*Plain leather rein*

*Laced leather rein*

*The reins fastened to the bridoon bit are wider than the curb reins so that you can tell them apart without looking.*

*Tack tips*
* To make the bridle really glossy, use boot polish the same color as the leather to clean the top side of each strap, instead of saddlesoap. Only do this for shows.
* Don't oil the outer surface or the lining of the saddle or you will stain your jodhpurs and the pony's back.

### TACK YOU WILL NEED

| | |
|---|---|
| * Plain girth <br> * Straight-cut show saddle <br> * White fleece saddle pad <br> * Snaffle bridles preferred <br> * All plain tack | * Avoid colored items, such as patterned browbands <br> * Martingale allowed for any class that includes jumping |

# YOUR CLOTHING

Don't forget to make sure that you are correctly dressed for whichever class you enter. Although the judge is mainly judging the pony, your appearance counts as an important part of the overall effect, and also shows that you have taken the effort to prepare seriously. Check the rule book for your class to see what to wear: two possible outfits are shown here. If you wear yours to the show, put a tracksuit over it until you go into the ring.

This picture shows two neat showing outfits. Below and opposite is a list of things you should wear:

Black velvet hard hat with harness

Grey, navy or dark green riding jacket

White or striped shirt - ratcatchers preferred for girls in the US

Plain or spotted tie - choker preferred for girls in the US

Beige or canary breeches or jodhpurs

Black or brown paddock shoes with jodhpurs

Black dress or field boots with breeches

Some girls have braided hair with colored ribbons at the end

# OTHER IMPORTANT DETAILS

## Hairstyles
Keep your hairstyle as simple as possible and make sure it looks clean and tidy. If it is long enough to show under your hat, either put it in a hairnet, or tie it up neatly as shown in these pictures. Bright ribbons are fine for Show or Riding pony classes but for Working classes, only use dark ones.

A single braid with a ribbon is a neat way of tying up long hair.

Bunches with ribbons are allowed for younger children in the UK.

## Ties
Wear a tie - not a stock - that is nice and not too bright or distracting. Small white spots on navy, green or burgundy are ideal.

## Crops
Carry a plain black or brown leather show cane. This is for ornament only (do not use it!)

## Tie pins
You should fasten your tie with a small tie pin. Avoid other jewelry though: the judge is looking mainly at your pony, not at you.

## Gloves
Wear black, brown or navy leather gloves to match your jacket. Make sure they grip well.

# BRAIDING

Braiding your pony's mane improves his looks and shows that you have taken care to turn him out nicely. A well-braided tail is a nice finishing touch, although for many classes you can just thin, or "pull", the tail if you prefer. Braiding is awkward, so try it out before the show, and bandage the finished tail (see page 89) to protect it on the journey.

## WHAT YOU NEED

*A clean bucket with fresh, warm water*

*A sponge for damping the forelock*

*A stiff brush for damping down the mane*

*A short pair of blunt-ended scissors*

*A stool for standing on*

*A large blunt needle for sewing braids*

*Braiding thread the same color as your pony's hair*

*Rubber bands*

*A mane comb*

### Before you start
* Wash the mane or tail a few days before so the hair is not frizzy or "fly-away".
* Manes need pulling for braiding, but tails should be left full.
* Braid on the day of the show. Allow lots of time.
* Thread your needle with enough thread for several braids. Stick it in your jacket or shirt.
* Dampen the hair.

### NATIVE PONIES

If you have a Native pony (see page 67), never braid or trim his hair, or brush it much between shows. Don't comb it, as this thins it out. Pick out pieces of bedding regularly, and wash and brush the hair a few days before the show. Contact your breed society to find out exactly how to show him.

*The pony's head and neck are very important features. Braiding shows them off more clearly.*

# BRAIDING THE MANE

Poll

Starting at the poll, split the mane into 2-5cm (1-2in) sections, going along the neck. Each length will make one braid. Comb and fasten each with a rubber band.

Remove rubber band before braiding.

Take up the section nearest the head and split it into three equal parts. Braid them tightly, making sure that the top of the braid is very firm and even.

Braid down to the end and pinch it together. With your threaded needle, sew up through the end of the braid. Wind thread around it and sew through it again.

Push needle up through middle.

Fold the braid under so that its tip touches the roots of the mane. Sew up from underneath and back a couple of times to hold the looped braid well in place.

Cut thread so no loose ends trail.

Fold the braid under again so that it makes a firm ball, snug to the neck. Sew back and forth through the middle as before, until the braid is secure.

Braid the forelock last. For this, take in any stray hairs as you go, as you do for a tail braid (see page 86). Sew, roll and secure the braid as for the mane.

# MANE TRICKS

*Lots of little braids make a neck look longer.*

*Fewer, thicker braids make a neck look shorter.*

*Braids rolled high to sit up along the top, make a neck look wider.*

*Braids sewn down flat make a thick neck look narrower.*

*An odd number of braids looks best; an even number can make the neck look "split" in half.*

# BRAIDING THE TAIL

Take out any stray pieces of bedding from the tail. Brush or comb through it carefully, especially at the sides, which you will use to make your braid.

Take a section of hair from each of the sides, under the top. Cross the left one over the right. Then take a third section from the right and cross over as shown.

A well-braided tail adds a nice finishing touch to your pony's turnout, and helps to keep the tail tidy for the show.

Braid the three sections, pulling them tight each time. Whenever you cross a section of hair over another, take in a little more hair from that side.

Braid like this to three-quarters of the way down the tail bone. Then work what's left of the three sections into an ordinary, plain, thin braid.

## UNDOING BRAIDS

Don't leave braids in overnight after a show. Snip out the thread at the top of each braid, then unroll it and cut the thread at the bottom. Wetting braids with a sponge after you cut the thread makes them come out almost immediately. Use your fingers to unpick the braid gradually.

Sew through the end of the braid, then wind thread around and sew it tight. Fold the braid under itself until the tip is where the main braid finishes.

Sew the tip in place and secure it at the end. To make the loop lie flat, sew through both halves all the way down the middle with small stitches.

# BOOTS AND BANDAGES

To make sure your pony arrives at a show looking his best, he needs the right type of clothing for the journey to keep him clean, comfortable and well-protected. You should also put him in stable bandages and a tail bandage (see page 88).

## USEFUL PONY CLOTHING

Make sure you get your pony used to being dressed and bandaged well before a show, or he may panic on the day.

Blankets (see checklist below). Use a sweat sheet under a summer sheet if warm, or a blanket or wool cooler if cold. Take spares as it may be very cold outside at the show.

A head bumper fits over the ears. It is made of padded leather or foam. It stops the pony from bashing his head in the trailer.

A tail guard is made of strong, soft fabric. It fits over a tail bandage to protect the tail when traveling. It must be soft so that it doesn't rub the skin at the top of the tail.

Tail bandage (see page 89).

Stable bandages (see page 88) (or shipping boots, see below).

Hock boots are thick leather pads that fit over the hocks. They protect the hocks from bumps.

Knee boots are like hock boots, but fit over the knees. These and hock boots are usually worn with bandages.

Summer sheet

Sweat sheet

Bell boots are made of rubber. They pull on over the hooves or fasten with Velcro tapes. They protect the heels from being kicked by the hind feet.

*Blanket checklist*
* Make sure that blankets fit and that they are correctly fastened.
* Choose blankets according to the weather, the number of ponies traveling with yours (he will be warmer in company), and what he is used to wearing.
* It is best to put layers of blankets on. You can take one off if he gets too hot.

*Shipping boots*
These are padded wraps to protect the lower legs. Use instead of stable wraps, but only for traveling as they don't give support and are rather bulky.

## BANDAGES

A tail bandage stops your pony's tail from getting rubbed when he travels, and keeps it smooth and flat. Stable bandages keep his legs dry, warm, protected and clean the night before and on the way to the show. You need to take them off before you go into the ring.

*Stable bandages are made of closely knit wool or cotton, and you should always put padded cotton quilts underneath them.*

## HOW TO PUT ON A STABLE BANDAGE

Wrap a cotton quilt (available from tack shops) around his leg. It should reach from his knee to the top of his hoof. Make sure it lies flat and fits snugly.

Holding the quilting in place, unroll about 5-7cm (2-3in) of bandage. Leave the end free and wind the bandage once around the leg, just below the knee.

Fold the end down. Wind the bandage around again, covering the loose end to hold it in place. Make these turns firm, otherwise the whole bandage will slip.

*Don't stretch the bandage as you wrap it.*

Coil the bandage around and around the leg. Each time pass from front to back and cover half of the previous width, so that there are no gaps.

Fetlock

Once you have covered the fetlock, start to bandage back upward again until you get to the strings, which you should find are near the pony's knee.

*Strings or Velcro fasten on outside of leg, at side, so pony can't trip up or pull them off.*

Fasten the bandage, using its strings or Velcro strips. Strings should be flat and tied in a bow which is no tighter than the bandage. Tuck the ends in neatly.

# HOW TO PUT ON A TAIL BANDAGE

Dampen the top of the tail. Unroll about 5-7cm (2-3in) and slip the bandage under the dock. Hold one end out of the way, then coil the bandage once around the tail.

Fold the spare end down and make another turn with the bandage so that it covers the loose end. Make this turn firm to keep the bandage secure.

*Tuck stray ends under bandage.*

Wind the bandage around the tail until you get all the way down the tailbone (dock). Go back up, then part the strings and tie them in a bow on the outside.

To finish, put one arm under the tailbone and with the other, gently bend the tail over so that it makes a natural-looking curve.

*Bandage tips*
* To take off a tail bandage, undo the strings, grip it firmly at the top of the tail and slide it down. If the tail is braided, unwind the bandage carefully to avoid spoiling the braid.
* To take off stable bandages, undo strings and unwind bandage from hand to hand.
* For stable bandages, you should be able to fit a fingertip inside any coil of bandage and pull it slightly away from the leg.
* Don't leave stable bandages on for more than 12 hours, or tail bandages for more than five, as this is bad for the circulation.

## KEEPING CLEAN WITH A HOOD

If you have a grey or cream pony, and want to keep him clean the night before the show and while you travel, you could put him in a hood like the one shown here. Make sure it fits really well, and don't leave it on any longer than necessary.

*Make sure the hood fits snugly around his ears and won't slip over his eyes and frighten him.*

*It should fit securely around the pony's neck but not press on his throat when fastened.*

# TRAVELING TO THE SHOW

To arrive at the show looking your best and ready to start, you need to travel by horse trailer. This needs careful planning. Traveling cooped up in a trailer is unnatural and can be worrying for ponies. So make sure you know what to take, that the vehicle is safe, your driver is experienced, and that you know how to load and unload your pony.

## GETTING READY FOR THE JOURNEY

If your pony is not used to loading, make sure you practice a few days before the show. If you have problems with him you will need to leave plenty of time on the day. Before you get your pony, make sure everything else is ready (see checklist on page 91). Once loaded, you don't want to keep him waiting any longer than necessary, or he may get restless and start to act up.

## LOADING A PONY

*Fasten this breast bar before you load.*

*Be careful not to distract or frighten him.*

*Tie him up fairly short.*

Lead the pony straight up the ramp. Don't go ahead or pull him. For better control feed the lead rope through the halter rings and over your pony's nose.

As you go up the ramp, the helpers should stay on each side, slightly behind the pony, encouraging him forward. Take your time and praise him as you go.

Lead him into the trailer. A helper should fasten the strap behind him (the "tail" strap). Duck to the other side of the bar and tie him up.

*The jockey door gives you easy, quick access to your pony.*

*Tail strap*

### Loading tips
* Keep calm, don't rush and be patient.
* Never hit, shout or wave things at the pony. If he gets upset he won't go in.
* Don't blindfold him. It may get him up the ramp, but he might fall off or bash into the vehicle.
* Never ride him in.
* Don't fight him on the ramp: you won't win, and will only upset him more.
* Give him plenty of time to see where he is going.

Check that the breast bar is securely fastened. Then leave the trailer through the small side door, called the "jockey" door. Shut it behind you.

An adult should now raise the ramp and lock it. Check that the vents are open, all doors are tightly shut and the trailer hitch is secure before you drive off.

90

*If he won't go in, try tempting him up onto the ramp with treats.*

*Preparation checklist*
* Clean out and check horse trailer thoroughly.
* Make sure the floor is covered either with rubber matting or deep, comfortable bedding.
* Fill a haynet and hang it safely in the trailer.
* Fill a container with plenty of fresh water.
* Pack show clothes, tack, grooming kit, spares and first aid kits.
* Pack vaccination certificates, show passes, map and route directions.
* Take a mobile phone or coins for a payphone and phone numbers.
* Dress pony for shipping (see page 87).

## DURING THE JOURNEY

If you are only going to a local show, you probably won't need to stop on the way. If you are going farther afield, organize the journey so that your only stops are to check on the pony. You must always stop whenever you make a check, even if you are using a horsevan rather than a trailer. It is illegal, and very dangerous, to enter the van while it is moving. Stop in a safe place such as a service area. Keep stops short and try not to unsettle the pony, but on a long journey, make sure you stop often to offer him small drinks.

## UNLOADING A PONY

Go into the trailer through the jockey door. Untie him and put the the lead rope through his halter as before, for more control. Then duck under the breast bar so that you are beside him. A helper should now lower the ramp and make sure it is stable.

Make sure the helper stands at the side of the ramp as for loading. Then undo the breast bar and walk down the middle of the ramp, staying beside the pony. If you are taking him down a back ramp, undo the tail strap. Then gently push his chest and say, "Back".

# AT THE SHOW

From the moment you arrive at a show, as well as unloading and preparing your pony, there are lots of other things to remember. Once you have competed a few times you will quickly get into the swing of what to do.

## WHEN YOU ARRIVE

Try to park near friends, so you can keep an eye on each other's ponies. Don't tie the ponies up together, though, or they may make a fuss when one of them has to leave to go into the ring. At big shows, announcements are made over a loudspeaker, so park where you can hear when your class is called. Find out which class is in progress so that you know how much time you have to get ready.

Go to the Secretary's tent and check in. You will be given your show number which you must tie onto your back before going into the ring.

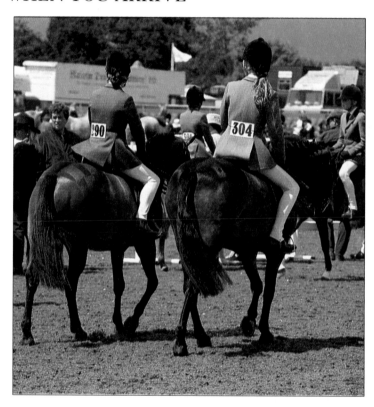

If you have time, ride your pony around the showground before you go into the ring, so that he is not fazed by all the sights and sounds.

### Settling your pony

* Unload your pony as soon as you arrive, unless the weather is very bad, when he will be better off waiting in the trailer while you get your number (see above).
* He may be a little stiff and unsteady from standing during a long journey, so give him a short walk around to relax and loosen up. Be careful not to tire him out, though.
* Settle him in a shady spot out of the wind. If it is cold and wet, keep him under cover.
* Tie him securely to a ring on the trailer with a slip knot.

* If you have ridden to the show, unsaddle and give your pony a small haynet, as long as you are not going straight into the ring.
* Check which ring your class will be held in, and find out where it is.

# WARMING UP BEFOREHAND

*Warming up is very important so allow plenty of time for it.*

The amount of time you spend warming your pony up, or "working him in", depends on his temperament: some ponies only need about 20 minutes, others are so frisky that they need up to an hour. Find a quiet place away from the bustle of the crowd, and put him through his paces. Get him into his natural rhythm. Ride bends and transitions and canter on the correct lead (see pages 72-75).

## GETTING READY FOR YOUR CLASS

Wear a tracksuit and spare boots over your showing clothes so that you stay clean while you get your pony ready. Take off his bandages and put the finishing touches on his grooming, such as quarter marks (see page 79). Pick out and put hoof oil on his feet. Then tack up, checking that the saddle and bridle are on properly and securely. Take off your tracksuit and put on the rest of your outfit including clean boots. Get a friend to tie on your number so that it can be clearly seen. You could trim the corners off it to make it look neat.

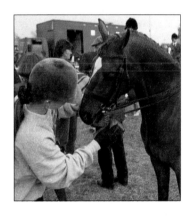

*Dab a little baby oil around his eyes and muzzle to highlight them.*

## USING THE WARM UP RING

The warm up ring is often very crowded and chaotic, so warm up elsewhere if you can. Use it just for putting last-minute touches to your turnout, such as getting rid of any grass in or around your pony's mouth.

For Working classes, you will have to use the practice jump in the warm up ring. Make sure you jump it the right way, and be careful not to get kicked or barged in the crowd.

*Health and safety tips*
* Don't leave your pony, tack or equipment unattended.
* Try to keep your pony in the shade so that he doesn't get too hot.
* Keep checking to make sure he does not get a chill standing around. Put extra blankets on if necessary.
* Offer him water often, but don't use troughs at the show: bring your own water and containers to avoid the risk of infection.
* For the same reason, don't let your pony touch muzzles with unknown ponies.

# RINGCRAFT

In under saddle classes, you ride around as a class to start with. Then you are called into a line. Each of you is asked in turn to run up in-hand. Then you saddle up again. Think about how to position and manage your pony in advance to increase your chances of doing well.

## RIDING AROUND THE RING

Riding in a group needs some skill to make sure that you give the judge the best chance to have a good look at your pony. First impressions count, so follow these tips.

Make any corrections to his action as you come around to the side of the ring that the judge isn't watching.

Space out carefully so that you are not too close to the pony either in front or behind. Your pony needs plenty of room to move freely and show off his action.

The judge usually watches one side of the ring. Get your pony going well for that side.

Be alert and keep an eye on the ring master: he gives the instructions. He has no say in the placings though.

Stay in your space. If you have to pass, do so on the inside, so that the judge can still see your pony.

Try to feel how he is moving so you don't have to look down. You want to appear confident.

The judge gives the marks and placings.

Use your legs to keep your pony moving forward steadily. Focus on him but be aware of others.

# SHOWING YOUR PONY IN-HAND

Take off the saddle and martingale if your pony wears one. Put it behind the pony, well clear of his hooves. Bring the reins over his head.

Your helper, who must be nicely dressed, should now bring your brush and cloth and neaten the pony up quickly: this is not a full grooming.

When it is your turn, lead your pony out boldly. Make him stand with all four feet firmly on the ground, his front feet parallel, but the back ones slightly apart.

Stand in front of the pony and give him a little grass to make him arch his neck and improve his top line. The judge looks at him from the side, front and back.

When asked, walk the pony away from the judge, going as far as the end of the line. Make sure he moves alongside you without pulling or lagging.

Turn the pony around and trot him back straight toward the judge. Go past her, then behind the line-up and back into your original place.

## MANNERS IN THE RING

Manners are a crucial part of how well you do in the show ring. Judges and stewards are experienced people who are used to being treated with respect. Just as your pony will lose marks for bad behavior, so will you if you are rude, flashy or uncooperative. Most judges make allowance for some nerves, but not for arrogance or an unsportsmanlike attitude. No matter how upset you are, never argue.

*The judge expects you and your pony to have perfect manners.*

## IF THINGS GO WRONG

Don't be disappointed if your pony doesn't get a prize. He is not a machine, able to perform to exactly the same standard every time. If he is off form, try to think why. A common mistake is if you have to rush. This puts him under stress and means you may not have warmed him up well. Ask the judge politely how you could improve. Have a good look at the winners, too.

# JUMPING

## Contents

# ALL ABOUT JUMPING

It may surprise you to know that horses and ponies are not natural jumpers. In the wild they only jump to escape from something, and most would opt to go around an obstacle if given the choice. It's fairly easy to train horses and ponies to jump, however, and most enjoy it once they have learned.

## NATURAL ABILITY AND CONFORMATION

Although all ponies are able to jump, some are naturally better at it than others. One of the things that influences a pony's natural jumping ability is his conformation, which means the shape and proportions of his body.

Jumping is a strenuous sport and a pony with good conformation is less likely to suffer strain or injury. His natural jumping style is also likely to be better, which should enable him to jump higher and with less effort than one with poor style.

The picture opposite shows some good points of conformation that can influence a pony's natural jumping style and ability.

Large, sound hocks, free from any heat, lumps or swelling.

Well-proportioned forehand (head, neck, shoulders and front legs).

Strong hindquarters - all the power for the jump comes from here.

Neck not too short, slightly arched - helps him balance and keep a rounded shape in the air.

Medium-length back.

Sloping shoulders means a smoother stride and less shock on landing.

Deep girth allows room for heart and lungs to work well under strain.

Short, strong cannon bones.

Large, flat knees.

Large, sound fetlocks.

Sloping pasterns absorb shock on landing.

## LEARNING TO JUMP

Jump training for pony or rider starts on flat ground.

Poles on the ground are an introduction to jumps.

A variety of small jumps are introduced gradually.

When learning to jump, the training process is quite similar for pony and rider. However, an inexperienced rider should never try to learn with an equally inexperienced pony.

As with any training partnership, the beginner will learn from the more experienced. Confidence is essential to jumping and two beginners are likely to make each other nervous.

In order for pony or rider to gain confidence, it is important to progress steadily. This book shows some of the stages and exercises of early jump training.

# TYPES OF JUMPING

*Cross-country riders face a variety of formidable obstacles.*

Once you know the basics of jumping there are many different types of fences and courses to specialize in. Show jumps are brightly painted fences set out in an enclosed arena. Top level show jumps are built to test how high and wide a horse can jump, but they will fall if knocked.

Cross-country jumps are solid obstacles set in the countryside with long stretches of gallop in between. Steeplechase and point-to-point fences are designed to be taken at speed, and although you won't be encouraged to race over fences while learning, the basic technique is the same. This book includes fences typical of Great Britain as well as America, so you will find plenty of ideas for setting up your own jumps or course.

*A top show jumper needs perfect style and precision to clear large fences cleanly and neatly.*

*Steeplechase and point-to-point races are restricted to adults but they are still fun to watch.*

# TACK AND EQUIPMENT

Jumping can be dangerous. You are often working at faster speeds, so if you do have a fall you are likely to fall harder. That's why it is doubly important to wear protective clothing and check all your equipment carefully. Make sure your tack fits well too, for comfort as well as safety reasons.

## A PONY AND RIDER EQUIPPED FOR JUMPING

Crash hat with chin straps. It must meet current safety standards.

Gloves for protection and a better grip on the reins.

A bridle of reasonably thick leather. Showing bridles made of thin leather can easily break.

Riding boots with smooth soles, pointed toes and small heels.

A running martingale is often used for jumping. It stops the pony from lifting his head and getting out of control. Make sure it's correctly fitted (see below).

A body protector that meets current safety standards is essential for all jumping.

Long sleeved shirt or sweater.

Comfortable numnah, made of natural fiber such as cotton or sheepskin.

Forward-cut saddle (see below).

Jodhpurs or chaps.

Correctly fitting stainless steel stirrup irons.

Boots to protect legs.

## Checking the fit of a running martingale

You should be able to fit a handspan between the rings and the withers.

Rubber stops prevent the rings slipping down to the bit.

Girth attachment

## Different types of saddles

A jumping saddle is very forward-cut, specifically for use with shorter stirrups. It helps you keep a good position.

A general-purpose saddle is less forward-cut, but still fine for early jumping practice.

A straight-cut saddle, such as a dressage saddle, is designed for use with long stirrups and makes it hard to adopt a good jumping position.

## Equipment checklist

* Check all stitching on the girth, stirrup leathers, reins and cheekpieces.
* Check all leather for cracks or signs of wear.
* Check the numnah is not pressing on the pony's spine, by pulling it up into the gullet of the saddle.
* Make sure any boots or bandages are correctly fitted and firmly fastened.
* Check the girth is done up tightly.
* Make sure the safety catches on the stirrup bars are down.
* Check that all tack and equipment fits correctly.

# BOOTS

There are various types of boots, all designed to protect your pony's legs in some way. They must be put on correctly and fastened securely so that they do not come loose. Buckles fasten on the outside, pointing to the back.

*Brushing boots protect the legs from knocks and stop them from brushing against each other.*

*Over-reach boots protect the front heels from being trodden on by the back feet.*

*Tendon boots protect the back of the leg. They should fit the shape of your pony's leg.*

*Open-fronted tendon boots are useful for show jumping. They protect the tendons but a pony can still tell when he hits a pole.*

# BANDAGES

Exercise bandages protect the legs and give them some support. They are slightly elastic and must be put on correctly with even tension and padding such as gauze bandage. They must be tight enough to stay firmly in place, but not so tight that they stop the blood in his legs. If you put them on yourself, make sure an experienced person checks your work.

Wrap gauze bandage around the leg. Start bandaging just below the knee (or hock). Fold the loose end down and bandage over it as you go.

*Loose end*

Continue down the leg to the fetlock. Check each turn is of an even width and tension. Work back up toward the top, until you get to the tapes at the end of the bandage.

*Tapes*

Fasten these tapes and tuck under a fold. For extra safety, add plastic tape or sew over the fold. All tape must be no tighter than the rest of the bandage.

*Plastic tape*

# STUDS

Studs are like small screws which are added to your pony's shoe to stop him from slipping. They are very useful on wet ground. The farrier includes special holes for them in your pony's shoes.

*Thick studs are used for wet ground.*

*Smaller, pointed studs are for hard ground.*

You will need an experienced person to help you put them in using a special stud key. Studs are taken out after jumping and the holes filled with cotton coated with vaseline (or with special keepers).

*Stud key*

*This part is used to restore the "thread" inside the stud hole.*

*This part is used to screw in studs.*

This prevents them from getting packed with mud.
When not in use, keep studs in oil to stop them from getting rusty.

*Stud holes are usually on the outside of each shoe.*

# ARE YOU READY TO JUMP?

Before you learn to jump you must have a secure riding seat, and be able to control your pony well in all three gaits. Make sure that you can ride turns, circles and transitions confidently, and with balance, rhythm and impulsion. A warm-up of at least twenty minutes is essential before any jumping session.

## BALANCE, RHYTHM AND IMPULSION

These three words crop up over and over again in jumping lessons. Having your pony going forward with rhythm, impulsion and balance is the key to a good approach, and a good approach is the key to a good jump.

Balance means that you and your pony have your weight well distributed. If too much is on the forehand it will be harder to take off.

Rhythm means that the pace is steady and constant. On hard ground you may hear the regular hoof beat.

Impulsion means that your pony is moving forward willingly and easily, with lots of energy. His energy comes from his hind legs so they need to be beneath him, not trailing behind. He shouldn't be going too fast and must be under control.

*Pony is unbalanced, with too much weight on his forehand.*

*Back is flat.*

*Hocks are trailing behind.*

*Nose is sticking out.*

*Mouth is resisting the bit.*

*Pony is well balanced, going forward with impulsion and rhythm in working trot.*

*Back is rounded.*

*Hocks are beneath him.*

*Rider has light rein contact.*

*Pony is accepting the bit and holding head correctly.*

## TRANSITIONS

| *Walk to trot* | *Trot to canter* | *Canter to trot* | *Trot to walk* | *Walk to halt* |

A transition is a change of gait, for example, from walk to trot or from walk to halt. Working on your transitions is the best way to improve the aids you use to tell your pony what to do and test his obedience. Practice changing gait at markers around the arena. Start from walk to trot, then back to a walk and then halt. Eventually you can try from halt straight into trot.

# IMPROVING YOUR BALANCE

A good way to improve your seat and balance is to work without stirrups or reins. You can practice without stirrups yourself but for work with no reins you need to be on a longe (a long line that goes from a special noseband to an instructor in the middle of the arena). The instructor controls the pony, while you concentrate on your position.

It may help to hold onto the pommel of the saddle at first when you trot. Relax your body and sit deep in the saddle to stop yourself from bouncing around.

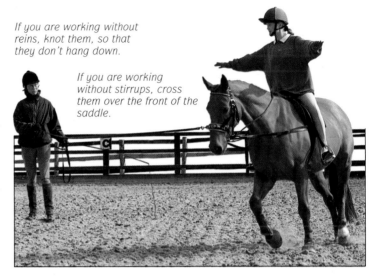

*If you are working without reins, knot them, so that they don't hang down.*

*If you are working without stirrups, cross them over the front of the saddle.*

*Arm exercises help you to relax your body and stay balanced. The girl here is twisting to each side with her arms held out to the sides.*

## TURNS AND CIRCLES

Work on turns and circles will improve your pony's suppleness. It's also good practice for his, and your, balance. Make sure you practice each way so that your pony does not become stiff on one side. If he does have a more supple side work this side first, then work the stiff side.

Start with large circles, using half the ring. As your pony warms up try smaller ones. Use sitting trot for these. Figures-eights and serpentines (see below) work both sides in turn.

*This pony is bending nicely around the rider's inside leg.*

20m (66ft) circle
15m (49ft)
10m (33ft)

Serpentine
Figure of eight

## WARMING UP

⁕ Walk on a long rein in both directions. Allow your pony to stretch out.
⁕ Pick up contact with the reins and use your legs to tell your pony to start walking more actively.
⁕ Practice transitions from walk to halt, then back to walk, and finally into trot.
⁕ Establish an active working trot. Concentrate on getting him going with rhythm, balance and impulsion.
⁕ Practice plenty of turns and circles on each rein, to get him bending correctly.
⁕ Canter on each rein, making sure your pony is leading with the inside leg.
⁕ Finish by walking quietly on a long rein and shorten your stirrups ready to jump.

103

# YOUR POSITION

When jumping, it is important to make your pony's task as easy as possible. To do this you need to move your weight forward, off his back, in the position shown below. Shorter stirrups will help you keep your balance in this new position.

## THE FORWARD POSITION

This picture shows you the correct position for jumping. Practice it at a standstill first. Then try it at a walk, trot and finally over trotting poles (see page 108).

*Body folds forward from the hips, so that your weight is just off the pony's back. It should feel as if your stomach leads and your shoulders follow.*

*Head is up and looking straight ahead, between pony's ears. This helps keep your weight even, and lets you see where you are going.*

*Back should be straight, so that you bend from the hips not the waist.*

*Arms stretch forward to go with the pony's head.*

*Legs are more bent than in a normal riding position, which means shorter stirrups, see opposite.*

*Knees and ankles take all your weight and act as shock absorbers.*

*Lower legs remain straight and in contact with the pony's sides, so that you can still use them to give commands.*

*Heels point down. If your weight is in your toes, you will fall forward.*

## SHORTENING YOUR STIRRUPS

In the forward position, your weight is no longer in your seat. It goes through your knees and ankles to the stirrups, and you will find it easier to balance with shorter stirrups. Two holes shorter is usually about right, but try whatever feels comfortable for you. To shorten them while mounted, keep your feet in the stirrups and put the reins into one hand.

Take your leg away from the saddle and pull out the stirrup buckle with your free hand.

Pull the free end of the stirrup leather upward so that the pin of the buckle pops out.

Use your index finger to guide the pin into the new hole. Pull the leather back to its original position.

# ALL ABOUT BALANCE

When you work your pony on flat ground, his center of gravity is through his girth, so you sit upright.

When jumping he has to balance on two feet, and his center of gravity moves forward over his withers.

By using a forward position, you place your weight over his center of gravity which helps him stay balanced.

## COMMON MISTAKES

*Bent waist and rounded back stops you from going forward with the pony.*

*Tipping forward too much, too early puts weight on your pony's forehand, making it harder for him to take off.*

*Collapsing on landing is uncomfortable for your pony and means you're not ready for the next fence.*

*Lower legs back make your position insecure.*

*Looking down and leaning to one side unbalances your pony.*

**BEGINNER'S TIP**

*Neckstrap*

A neckstrap is useful for novice riders with less than perfect balance. Hold onto it as you approach the fence to prevent yourself from accidentally pulling on your pony's mouth.

*Getting left behind unbalances your pony and means you may pull on his mouth.*

*If your hands are fixed you will pull on your pony's mouth.*

# HOW A PONY JUMPS

Once you understand how a pony jumps, it's easier to see how
you can help. You can learn a lot by watching top jumpers in action.
They make sure that their horse or pony has a good straight approach,
but interfere as little as possible while he actually jumps the fence.
The jump can be broken down into the five phases shown below.

## APPROACH

As the pony approaches the
fence he sees it for the first
time, so this is where the
rider can be of most help. If
the approach is straight and
controlled, the pony has
more time to study the
fence he is about to jump.

The rider below is sitting
slightly forward, but not too
far in case she needs to sit
down in the saddle and
urge her pony on at the last
moment. Her lower legs are
straight, close to the pony's
sides, and her hands are
firm enough to keep the
pony straight, but ready to
move forward as he takes a
good look at the fence.

### Your pony's sight

Did you know that your
pony has a blind spot?
He can't see things
immediately in front.
This means that at the
moment of takeoff, he
cannot see the jump!

Blind spot

## TAKEOFF

The pony bends his knees
and lifts his front legs to
take off. His neck arches
which makes it look shorter,
and his hindquarters come
beneath him, ready for an
upward spring.

The rider has let her
hands move with his head,
and as he lifts his
shoulders, she folds farther
forward from her hips, to
take her weight off his back
and stay in balance with
him. If she did this too
soon, she would make it
harder for him to take off.

*Rider bends forward from
the hips, to remove weight
from pony's back.*

*Hands have a light contact
with the mouth, just enough
to keep him straight.*

*Rider sits lightly in saddle,
ready to urge him on.*

*Forelegs lift up.*

*Hind legs are
underneath, ready
to push off.*

*Pony stretches
neck to look at
fence.*

## IN THE AIR

All four feet are in the air, and the pony's head and neck are stretched forward. His back has rounded into a nice curved shape which is called a "bascule" (see the diagrams on the right). His hind feet are stretched out behind, toward the point he took off from.

The rider has stayed still in the forward position, with her weight off his back. By looking ahead and keeping her lower leg straight, she is staying in balance with her pony.

*See how the pony's neck goes forward. This is why it's important to move your hands forward with the reins.*

## LANDING

The pony's forelegs stretch out to touch the ground, one at a time. He brings his head back up to help him balance and to minimize the shock on his forehand. His back legs are tucking neatly in behind. If they didn't he might catch the top of the fence.

The rider absorbs all the shock of landing through her ankles and knees. If she fell back into the saddle it would be uncomfortable for her pony and throw him off balance. Her hands are light so that she doesn't jab him in the mouth.

*By looking ahead the rider keeps the pony straight, as well as seeing what's coming next.*

## GETAWAY

As soon as his front feet touch down, the pony brings his back feet underneath him to take the weight off his forehand. Now he is ready to move into the first new stride.

The rider returns to her position for approach, and concentrates on a good rhythm, so that they are ready for the next fence.

### Bascule

*Jumping with good bascule.*

*Jumping with a hollow back.*

*Hind legs tuck in underneath to clear fence and be ready to land.*

*Rider sits more upright. Her weight is in the stirrups, not the saddle.*

*This leg takes all the weight for a brief moment.*

# POLEWORK

Working over poles on the ground is an excellent introduction to jumping for you and your pony. It will give you both confidence, and improve your rhythm and balance. Ideally, you should practice all these exercises with an instructor who can help you correct your position as you work.

## FIRST POLES

### About the poles
* Use solid, rounded poles that will roll if the pony knocks them.
* They should be about 10cm (4in) thick and 3-3.5m (10-12ft) long.
* Paint them in bright stripes so that your pony can see them easily and get used to bright jumps.
* Have someone on the ground to help you move the poles around.
* Place them against a wall to help you keep straight and stop your pony from running out (see page 117).

Start by placing a single pole on the ground, at the edge of the arena. Walk over it a couple of times in each direction. Let your hands move forward slightly as your pony stretches his neck.

Now try trotting over it. Concentrate on keeping a good rhythm and plenty of impulsion, so that your pony does not knock the pole. Add more poles around the arena, keeping them spaced well apart.

## TROTTING POLES

*Raise alternate ends of each pole.*

Place three poles in a row, with about 1.35m (4½ft) between each one. Get your pony going steadily at a rising trot, and then ride over the poles. Count, "one-two, one-two" out loud as you go, to help your rhythm.

When your pony is trotting rhythmically over these, add an extra pole. Keep adding, until you have a line of six poles. To test your balance, try riding over them in your jumping position (see page 104).

For more advanced work, raise the poles slightly off the ground, to make your pony lift his knees and hocks higher. Place a low block or brick under alternate ends so that he trots over the middle.

108

## Tips for trotting poles

* Always look straight ahead to help you keep a straight course.
* Be careful not to jab your pony in the mouth. Use a neckstrap if necessary (see page 105).
* Don't overdo this work. Stop while your pony is doing well, and before he gets bored.
* Never use only two poles. Your pony may think he has to jump them.
* Make sure you ride over the poles from both directions, so that you work your pony on each side.
* Always ride exactly in the middle of the poles.
* If your pony gets over-excited, turn him in a large circle in front of the poles until he calms down.

*Keep your pony going with impulsion and a good rhythm, so that he lifts his feet and avoids knocking the poles.*

## HOW TO MEASURE DISTANCES

It's important to get the distances correct between trotting poles. In lessons your instructor will place the poles for you, but if you set up your own, you need to work it out for yourself.

To do this, count how many footsteps, placed heel to toe, fit between the poles set up for you in a lesson.

When you start jumping, it is equally important to measure distances correctly. As they are longer, it is more useful to use strides.

All the distances given in this book are about right for a 14.2hh pony. Tables like the one on the right give approximate distances for smaller ponies.

| Trotting pole distances | |
| --- | --- |
| Pony's height | Distance |
| 12.2hh | 1m (3½ft) |
| 13.2hh | 1.2m (4ft) |
| 14.2hh | 1.35m (4½ft) |

*Counting footsteps between poles.*

*The correct distance always depends on your pony's size and length of stride.*

*Counting strides between jumps.*

If the distances are correct your pony should step in the middle, between the poles like this.

# FIRST FENCES

Once you can trot confidently over a line of poles and keep a balanced jumping position, you should be ready to try your first fence. Start with a low cross pole. As you improve, try different types of fences, but always keep them low and never do too much in case your pony gets bored and misbehaves.

## CROSS POLE

A low cross pole is the simplest fence to jump. The cross helps your pony aim for the center. If you are with others, jump toward them, as your pony will be happier going toward his friends.

Approach at a steady trot initially, exactly as for the trotting poles. It can be helpful to use a placing pole at first (see below).

### Reasons for a trot approach
* You have more control.
* You have more time to prepare for the jump.
* Your pony has more time to look at the jump.
* The trotting stride is shorter, so it's easier to reach the correct point for takeoff.
* A slower pace makes it easier to keep balance and rhythm.

## USING A PLACING POLE

*The placing pole helps you judge the distance to the jump.*

A placing pole will encourage your pony to take off at the right place, making the jump more comfortable for both of you. It should be placed about 2-2.7m (7-9ft) in front of the jump for a trotted approach.

Your pony will trot over the pole and then jump the cross. Make sure you do not jab him in the mouth as he takes off. Use a neckstrap (see page 105) if you find it difficult to balance.

You could also try jumping a cross pole after a line of trotting poles. It's good practice for you (it helps your balance and rhythm) and for your pony (it makes him more supple and improves his technique).

# ALL ABOUT GROUND LINES

A pole placed in front of a fence, makes a clear ground line.

A ground line on the wrong side of a fence will cause a pony to take off late.

A pony judges a fence from the ground up, so the "ground line", which refers to the part of the fence which is nearest to the ground, is what he uses to judge when to take off. Ideally it should be slightly in front of the fence.

A false ground line is when the base of a fence is behind the front part. It is very confusing for a pony and will cause him to take off too late, knocking the fence or even falling. Avoid practicing over fences like these.

## JUMPING SPREAD FENCES

In a spread, one or more higher poles are added behind the first. Spreads usually slope upward from the ground which means they can only be jumped one way. If jumped the wrong way, they give a false ground line (see above).

They may look bigger to you, but in fact their shape helps your pony to "bascule" as he jumps (see page 107).

## JUMPING UPRIGHT FENCES

An upright fence is one where all the poles are set directly above one another.

It's quite hard for the pony, as he has to judge the height immediately and take off a suitable distance away to clear the fence. For this reason it is especially important to approach an upright fence straight, in good control and with plenty of impulsion.

You can make an upright easier, by placing a pole on the ground slightly in front of the fence.

# INTRODUCING GRIDS

Gridwork is similar to polework, but with jumps instead of poles on the ground. It is a great way to build up confidence and introduce new jumps. The distance between jumps is important so that your pony gets the correct takeoff point each time, so it's best to practice with your instructor. She can set up all the jumps for you too.

## BUILDING UP A GRID

Always build up your grid gradually, and make sure that you are comfortable at each stage before going on to the next. Keep the hardest jumps to the end.

### Double cross pole

Two strides
9m (30ft)

One stride
5.4m (18ft)

Start with a placing pole and two cross poles, about 9m (30ft) apart. Your pony will land over the first cross, take two strides and then take off for the second.

When ready, move the second cross pole closer (5.4m (18ft) from the first). This will allow your pony only one stride between the cross poles.

*Benefits of gridwork*
* It improves your rhythm.
* It makes your pony more supple.
* It's good practice for your balance.
* It encourages you to jump in a straight line.
* It makes you practice a good position.
* It's an excellent way of building up confidence over low fences. You can make the last fence bigger, but always keep the first ones small.

### Treble cross pole

One stride
5.4m (18ft)

Two strides
9.9m (33ft)

One stride
5.4m (18ft)

One stride
6.4m (21ft)

Add a third cross pole, two strides on from the second (9.9m (33ft)). Then close the gap to allow only one stride (6.4m (21ft)).

Note that with the third fence the distances increase slightly, as your pony will lengthen his stride as he jumps.

### Varying the fences

5.4m (18ft)
6.4m (21ft)

5.4m (18ft)
6.4m (21ft)

Upright

Upright

Spread

When you are confident over this, try varying the last fence. Raise one end of the last cross pole, to make an upright.

Then add a pole behind to make a spread. Finally change the second fence to an upright. Always have the biggest fence last.

# BOUNCE FENCES

A bounce fence is when a pony jumps one fence and then takes off for the second one as soon as he lands, with no strides in between.

Practicing over this type of fence is good for your pony's suppleness and for your balance. Make sure you have warmed up over a few easier fences first.

Start with two small cross poles about 3m (10ft) apart. Add on fences one at a time, increasing their distance apart by about 30cm (1ft) each time.

*A grid including bounce fences is a good test of your balance and your pony's suppleness. Always build up gradually.*

## LEARNING ABOUT YOUR PONY'S STRIDE

For more advanced jumping you need to be able to judge the length of your pony's stride. Gridwork is a good chance to learn more about this.

When practicing with a class of similar-sized ponies, compare to see whether yours has a short stride (does he have to stretch to make the second part of a double?) or a long stride (does he get too close to the second part?).

The distances in the table are for ponies with average strides, which is how fences are usually set up in a competition. If your pony's stride is short the fences may be too far apart; if long, they may be too close.

*What influences a stride?*
* Size – bigger ponies tend to have longer strides.
* Pace of approach – the faster it is, the longer his stride will be.

* Number of fences in a row – a pony needs more room as he progresses down a line.
* Ground conditions – if soft, the stride will be shorter.

| Approximate distances for grids approached in trot | | | | | |
|---|---|---|---|---|---|
| Pony's height | Placing pole to fence 1 | Fence 1-2 | | Fence 2-3 | |
| | | 2 strides | 1 stride | 2 strides | 1 stride |
| 12.2hh | 2.1m (7 ft) | 8.5m (28ft) | 4.8m (16ft) | 9.4m (31ft) | 5.8m (19ft) |
| 13.2hh | 2.4m (8ft) | 8.8m (29ft) | 5.1m (17ft) | 9.7m (32ft) | 6m (20ft) |
| 14.2hh | 2.7m (9ft) | 9m (30ft) | 5.4m (18ft) | 9.9m (33ft) | 6.4m (21ft) |

# TOWARD A COURSE

As your jumping improves, you can practice jumping several fences together from a canter. It's still essential to keep good impulsion, rhythm and balance and it's important to plan your route carefully so that your approach to each fence is straight. Once you can do all this, you'll be ready to tackle a complete course.

## JUMPING FROM A CANTER

Circle here if necessary.

Make sure the inside leg is leading.

When jumping from a canter, make sure your pony is leading with the correct leg (the inside leg). Otherwise he will be off-balance. The best way to do this is to ask him to canter at a corner when he is bending the right way. If he is wrong, go forward into trot and circle until you get him going correctly.

Count out the last three strides into the fence. This will help you become familiar with your pony's stride. Practice this over a pole on the ground first.

## CHANGING DIRECTION

When working at canter, you need to change the leg your pony leads with each time you change direction.

The easiest way to do this is to go forward into trot, then ask him to canter again once you have changed direction. This picture shows how to set up your jumps to practice this.

Have your pony cantering on the left leg for fence one. Go into trot at F and canter on the right leg just before or after A. Trot again after fence two and canter on the left leg just before or after C.

If necessary circle at A or C until your pony settles or strikes off on the correct leading leg.

A

F

Canter
Trot    with the right
leg leading.

K

B

1

2

E

M

3

Canter with
the left leg
leading.

Trot

H

C

114

# PRACTICING A STRAIGHT APPROACH

When you jump away from the sides of the arena, it's harder to keep straight. You need to plan your approach carefully so that you don't turn into the jump too soon or too late.

*The red line shows a good approach. The blue lines show poor ones.*

*The key to a good straight approach is to keep looking ahead. This rider is already looking ahead to the fence as she turns into it.*

# PLANNING A GOOD ROUTE

Although it is helpful to turn a circle before a jump when training, it is not allowed in competitions.

You must plan a careful route with long, flowing turns that lead to a straight approach for each fence.

It's a good idea to walk the route yourself first on foot. Then ride through it with the poles on the ground.

This picture shows a well planned route over five jumps. The first two fences are in line and so fairly easy, but you must plan a careful approach to the third. Make a wide loop and don't let your pony cut the corner.

The best route to fence four is around fence one. If you cut in front of it, the turn will be sharp and you won't have time to change legs. Check that your pony is still cantering on the right leg after fence four (some change legs as they jump). Don't race home over the last. Keep a steady pace.

*Be prepared to stop your pony from trying to leave the arena as he passes the entrance.*

*Change to canter on the right leg here.*

*Canter on the left leg to start.*

*Check your pony is leading with the right leg here.*

# WHEN THINGS GO WRONG

The most common reason for jumping mistakes is bad riding, but once a pony knows he can get away with something he is likely to continue being disobedient. Keep taking regular lessons so that your instructor can straighten out any problems right away.

## WHY PROBLEMS HAPPEN

| Problem | Cause | Solution |
|---|---|---|
| He's afraid. | *The fence is too big.*<br>*It's new and spooky.*<br>*He hit it hard last time.*<br>*He's had a bad fall.*<br>*The ground is wet and slippery.* | *Go back to small fences.*<br>*Follow another pony over.* |
| He's in pain. | *You are hurting him.*<br>*His tack is uncomfortable.*<br>*His feet or legs hurt - it could be that the ground is hard.* | *Ask your riding instructor for advice.*<br>*Have a saddler check his tack.*<br>*Ask the farrier to check his feet and legs and avoid jumping on hard ground.* |
| He's bored or tired. | *You've been jumping the same fences over and over again.*<br>*He's out of shape.* | *Take a break from jumping. When you start again do a little at a time and practice a variety of fences.* |

## RUSHING FENCES

Rushing is when a pony suddenly speeds up as soon as he sees the jump. It can be that he's too eager, but it may also be that he's scared and wants to get over it as quickly as possible.

Build up his confidence over small fences, and try not to pull on the reins as this usually makes things worse. If you are tense, try to relax and concentrate on improving your rhythm.

### Tips for correction
* Circle in front of the fence until he settles.
* Work over trotting poles and low grids to slow him down and improve rhythm.
* Approach in a walk, only breaking into trot a couple of strides before takeoff.
* Vary his work. Do a couple of jumps, then go out for a ride or train him flat ground.
* Keep the approach short.

# KNOCKING DOWN FENCES

This is often caused by rushing, or a poor approach that leads to a poor takeoff.

If a rider catches the pony in the mouth on landing, the pony may pull his head up and drop his hind legs at the same time.

*Pony takes off too late and catches pole with front legs.*

*Pony takes off too early and catches pole with back legs.*

## Tips for correction
* Concentrate on rhythm, balance and impulsion in the approach.
* Use bright poles and fillers (see page 118), to make him pay more attention to the jump.
* Practice over a variety of jumps, particularly spreads.
* Do plenty of gridwork.

# REFUSALS AND RUNNING OUT

A refusal is when a pony stops dead and refuses to jump. Running out is when he runs to one side of the fence. If a pony starts to do either, find out why before it becomes a habit. Check all the things in the table on page 116 and ask your instructor for advice.

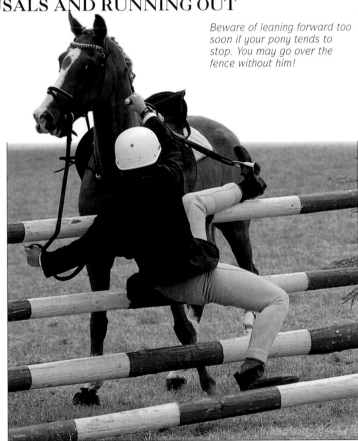

*Beware of leaning forward too soon if your pony tends to stop. You may go over the fence without him!*

## Tips for refusals
* Ride strongly into the jump, keeping both legs firmly against his sides.
* When he does jump, make sure that your hands move forward with his head.
* Follow another pony over.

## Tips for running out
* Keep the approach slow but active and very straight.

*Wings*

*Guide poles*

* Use wings on fences, and add guide poles to the sides of the jump.
* Place jumps against the side of the arena.

* If he runs out to the right, make him turn back to the left, and vice versa. Try to stop him before he goes beyond the fence.

* Carry a whip. Have it on the side he runs out to.
* Keep fences wide – narrow ones are easier to run out at.

# BUILDING JUMPS

If you want to build your own jumps to practice over at home, you'll need to collect a lot of good-quality equipment. Always build practice jumps in a safe place, and only use materials that won't damage your pony's legs if he hits them.

## EQUIPMENT FOR SCHOOLING FENCES

Solid, round, wooden poles, as described on page 108, are best but they are heavy. Plastic ones are cheaper and lighter, and so easier to use at home.

*Rustic poles   Painted poles*

Cups fit onto a stand. Plastic ones are safest. Metal ones must never be left on the stand without poles, as they can cause injury.

*Cups are curved so that a pole will roll off, if knocked hard.*

Stands must be solid, strong and stable. The best are the purpose-built wings which help frame a jump and discourage ponies from running out.

*Simple stand*

*Jump wing*

Plastic blocks can be used instead of wings and cups. They are light and can be stacked on top of each other easily to make different jumps.

## BUILDING SCHOOLING FENCES

*This fence looks flimsy and your pony will find it harder to jump.*

*Adding extra poles, a ground line and wings makes it more inviting.*

*Fillers like these, make a fence look more solid.*

The best place to set up practice jumps is in an enclosed arena or a small field. It should be at least 20 x 40m (65 x 130ft), bigger for several jumps.

Make sure the ground conditions are good. Wet, slippery, hard or rutted ground may frighten a pony and can be dangerous.

If jumping in a field,

choose a flat, grassy area that is well-drained. Avoid jumping in the field your pony lives in, as it will ruin all his grass.

Try to make fences look as solid as possible by adding poles or special fillers. You can buy a variety of these or use things like bales or barrels as shown on page 119.

### Safety checklist
* Build solid-looking jumps.
* Avoid flimsy materials.
* Include a ground line.
* Keep jumps wide.
* Check the ground on each side of the fence.
* Make sure there are no sharp edges.
* Keep all jumps in good condition and stack away neatly after use.

# OTHER TYPES OF JUMPS TO BUILD

## Tires

Tires threaded onto a pole make a well-shaped jump and won't hurt your pony's feet if he knocks them. Ask your local garage if they have any old ones that you could have.

## Straw bales

Stack them up in various different ways and use extra ones to make wings. Make sure there is no loose string that your pony could catch a foot in. Remember to put them away at night if you intend to use them later.

## Logs

Fallen trees can be excellent jumps. Make sure the ground is safe on either side before you jump, or arrange to have the trunk moved to a suitable spot. Ask an adult to saw off any sharp edges or branches that stick out.

## Empty oil barrels

Only use barrels in good condition with no rust. Paint them if you like. If you use them on their sides, put pegs in the ground to stop them from rolling. When knocked, they make a loud noise which can scare a pony, so it's best to add a pole above them.

## STORING JUMPS

Stack unused jump materials neatly in a fenced off area of the field or a spare shed. Never leave cups lying around.

# SHOW JUMPING

Show jumping competitions take place in indoor or outdoor arenas. The jumps can be quite high, but they are built so that they fall if knocked hard. There are plenty of novice events organized by Riding and Pony Clubs that you can take part in, as well as the more professional ones.

## WHICH CLASS TO ENTER?

Classes can be limited by the height of your pony (for example 13.2hh and under), by your age (for example under 14) or by experience.

Beginner classes are for ponies and riders who have never won anything, whereas an Open Class has no restrictions. Novice and Intermediate are somewhere in between. Don't be too ambitious. Opt for an easy class to begin with.

Some shows have "Clear-round" classes which are excellent for beginners. Competitors ride the course once only and get a rosette if they jump clear.

Equitation jumping is also good practice. You are judged on style as well as a clear round.

*This picture shows some of the common obstacles found in a show jumping ring. The red line indicates a shorter "second round" version of the same course (see right).*

*3. Spread fence with shark's teeth fillers – can be spooky.*

*4. Gate – an upright that is easily knocked as it hangs on flat cups.*

*5. Ornamental wall – looks solid but some ponies find it spooky.*

*6. Planks – these also hang on flat cups and fall easily.*

*7. Parallel bars – one of the hardest types of spreads, as the front pole is as high as the back one.*

*Entrance from practice ring – pony may try to turn home.*

*Be careful here to be straight and change leading legs.*

*2. Upright poles – looks quite airy so make a steady approach.*

*Go around fence 9.*

*8. Double including a spread (A) and a palisade(B).*

*1. Brush with rustic poles – all natural materials, so not spooky.*

*9. Stile – narrow, so needs an accurate approach.*

# WALKING THE COURSE

Before your class starts you will be allowed into the arena on foot to take a closer look at the fences. Make sure you are nicely dressed. There is usually a map showing which order you jump the fences in, but they will also be numbered.

*If there is time, watch the first few riders jump the course.*

*Note where problems occur and be ready for them.*

*Decide on how best to approach each fence.*

## Tips
* Walk the exact route you plan to ride.
* Figure out where you must change leading legs.
* By all means take a friend for advice, but don't get distracted.
* Check what the ground is like and look for any slight slope that may alter your pony's stride.
* Pace out the distances in any doubles or triples.
* Look out for any spooky objects around the ring.

# COMPETITION RULES

Most competitions have two rounds. In the first, the goal is to jump clear. For each mistake you make, you will get the penalty points listed below.

Competitors who go clear then jump a second round, which is usually a shorter course of higher jumps and is often "against the clock". This means the fastest clear round wins.

## Penalty points
* 3 for first refusal, run-out or circling in front of a fence.
* 4 for a knock-down.
* 6 for second refusal.
* 8 if you fall off.
* Elimination for third refusal, taking the wrong course, starting before the bell or failing to pass through the start or finish.

# CROSS-COUNTRY

Most early jump training is done over schooling fences in a flat, enclosed arena. Cross-country jumps are set in the open across all kinds of different terrains. They are built from natural materials but include many natural obstacles which some ponies find as spooky as brightly painted poles.

## JUMPING UPHILL AND DOWNHILL

Before you tackle jumps on a slope, practice trotting and cantering up and down gradually steeper hills. As a pony has four legs, it is easier for him to go directly up or down. If he zigzagged downhill, as we might, his hindquarters would swing out, overtake his front legs and throw him off-balance.

Going downhill is less effort for your pony but he will take longer strides and have more problems keeping his balance. When jumping downhill you need

*Riding downhill needs good balance.*

*Ponies need plenty of impulsion for uphill work.*

to approach slowly, in good control and balance. Don't lean too far forward. For more about downhill jumps, see the section on drop fences below.

Going uphill, he will take shorter strides and use lots of extra effort. If jumping uphill he needs lots of impulsion, so approach in a short bouncy canter.

## DROP FENCES

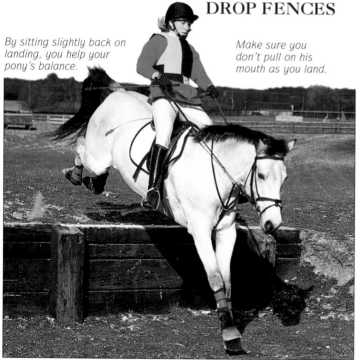

*By sitting slightly back on landing, you help your pony's balance.*

*Make sure you don't pull on his mouth as you land.*

A drop fence is one where the ground on the landing side is lower than it is on the takeoff. Often this means that a pony cannot see where he will land and so has to trust you.

Try a small step down first. If necessary let him stand on top and look but don't let him turn away. Keep your leg on the girth and your body balanced.

Approach larger drop fences at a steady pace but keep the pressure of your legs against his sides. This encourages a longer stride, so that he jumps out well. Sit slightly back on landing.

## WATER

Some ponies are terrified of water and will refuse to go near it. Others adore it, will splash around in it, and even try to roll. You may have a hard time getting them out again.

Try to introduce your pony to water while out on a ride. If necessary follow another pony in. Let him paddle and get used to it.

Once he is happy in water, try a small jump just after it. Let him take off from dry land at first. The water will slow him down, so you need to approach with plenty of impulsion.

Jumping down into water can be nerve-racking for your pony. He has no idea how deep it is. While building up his confidence, allow him to land on dry land first and then step into shallow water.

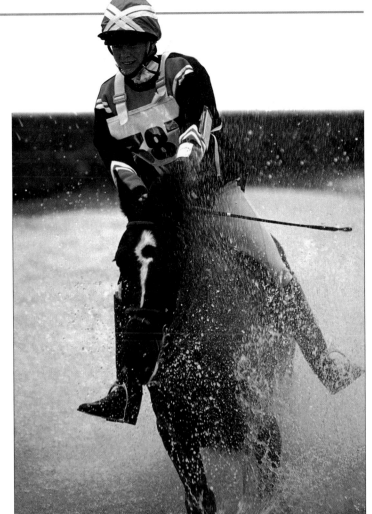

*Water is one of the most difficult obstacles for some ponies.*

## TACKLING DITCHES

*A natural ditch*

*A trakhener*

*A coffin*

Many ponies find ditches really frightening. To them, they look like a big black hole in the ground.

Try your pony over a small, natural ditch to start. You may come across one out riding, but make sure the ground is safe on both takeoff and landing sides.

If you sense your pony stopping as he spots the hole, squeeze with your lower leg to urge him on. Be ready for a large leap.

Two British cross-country jumps that include a ditch are a "trakhener",

which is a ditch with a rail over it, and a "coffin", which has a ditch between two other fences. The approach to the first part of a coffin is slow, so that the pony can see what's in the middle, but the impulsion is kept up in case he hesitates.

# RIDING A CROSS-COUNTRY COURSE

A cross-country course is spread out over several fields. The jumps are solid, with no top pole to fall off when knocked hard. For this reason they are only suitable for more experienced ponies and riders.

*This picture shows a variety of cross-country jumps. On a real course they would be spaced much farther apart than shown here.*

There are courses of varying standards around the country that you can arrange to practice over. Make sure you pick one of your level. Regular competitions are held over these courses too, as long as the ground conditions are good.

If competing, you need to walk the course first in order to study each jump,

plan your approach, and figure out the correct route. This may take some time, but it is usually possible to visit the course the night before. The list on page 125 shows some of the things you need to consider.

If you are jumping late in your class, you may have time to go back onto the course and watch a few riders over the more difficult fences.

*Log pile*

*Bullfinch – looks high but the top part is thin so you can brush through it. Some ponies however, will try to jump the whole height.*

*Post and rails*

*Ski jump – a solid fence going downhill. Difficult, as your pony cannot see the landing.*

*Steps down into water – like a small series of drop fences which require good balance.*

### Competition rules
* Penalty points are given for refusals, run-outs and falls.
* Elimination is for three refusals or run-outs at one fence; a second fall; taking the wrong course; jumping to the wrong side of the flags.

* Often there is a set time and penalty points are given for being faster or slower than the set limit, or there may be a timed section which you have to ride as fast as possible. Don't rush it; a clear round is more important.

## Walking the course

* Check the ground conditions – are they soft or hard? If soft, takeoff and landing may get difficult for those jumping later.
* Plan your pace. Try and maintain a steady, balanced canter throughout the course so that your pony does not tire at the end.
* Think about the hills. An uphill section at the end will be tiring, so take the first part steadily.
* Some jumps may have several options. Consider which route your pony would jump best.
* Slow down to a trot in wooded sections with narrow, twisting paths.

*Watch out for jumps into and out of woods or shaded areas. The change in light conditions will make it harder for your pony to see the fence well.*

Stone wall

Stile

Fallen log

Steps up

Tiger trap – there may be a ditch beneath it.

Feed trough – some ponies stop to check it for food!

Corner fence – you can either jump in and out of the wide end, or do one big jump over the pointed end, which needs a very accurate approach.

# OTHER EVENTS

Whether you are trying for the top competitions or simply enjoy jumping for fun, you'll find a great variety of events to take part in. Keep watching too. You can learn a lot from the top riders, whether you see them on television or at a national show.

## ONE, TWO, AND THREE-DAY EVENTS

These competitions consist of three separate sections: dressage, cross-country and show jumping. They test a horse and rider's all-around skills and stamina.

At Pony and Riding Club level, the event lasts one day. The dressage is a memorized test, where you are judged on performance, style and obedience. Your score is given as penalty points (so the lower it is, the better) and is added to your jumping scores.

The cross-country course must be completed clear, and within a set time to avoid penalty points. In the show jumping, your goal is to jump clear, too, as there is no timed round. At the

*The cross-country course tests stamina and courage.*

end of the day the pony and rider with the fewest penalty points win.

More experienced riders and horses take part in two- and three-day events, which have two extra sections before the cross-country:

the roads and tracks, and the steeplechase. The roads and tracks section does not include jumps, but it does test the horse's stamina. The steeplechase is a course of brush fences which has to be ridden with speed.

*Show jumping tests accuracy and ability.*

*Dressage tests obedience.*

# TEAM EVENTS

Both cross-country and show jumping events often include pairs classes. In show jumping, one pony and rider jump first and then hand a baton to the second pony and rider at the end of their round.

In cross-country, the two ponies and riders go around the course together. You can choose who gives the other a lead over most fences, but there may be a few where you are meant to jump side by side.

*Wear the same colors to look good as a pair.*

*In "team chase", an experienced horse can lead a novice over the fence.*

Pairs classes are a good chance for a young pony to gain confidence from a more experienced one.

Team chasing is an exciting event which is usually only for senior riders. A team of four riders and horses follow each other around a cross-country course. The scores of the first three riders home are usually the ones counted.

# NOVELTY CLASSES

Shows often have novelty events that you can take part in for fun, such as Chase-me-Charlie or Horse and Hound. You can usually enter on the day, so wait to see how tired your pony is from other classes first.

In Horse and Hound, you jump with your pony first and then do a second round with your dog! (See right.)

In Chase-me-Charlie, ponies and riders take turns jumping just one fence which is gradually raised higher and higher. You drop out once you knock it down or have a refusal.

The adult version of this is called the "Puissance", and usually includes three jumps of up to 1.8m (6ft) or more.

127

# PONY GAMES

## Contents

# WHAT ARE PONY GAMES?

Pony games, most often called gymkhanas, are riding competitions which involve different races and games. They are often part of larger shows where other events such as jumping take place. The games may look simple, but each one is designed to test you and your pony's skill and training. Taking part is a lot of fun, and a good way to improve your riding skills.

## GYMKHANA COMPETITIONS

### Why enter gymkhanas?

- Taking part in gymkhanas is a good introduction to competitive riding.
- You will have the motivation to train and practice regularly.
- You will have clear goals to work toward.
- Your riding skills will improve.
- You and your pony will get in better shape.
- You may meet new friends who have the same interests as you.

There are many different types of gymkhnanas. Originally they were held in farmers' fields, for people of all ages. As other more specialized events developed, such as dressage and three-day eventing, gymkhanas became popular with younger riders on ordinary ponies. Local gymkhanas still exist, but there are also more serious competitions which require excellent riding skills. Some competitions are open to individuals, while others are for teams.

Because there are so many types of gymkhanas, it means that there's something suitable for everyone, regardless of age or experience.

*In Great Britain, Pony Club teams compete for the Prince Philip Cup, one of the most highly prized gymkhana trophies.*

# FINDING OUT MORE ABOUT GYMKHANAS

Your local riding school may run an annual gymkhana which riders can enter on school ponies. Joining your local branch of the Pony Club is also an excellent way to find out about gymkhanas. You can sometimes pick up information about local gymkhanas from feed stores and tack shops.

Gymkhanas are normally divided into classes according to age group. Each class has a number of different games. The gymkhana schedule will tell you if you have to send an entry form to the organizer in advance, or whether you can simply enter on the day.

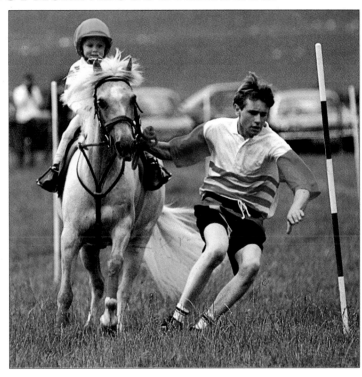

*Young riders can enter the games in a lead rein class.*

# ENTERING A GYMKHANA

It's a good idea to go to watch a few gymkhanas before you enter one. This will give you the chance to see the kinds of games which are included.

When you've watched a few, try entering one or two games in a small, local event. One of the officials should explain the rules before each game begins, but if you are unsure about anything, don't be afraid to ask questions.

*In speed games you have to ride as fast as you can, often tackling obstacles on the way.*

*Precision games involve an element of skill, such as picking up and balancing objects.*

# GAMES PONIES

Games ponies come in all shapes and sizes. There is no particular breed which does better than others, and a good temperament is more important than the way a pony looks. Experienced games ponies that have won a lot of competitions are very expensive, but every pony has the potential to do well at gymkhnana games.

## YOUR PONY'S TEMPERAMENT

If a pony is going to be successful, he must have a good temperament. This means that he behaves well, and has a good attitude toward other ponies and riders.

### Calmness

Your pony should be able to stay calm, even when equipment is being waved close to his head. Timid, nervous ponies won't cope with these conditions.

### Willingness

He should enjoy competing as much as you do, and be willing to learn. Lazy ponies don't enjoy gymkhanas and they don't usually win many ribbons.

### Good behavior

It's important that he's well behaved around other ponies and enjoys their company. He should also be easy to handle, load, shoe and catch.

### Intelligence

As you become more experienced, it's important that your pony is intelligent. An intelligent pony will enjoy the different games and will watch the starter's flag as eagerly as you do.

### Tolerance

He should be able to put up with you moving around in the saddle as you reach out for pieces of gymkhana equipment. He shouldn't mind if, in the excitement of the gymkhana, your riding is less than perfect.

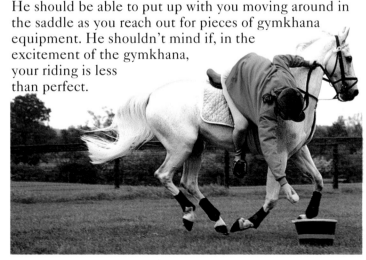

# HOW OLD IS YOUR PONY?

You can tell a pony's age by looking carefully at its teeth. A young pony will have small, white, straight teeth, while an old pony's teeth will be long, discolored and sloping.

An ideal first games pony can be any age from eight to eighteen. Some ponies even continue to compete when they are well into their twenties or beyond. The only hard and fast rule is that ponies under five years old cannot be entered. This is because competing would be too stressful for them, and could strain their developing muscles and bones.

 5 year old

 7 year old
*Hook appears.*

10 year old
*Hook goes and groove starts.*

 20 year old
*Groove lengthens.*

## YOUR PONY'S SIZE

You will have chosen your pony so that he's big enough to last you for a few years, but not so big that he's too strong for you.

It's worth bearing in mind the size of your pony when you choose which games to enter. A larger pony will tend to be faster, while a smaller pony will

*The withers are the highest part of a pony's back.*

be more agile and easier to mount and dismount. Ponies are measured in hands and inches from the ground to the withers. A hand is 4in (10cm).

In Pony Club mounted game competitions, there are three divisions of pony size and corresponding rider weight.

## YOUR PONY'S CONFORMATION

Your pony's conformation is his shape and the way he is made. A games pony doesn't need to have the kind of conformation which would win him first prize in a showing class, but there are a few important points to look out for.

*A good games pony will look athletic, supple and alert.*

*He should have muscular hindquarters as this is where his speed mainly comes from.*

*He should have strong legs and healthy feet to take the impact of his movement.*

*He needs a broad chest and deep girth to allow plenty of room for his heart and lungs.*

# TRAINING YOUR PONY

Good games ponies can stop and start easily, stay completely still on command and turn tight corners quickly. Normal schooling won't develop these skills, so ask your instructor to help you, and do plenty of practice. The amount of training and practice you'll need depends on you and your pony's experience, and levels of fitness.

## BUILDING UP FITNESS

Before you start training your pony, you must make sure he is fit. Sudden stops, starts and sharp turns put strain on his legs, so it's important they are strong. Cantering makes his heart and lungs work hard, so, just like a human athlete, he needs exercises that will build up his fitness gradually.

When your pony is in good shape he will be able to compete in gymkhanas without getting too hot or puffed out.

*Gymkhana games test your pony's physical fitness and training.*

*Fitness program*
- If your pony has not been working, it will take at least 8 weeks to get him fit.
- Spend weeks 1 to 3 just walking. Build up the distance until you can ride him for two hours.
- In week 3 start trotting work. Gradually increase the distance.
- In week 5 introduce short canters and begin schooling work (see below and right).
- In weeks 6 to 8 increase the speed and distance of canters, and schooling.

## EXERCISES FOR SUPPLENESS

When your pony is reasonably fit, circling exercises will improve his suppleness and help him to turn quickly. Start with large 20m (66ft) circles. Gradually decrease the size of the circles to 10m (33ft). Start with the slower paces and keep your aids light but clear. Circle in both directions, so your pony doesn't become stiff on one side.

*Work on controlling your pony's hindquarters as he turns, so that he doesn't knock equipment with his hind legs.*

*Put your inside leg on the girth to encourage your pony to bend.*

*Put your outside leg behind the girth to control his hindquarters.*

134

# TRANSITION EXERCISES

A games pony has to stand still at the start of a race, or a false start may be given. He should then move forward at a canter, and be able to stop when you ask him. These changes of pace are called transitions. You need to practice them until your pony responds to the slightest aid. Start with easier transitions such as halt to walk. Try practicing while you're out riding as well as in the ring.

*For a halt to canter transition, lean forward to prepare for the burst of speed. Use your inside leg on the girth and your outside leg just behind it. Keep the contact on your pony's mouth very light.*

*For a canter to halt transition, sit taller and deeper in the saddle. Keep your heels down and use your seat to slow your pony down. Close your fingers on the reins and squeeze on his mouth.*

## VOICE AIDS

Don't forget to talk to your pony. Most gymkhanas allow you to use your voice, so reinforce your leg and hand aids with simple commands such as "Whoa" and "Stand". A clever pony will soon learn to listen. Always talk to him quietly. If you shout he may become alarmed.

# IMPROVING BALANCE

A games pony needs good balance to perform well. The circling and transition exercises described above will help to improve your pony's balance. While you do them, encourage him to work actively and not "slop along". By keeping your legs closed gently on his sides and a light contact on his mouth, your pony should engage his hocks. This means he will push himself along with his back legs. Keep as still as you can on his back while you are practicing. Any unnecessary movements may confuse him because he'll have to try to balance you as well.

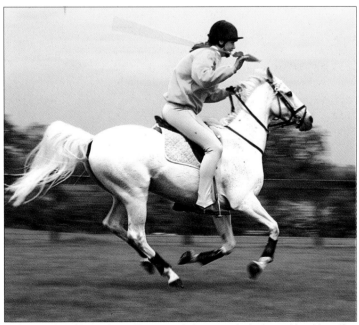

*This pony has his hocks well engaged. As a result, he is pushing himself forward with plenty of energy.*

# TRAINING WITH EQUIPMENT

Games equipment may be scary for your pony at first, but you can show him there's nothing to worry about. Set out equipment such as barrels, sacks and flags in your schooling area and work around them. Keep both hands on the reins and be ready in case he shies away. Get a helper to show your pony the equipment while you are riding him and talk to him in a reassuring voice. If he seems unworried, ask your helper to pass the equipment to you. Your helper should be ready to hold his head if necessary. If he remains calm, then ride at a walk while holding the equipment. He's most likely to "spook" when you're leaning over to pick equipment up, so practice this movement. Be patient and never rush him.

## Equipment tips

● Start in an enclosed area with an experienced helper in case things go wrong.
● As you ride, keep the equipment still and low at first. He may panic if he sees it above his head.
● Try to keep his training as varied as possible.
● Some ponies are less confident in strange surroundings, so practice away from home too.

*Make sure your pony is familiar with all the equipment and situations he's likely to encounter.*

## NECK REINING

Neck reining is a way of controlling your pony with one hand. It's a useful technique to learn because it leaves your other hand free to hold equipment.

*Try not to jerk your hand or your pony will start to turn the other way. Always reinforce your neck reining with clear leg aids (see page 134).*

To neck rein, tie a knot in your reins above your pony's withers. Hold the reins with one hand over the knot and your palm down. Hold your hand higher than usual.

To ask your pony to turn to the left, move your hand smoothly over to the left, until he can feel the pressure of the right rein on his neck.

Practice making him turn to the right by moving your hand smoothly over to the right, until he can feel the pressure of the left rein on his neck.

## LEADING

You'll have to lead your pony in some races. Once he's leading well at a walk, try leading at different paces. Make sure he doesn't overtake you, as he'll become hard to steer. Teach him to stop when you say "Whoa". With practice, he'll naturally match his pace to yours.

### Tips for leading

* Stay by his shoulder to encourage him to keep up.
* Try not to let him follow behind you as he may run into you.
* Use your voice to urge him to "Trot".
* Try not to pull him, or turn to look at him.
* If your pony is lazy, tap him behind his girth to make him trot.

# RIDING SKILLS

Mounted games are fun, but hard work. You'll need to dismount and mount while your pony is moving, reach for equipment and run fast. In order to win, you should be as well trained and fit as your pony. Your first goal should be to improve your fitness with the exercises below, then practice riding skills, such as vaulting, which will speed up your performance.

## STRETCHING EXERCISES

Stretch your arms up, then bend to touch your right foot with your right hand. Stretch up again, then touch the other foot. Repeat with your left hand.

Stand up in the stirrups. Put one hand on the pommel to steady yourself and stretch up as far as you can with your other hand. Repeat with the other arm.

Bend slowly back until you are lying on your pony's hindquarters. Try not to let your legs slip forward, though. Return slowly to a sitting position.

With your arms stretched out, swing around to face one side, then the other. Try to do this with a smooth rhythm, keeping your legs as still as you can.

## IMPROVING YOUR BALANCE

Improving your balance will help you to keep the correct position in the saddle while you ride at a high speed. You can work on your balance by riding without stirrups or without reins. When you ride without stirrups, cross them over the front of the saddle, so they don't bump against your pony's sides. When you ride without reins, an instructor will need to control your pony using a longe line.

*Ask your instructor for a longe lesson. It will help you to improve your balance.*

*Sit deep in the saddle and relax into your pony's movement. Concentrate on your riding position.*

*Longe line*

*Hold the pommel at first, to steady yourself.*

# FLYING DISMOUNTS

As you approach a task or obstacle, you can save time by dismounting from your pony before he slows down. This is called a flying dismount. It's more usual to dismount on the nearside, but try practicing your flying dismount on the offside too.

Dismount normally, but push out strongly, so you land away from your pony.

As soon as your feet touch the ground, face forward and start running.

Keep your right hand on your pony's neck to steady yourself if you need to.

# LEARNING HOW TO VAULT

Vaulting is a way of mounting your pony while he is moving. Learning how to vault takes a little practice, but it's worth the effort because it's much quicker than mounting in the usual way. Make sure your pony is trotting or cantering before you vault, as it is this forward movement that will carry you into the saddle.

*This experienced rider is practicing her vault on the offside at a canter.*

Urge your pony into a trot or canter and run beside him. Hold the reins in the hand nearest his head. Rest this hand against his neck.

With the other hand, grip the far saddle flap. Watch your pony's stride. As his near front foot hits the ground, jump up.

As you jump, put your weight on the arm holding the saddle and swing your inside leg over the back of the saddle.

139

# TEAM TRAINING

If you've taken part in a few gymkhanas and enjoyed them, the next step may be to join a mounted games team. Most Pony Club branches and some riding schools have a team squad. The squad consists of a number of riders and ponies from which the team is selected.

## BEING IN A TEAM SQUAD

Being a member of a team squad is one of the best ways to improve your mounted games skills. You and your pony will become fit and well trained through attending regular practices, and you will learn useful tips from more experienced members. You will also get the chance to enter plenty of competitions, many of them on a more serious level than local gymkhanas.

*Training is often more fun when there are other people to keep you company and spur you on.*

## TEAM PONIES

If your pony enjoys being with other ponies, and doesn't kick or bite, then he'll probably work well in a team. It's also an advantage if he can wait patiently behind the starting line while other ponies are racing, and is willing to lead other ponies and be led. If your pony doesn't have all these qualities, don't worry. As long as he's good-natured, he will gain them with experience.

*Each team has five riders who are picked from the squad. The rider who races last wears a white hat band.*

# CHANGEOVERS

Many team games involve a changeover where equipment is handed from one team member to the next who then continues the race. It's worth practicing changeovers with your teammates until you can do them quickly and accurately. If you're fumbling with equipment, or trying to keep your pony under control, you may lose valuable time.

*Watch each other carefully. The incoming pony must have all four feet across the line before the changeover takes place.*

*Hold the equipment upright by one end so your teammate can take it easily.*

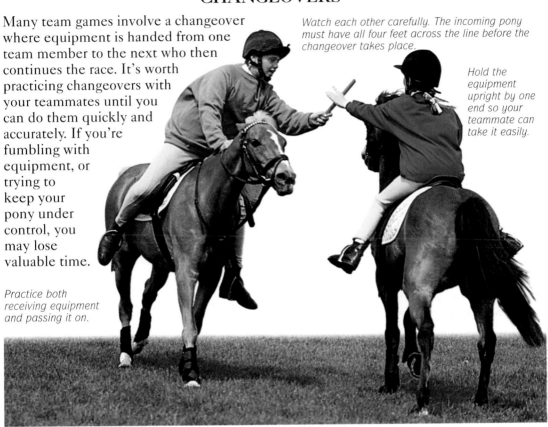

*Practice both receiving equipment and passing it on.*

## COMMON PROBLEMS WITH TEAMWORK

### Backing off

*Backing off can be a problem at changeovers.*

If your pony backs off when another pony approaches at high speed, keep him behind the starting line and walk him forward for the changeover. He won't be able to step back.

### Shying

*Ponies often shy because they lack confidence.*

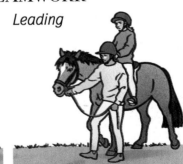

If your pony shies at the changeover, stand a steady pony alongside him. You won't be able to do this in competitions though. Ask the incoming rider to walk toward you at first.

### Leading

If your pony dislikes being led by another rider, ask a friend to lead him on a lead rope while you stay in the saddle. Push him on firmly with your legs. Urge him into trot and then a canter.

# EQUIPMENT

It's a good idea to build up a collection of gymkhana equipment, so you can practice whenever you want to. Many games use household items which are easily available. Other pieces of equipment, such as flags, are easy and cheap to make.

## USING BOTTLES

You can make equipment for the bottle race using plastic bottles. Part fill large empty plastic bottles with sand to weigh them down. You could cover the bottles with brightly colored insulating tape to strengthen them.

Wind tape around bottle.

Sand

In the bottle race you have to pick up plastic bottles from the top of an upturned bin.

### Picking up litter

In the litter race you have to pick up pieces of "litter" from the ground without dismounting.

To make the pieces of litter, use large empty plastic bottles, cut off at the "shoulders". To pick the litter up, use a 3ft. wooden dowel.

Hold the dowel about halfway along as it will be easier to control.

Bend as low as you can. Push the end of the dowel into the litter then bring the dowel up carefully so the litter stays on the end.

# MAKING YOUR OWN BENDING POLES

*Use 6 nails. They should stick out about 2cm (1in) from the pole.*

*Support the pole in the middle of the can until the cement starts to dry.*

Broom handles or 4ft. 6in. lengths of 1in. PVC pipe make good bending poles. Bamboo canes are not suitable, as they can snap and splinter. Metal posts can injure your pony. You will need five bending poles for a race lane, spaced between 7 and 9m (20-30ft.) apart.

If you use broom handles, ask an adult to help you bang nails into one end of each stick.

Set each pole in a 1 gallon paint can filled with wet cement. Leave until the cement has set.

Paint bright stripes on the poles. You can find out more about bending pole races on page 145.

## HOW TO MAKE FLAGS

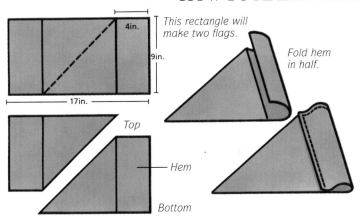

*This rectangle will make two flags.*

*Fold hem in half.*

4in.

9in.

17in.

Top

Hem

Bottom

*Tape secures the flag firmly to the dowel.*

To make triangular flags cut a 9in. by 17in. rectangle of fabric. Draw a straight line 4in. from each short side to make a square. Cut diagonally across the square to make two flags.

Fold each 4in. hem in half, as shown, then sew along the inside edges of the hems and along the tops. Leave the bottoms open so that you have a tube for the wooden dowels to fit into.

Insert a wooden dowel into the tube of each flag. Secure the flags to the dowels with tape. To make rectangular shaped flags attach 6in. by 8in. pieces of cloth to wooden dowels.

## A PRACTICE AREA

Set up your practice area in a small field, but not where your pony lives, as it will spoil his grass. Choose a flat, well drained area, as ground that is uneven or wet can be dangerous for your pony. Mark out a race lane 65m (71yds) long. If you're practicing with friends, the distance between lanes should be 7.5m (8yds).

*One long pace is about 1m (1yd).*

# SPEED GAMES

When you compete in a speed game, you will have to get from one end of the arena to the other and back again as fast as you can. The speed games described on these pages are traditional favorites, so it's likely that most gymkhanas or mounted games competitions would include at least one of them.

## STEPPING STONE DASH

This game involves riding to the end of the arena then back to a row of "stepping stones". You have to dismount, run along the stones then vault back onto your pony and ride to the finish. Dismount well before the stepping stones, so your pony is into a good trotting rhythm and you can quickly vault back onto him when you've run along the stones.

## SACK RACE

In the sack race, you have to ride as fast as you can to a marker at the end of the arena, then back to the center line where you dismount and get into a sack. You then have to run or jump to the finish, while leading your pony. It's worth practicing racing in a sack at home. Try jumping along, or sticking your toes in the corners of the sack and shuffling along.

*Keep the sack over your knees.*

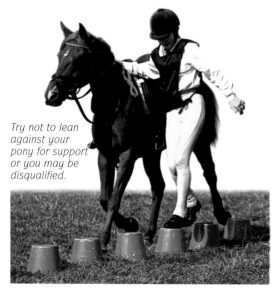

*Try not to lean against your pony for support or you may be disqualified.*

## CANTER, TROT AND WALK

In this game, you and your pony have to race up and down the arena, changing down through the paces when you reach colored markers. If you break the correct pace, you must circle on the spot before continuing. You will need good riding skills to make your pony stay at the correct pace in all the excitement of the race.

## ROPE RACE

The rope race is played in teams. You and a partner bend in and out a line of poles, each holding the end of a piece of rope. You should both be able to neck rein (see page 137) so that you can bend through the poles one handed. If you drop the rope, or miss a pole, you must return to the point where you made the mistake. When you reach the finish, one of you picks up another team-mate and starts again.

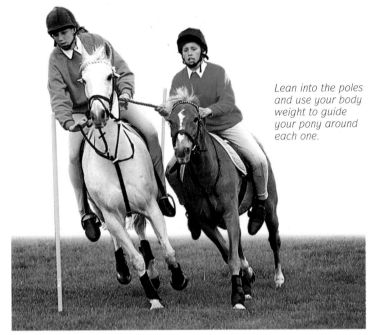

*Lean into the poles and use your body weight to guide your pony around each one.*

## BENDING RACE

*Go wide around the last pole, so that you can ride close to the first post on the return journey.*

In the bending race, you have to weave through five upright poles as quickly as you can. If you miss a pole, you must go back and correct your mistake, and if you knock a pole over, you must dismount and put it back up. The bending race forms the basis for several other games including postman's chase and the rope race.

## POSTMAN'S CHASE

Postman's chase is always played as a team game. The fifth member of your team stands at the far end of the arena, holding four cardboard "letters". You have to bend through the poles holding a sack, collect one of the letters and put it in the sack, then race back through the bending poles. You must then hand the sack to the next rider who races off to collect another letter.

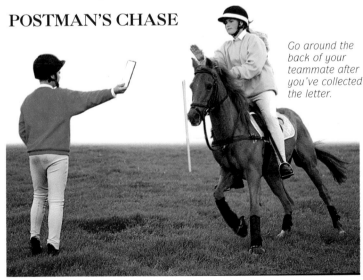

*Go around the back of your teammate after you've collected the letter.*

# PRECISION GAMES

Precision games involve more than just speed. You will also have to perform a skill, such as balancing a mug on top of a pole, or putting a ball in a bucket. Remember that if you make a mistake, you'll have to go back and correct it, so it's worth taking a little extra time to carry out the skill correctly the first time.

## THE FLAG RACE

This is one of the most popular gymkhana games, with several different versions. You will have to take a flag from one container and put it into another at high speed, without dismounting.

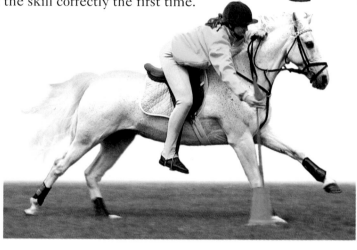

*When you collect the flag from the first container, change your grip so you're holding it like a sword. This will give you more control when you put it into the next container.*

## BALL AND CONE RACE

In this game you have to place a tennis ball on top of a plastic cone, or transfer it from one cone to another. You won't be able to balance the ball on the cone while your pony is cantering, so sit taller and deeper in the saddle and use your aids to slow him down.

*Pick the ball up with your palm facing backward, so that if you fumble, the ball will fall back into your hand.*

## BALL AND BUCKET RACE

In the ball and bucket race, you have to ride to the far end of the arena, dismount, pick up one of four tennis balls, then remount and ride to the center line to drop the ball into a bucket. You must then go get another ball. When all the balls are in the bucket you can ride to the finish.

*Lean down as far as you can. Let go of the ball gently so that it rolls down your fingers.*

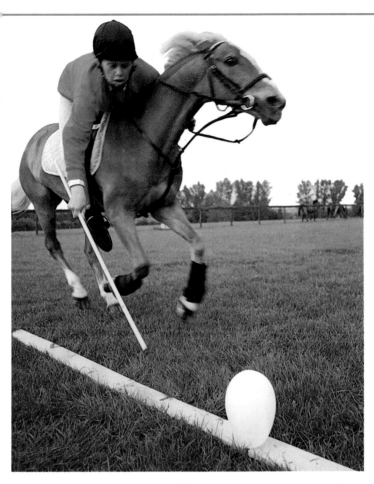

## BALLOON RACE

In this game, there is a board on the center line to which several balloons are attached. At the far end of the arena there is a bin containing a wooden pole with a pin attached to one end. You have to ride to the bin, get the pole, then ride back and burst all the balloons before you cross the finish line. You must remain mounted at all times. This game is often played in teams, with each rider bursting one balloon before passing the pole to the next team member.

*Make sure your pony is used to the sight and sound of bursting balloons before you enter the balloon race, otherwise he may become frightened.*

## MUG RACE

There are several versions of the mug race, one of which involves picking up mugs, one at a time, from an upturned can at the end of the arena, then placing them on top of a row of bending poles. Place each mug gently on the pole. If you slam them down too hard, they may bounce off when you let go.

*The mug race involves a lot of changes in speed. When you've collected a mug, canter as fast as you can to the poles, then slow down while you place the mug.*

## PYRAMID RACE

In this game you have to pick up sand-filled plastic boxes from one table and pile them on top of each other on another table. You don't have to dismount or vault back onto your pony in this race, unless you drop a box and have to pick it up.

*Use clear legs aids to keep your pony close to the table.*

# TACK AND TURNOUT

The Pony Club has firm rules about what you and your pony should wear for competitions. Local gymkhanas are unlikely to be so strict, but check the rules in the schedule. Pony Club games start with a tack (also called saddlery) and turnout inspection. Ribbons are awarded for the neatness and condition of pony, rider and tack.

## DRESS AND TACK FOR PONY CLUB COMPETITIONS

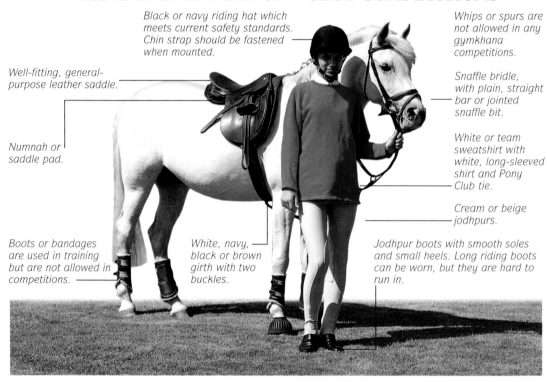

Black or navy riding hat which meets current safety standards. Chin strap should be fastened when mounted.

Whips or spurs are not allowed in any gymkhana competitions.

Well-fitting, general-purpose leather saddle.

Snaffle bridle, with plain, straight bar or jointed snaffle bit.

Numnah or saddle pad.

White or team sweatshirt with white, long-sleeved shirt and Pony Club tie.

Cream or beige jodhpurs.

Boots or bandages are used in training but are not allowed in competitions.

White, navy, black or brown girth with two buckles.

Jodhpur boots with smooth soles and small heels. Long riding boots can be worn, but they are hard to run in.

## CHECKING THE SADDLE

Check the fit of your pony's saddle regularly, as this is one of the things that tack inspection judges look for. A badly fitting saddle could also harm your pony. Make sure the saddle lies flat on his back with the weight evenly distributed.

Pommel  Seat  Cantle

Panel

Girth straps

Gap

You should be able to see a clear gap between your pony's spine and the saddle.

Pommel

You should be able to fit four fingers between the pommel of the saddle and your pony's withers.

148

# NOSEBANDS

There are several different types of nosebands. Apart from the cavesson (see below), most nosebands are pieces of corrective tack. They are designed to make a strong pony easier to control by preventing him from opening his mouth.

Always ask an experienced person for advice if you think your pony needs any kind of corrective tack, including nosebands. Cavesson, flash, drop or grakle nosebands are all allowed in gymkhana and mounted games competitions.

### Cavesson

### Drop

### Flash

### Grakle

Cheek-bone

Cavesson nosebands improve the look of a pony's head. They are available in different widths, to suit different breeds of ponies.

If you use a drop noseband, make sure it is fitted correctly. If it is too low, it could restrict your pony's breathing.

Make sure the top strap of a flash noseband is tight enough not to slip down and interfere with your pony's breathing.

A grakle noseband stops the pony from crossing his lower jaw. Make sure it does not fit too high or it may rub the pony's cheekbones.

## CHECKING THE FIT OF THE BRIDLE

Throat latch

The bit should stick out of your pony's mouth about ½cm (¼in) on each side. Make sure you can fit your forefingers between the ends of the bit and the sides of his mouth.

Browband

The browband should sit just below your pony's ears, but not touching them. It must fit closely, but make sure it is not so tight that it pulls the bridle forward.

When the throat latch is fastened, it should be loose enough to allow your pony to breathe easily. You should be able to fit your fist inside it.

You should be able to get two fingers between a cavesson noseband and your pony's face. The noseband should sit four fingers below his cheekbones.

# USING MARTINGALES

Running and standing martingales are pieces of corrective tack which prevent ponies from throwing their heads up and becoming out of control. You are allowed to use a standing martingale in gymkhanas and mounted games, but it will need to be fitted carefully, so ask an experienced person to help you at first. Remember that adding a martingale is not the cure for a problem and that good schooling with a qualified instructor is far better than corrective tack.

### Standing martingale

*The standing martingale strap should be loose enough to reach up to the throat.*

### Running martingale

Rings

Rubber stops

*Stops on a running martingale prevent the rings slipping toward the bit.*

*The rings should be one hand's length from the withers when you pull them back.*

# BOOTS AND BANDAGES

Boots and bandages protect your pony's lower legs from injuries and give them support. They can be worn when training but are not allowed in competitions. Boots should be fastened securely so that they do not come loose. Boot buckles fasten on the outside of your pony's legs, pointing backward. Bandages should be tight enough not to slip, but if they are too tight, they will be uncomfortable for him.

## Types of boots

Over-reach boots protect your pony's front heels from being stepped on by his hind feet.

Brushing boots prevent your pony knocking his opposite legs together. They also give general protection against bumps.

Tendon boots can be covered or open-fronted. They protect the pony's tendons at the back of his lower legs.

## Putting on exercise bandages

Wrap gauze padding around the lower leg. Start bandaging just below the knee (or hock). Fold the free end down and bandage over it.

Continue to wind the bandage evenly down to the fetlock. Work back up to the top, until you reach the tapes at the end of the bandage.

Tie the end tapes around the leg and tuck them under a fold. Sew over the fold or wrap plastic insulating tape around it, so the bandage can't come undone.

# STUDS

Studs fit into special holes in your pony's shoes and stop him from slipping on very hard or wet ground. You will need to ask the farrier to include the holes in your pony's shoes. Take the studs out after competing and fill the holes with keepers or cotton covered with vaseline to stop small stones from blocking them.

Stud hole

Outside edge of shoe

You use a stud key to fit studs into your pony's shoes.

Pointed studs are used for hard ground.

Square studs are only used when the ground is very wet.

# TAKING CARE OF TACK

It's important to clean your tack regularly, ideally after every ride. Wash, dry and rub the leather parts of the saddle and bridle with saddle soap to keep the leather soft and supple. Ordinary soap would make it hard and dry. Scrub fabric girths and halters with soap and water. Avoid detergents as they may irritate your pony's skin. Make sure your pony's saddle pad or numnah is clean too. Remove the bit from the bridle and clean it thoroughly in very hot water after every ride. Do not use soap, as your pony may react badly to a soapy taste in his mouth.

## Tack checklist
● Always keep your tack clean and in good repair.
● Check that the stitching on the girth, stirrup leathers, reins and bridle is not broken or frayed.
● Check all the leather for cracks and signs of wear.
● Check the bit carefully for any signs of roughness.
● Check that the saddle and bridle fit your pony (see pages 148 & 149).
● Make sure any boots or bandages fit your pony correctly and are firmly fastened.

*If you look after your tack carefully, it should last for many years.*

# GETTING READY

As the day of the gymkhana approaches, you will need to decide how to get to the showground. If the show is nearby, it may be best to ride there, but if it is far away you will need a horse van or trailer. Before you set off, prepare your pony and check that you have everything you'll need.

## PREPARING YOUR PONY

*Wash muddy legs with warm water then dry them thoroughly.*

Groom your pony thoroughly before the gymkhana, so that he looks his best.

Pick out his feet and use a dandy brush to remove mud and loose hair from his coat. Body brush him all over to remove grease and dirt, then sponge his eyes, nose and bottom with separate sponges. Brush his mane and tail in small sections to remove tangles. Finally, polish his coat with a stable cloth to make it shine and paint his hooves with plenty of hoof oil.

## RIDING TO THE SHOW

If you are riding to the gymkhana, plan your route well in advance. There are very few bridle trails in the country, so you will probably have to ride on the road for most if not all of your journey.

If possible, ask someone with a car to meet you at the show and bring the things you will need, such as your grooming kit. Allow plenty of time for your journey. If the showground takes more than half an hour to get to at a walk and steady trot, you should arrange to go by horse van or trailer.

*If you are not being met at the show, pack a small backpack with a halter, a lead rope, a blanket, a hoof pick, a body brush, a first aid kit and some money.*

### Road Safety tips

* Make sure your pony is used to vehicles before you take him on the road.
* Always keep to the right.
* Wear a reflective bib so you can be seen easily.
* Raise your hand, or nod and smile, to thank motorists who slow down.
* Wait for a clear road before passing any scary objects.
* Ride with an adult or experienced friend.
* Learn your Highway Code.
* Take your Pony Club riding and road safety examination.

# PROTECTIVE CLOTHING

When your pony travels in a horse van or trailer, he needs special clothing to keep him warm and to protect him against accidental knocks.

*A tail guard, with a tail bandage underneath, protects the tail.*

*Stable wraps should cover the fetlocks. You can also use shipping boots, which are padded wraps with velcro straps.*

*Thick leather hock boots protect the hocks from bumps.*

*Blankets keep the pony warm. Use a sweat sheet under a summer sheet if it's warm, or a wool day blanket if it's cold.*

*Knee boots protect the knees from knocks.*

# TRAILERS AND HORSE VANS

If your pony is traveling to the gymkhana in a trailer or horse van, practice loading and unloading him a few days before the journey. An experienced person will need to show you what to do and help you on the day. Make sure the floor is covered with bedding or rubber matting to prevent your pony from slipping. Hang up a haynet for him to nibble on the way and take a container full of water so you can give him drinks. Your pony needs lots of fresh air, so open the vents of the horse van or trailer.

*A horse van is a type of truck.*

*Living area*

*A horse trailer is towed behind a car.*

*Ramps*

## Tips for the journey

- Plan a long journey so the only breaks you need are to check on your pony.
- Stop in a safe place such as a service area.
- It is dangerous and illegal to be with the pony when the horse van is moving, so always stop the vehicle to check on your pony.
- Keep stops as short as possible and try not to unsettle your pony.
- On a long journey, offer your pony small drinks.

153

# AT THE GYMKHANA

Many gymkhanas are part of larger shows, where different events happen throughout the day. There is a lot to do when you arrive, so try to reach the showground in good time. Then you don't have to rush your preparations.

## LOOKING AFTER YOUR PONY

If you have ridden to the gymkhana, unsaddle your pony and settle him in the shade, out of the wind. If you have arrived by horse van or trailer, unload him as soon as you arrive. He may be a bit stiff, so lead him around to loosen him up and give him a chance to familiarize himself with his surroundings. Tie him to a piece of string attached to a ring on the trailer. If for any reason he panics and pulls back, the string will break and he won't injure himself. Bring your own water and containers to avoid the risk of infection from troughs at the showground.

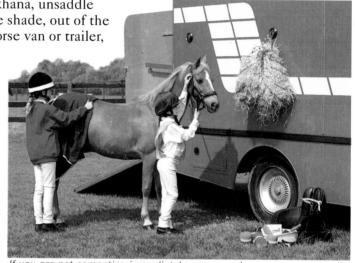

*If you are not competing immediately, you can give your pony a small haynet once he's settled.*

## FINDING YOUR WAY AROUND

When your pony is settled and happy, leave an experienced friend in charge, while you go to find the secretaries' tent. Fill in an entry form if you have not already done so, and check in. Make sure you know what time the first race in your age-class starts. Walk around the showground and find the gymkhana arena, practice ring and warm-up area. You should be aware of the ground conditions when you compete, as very short grass and wet grass can be slippery.

# WARMING UP EXERCISES

It's important to warm up before you compete, so that you and your pony are ready for racing. Warming up helps to prevent injuries, as warm muscles are less likely to strain than cold ones. Try the stretching exercises shown for ten minutes, then spend about twenty minutes warming up your pony.

If you rode to the gymkhana, your pony will only need about a ten minute warm-up. Don't work him too hard. You are trying to loosen his muscles, not wear him out.

*Stand up straight, then bend down to touch your toes. Straighten up slowly without bending your legs. Repeat five times.*

*Stand with your feet apart. Raise your left arm. Bend to the right and straighten up. Raise your right arm and bend to the left.*

*Rotate each arm in forward circles, then backward circles ten times. Finally, jog on the spot for a few minutes.*

*Warm up your pony with some transitions to put him through his paces. Then try a few stops and starts and do a couple of vaults and flying dismounts.*

## THE PRACTICE RING

Announcements will probably be made over a loudspeaker. Listen to them carefully, as you will be called to the practice ring before each of your races. Once you are in the ring, pay attention to the steward. He or she may call out people's names before each race to make sure all the contestants are there.

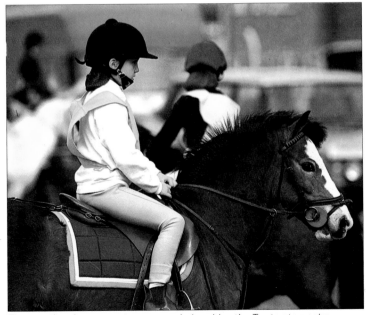

*The practice ring can get very crowded and hectic. Try to stay calm.*

### Tips before you start

- Try not to rush, as this puts you and your pony under stress.
- Relax. If you are nervous your body will be tense and you won't ride at your best.
- Be positive. Negative thinking isn't good for your confidence.
- Keep calm and don't panic, or your pony may become over-excited.
- Just before you go into the arena, close your eyes for a few moments and breathe calmly and deeply.
- Don't forget you're there to enjoy yourself!

# COMPETING

When you enter the arena to compete, all your skills and training are tested in just a few intense moments. During the games, concentrate hard on what you are doing and try not to get distracted by the other competitors. Most importantly of all, remember that you've entered the gymkhana to have fun and enjoy yourself.

## HOW THE ARENA IS SET OUT

Changeover line

Start and finish line

Judge stands here.

6 meter line

Exit to arena

Center line

Practice ring

Judge stands here.

Entrance to arena

## HEATS

If there are a lot of entrants, games are run in heats. The winner of each heat goes through to the final. Watch the other heats in your game, as you may pick up some useful tips. When everyone is ready on the start line, the starting official will lower a white flag to signal the start of the heat.

*If one of the riders moves off before the flag is lowered, the starting official will blow a whistle to signal a false start.*

## Tips for competing

- Remember that accuracy is more important than speed.
- Don't get distracted by other competitors. Concentrate on what you are doing.
- Always correct mistakes, no matter how long it takes.
- Always finish the game, even if you seem to be last. Another rider may be disqualified.
- Don't argue with the judge. His or her decision is final.
- Whether you win or lose, always remember to congratulate your pony.

## LINE STEWARDS

In Pony Club mounted games, each race lane has two line stewards, one at each end. At the end of the game, the line stewards tell the judge if an error has been made and not corrected and what that error was. The team is not informed, as this would be unauthorized assistance. Team members are responsible for telling each other if they have spotted an error.

*In the U.K., line stewards will notify the team if an error has been made, but this is not allowed in the U.S.*

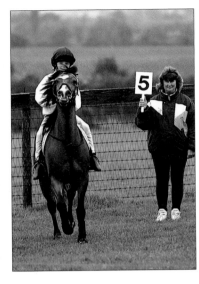

### Between games

- Between the games, try to conserve your pony's energy.
- Dismount, and keep him in the shade if it's hot.
- If it's cold, put a blanket over him.
- If there is a long gap between the games you have entered, take him back to the trailer or horse van for a rest.

## AT THE END OF THE DAY

Hopefully you will win some ribbons. If you don't, try not to be downhearted. Think about the events you did do well at. Also think about how your general riding skills have improved as a result of your gymkhana training. Pinpoint the weaknesses that let you down, so you can work to improve them before the next time. When you get home, check your pony's legs for any hot patches or bumps. Make sure that he has settled in well after the journey and that he eats a good dinner.

# POLO AND OTHER SPORTS

Gymkhana games are an excellent introduction to other competitive mounted sports such as polo and horseball. The skills you learn as part of a mounted games team are very similar to those used in these action-packed sports. Even if you don't get the chance to take part, mounted sports are exciting to watch.

## POLO

Polo was first played over three thousand years ago by the tribespeople of Persia and China. In more recent times, polo has become popular in Europe and the Americas.

The object of the game is to score goals by hitting a ball through the goalposts using a long polo stick. Polo is played in seven and a half minute periods called chukkas. The number of chukkas in a match can be between four and eight and is decided beforehand. Because polo is played almost entirely at the gallop, the players change their ponies after every chukka and no pony can play more than two chukkas in a match.

The four team members are given numbers called handicaps. High numbers are given to good players. The handicaps are added up to give the team handicap. This decides which tournaments the team can enter.

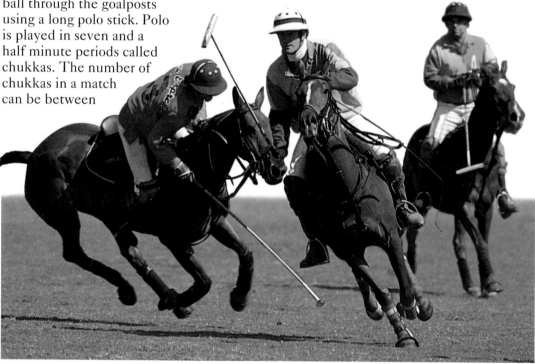

### Riding off

A polo player will often try to "ride off" an opponent. This means by neck-reining and using firm leg aids, the player pushes his or her pony toward the opponent, forcing him or her to move away from the ball.

*Above: Although riding off involves physical contact, penalties are given to players who ride dangerously.*

*Left: Polo players wear helmets and thick leather knee pads and boots.*

158

## HORSEBALL

Horseball is a mixture of rugby and basketball played on horseback. Two teams of six riders play against each other. Only four players from each team are allowed on the pitch at the same time, but substitutions can be made at any point. The game is played in two halves of ten minutes using a ball enclosed in a harness with six leather handles. Players use their hands to catch and pass the ball. Team members have to gain possession of the ball, then pass it at least three times within their team, before attempting to score by shooting the ball through a hoop.

*Horseball players learn how to lean out of the saddle in order to pick the ball up from the ground.*

*The fast pace of the game and the impressive shooting and passing skills of the players make horseball an exciting sport to watch.*

## POLOCROSSE

Many Pony Club members go on to play polocrosse when they become too old to take part in mounted games. Players throw and catch a soft foam rubber ball, using a long stick that has a net attached to its oval head. The Pony Club plays three divisions of games, divided by age group. The number of team members varies from 2 to 6 depending on the division. A goal is scored when an attacking player uses his or her stick to throw the ball into the goal.

*Polocrosse players use their sticks to catch the ball, or pick it up from the ground. They cannot use their hands.*

# UNDERSTANDING YOUR PONY

## Contents

# PONIES IN THE WILD

A domestic pony may seem very different from a wild one, but living with humans over the years hasn't changed ponies very much. They still have all the same natural instincts. So, to understand your pony well, it does help to know how he'd live in the wild.

## LIFE IN HERDS

Wild ponies live in herds which roam around, grazing. They never choose to live on their own, so any pony found on its own is probably sick or too old to keep up with the herd. Usually, a herd has one stallion, three or four mares and their foals. One of the mares makes decisions for the herd, and the stallion keeps other stallions away.

*Family members*

*Stallion - a fully-grown male.*

*Mare - a fully-grown female.*

*Foal - a very young pony of either sex.*

*Filly - a female pony under the age of four.*

*Colt - a male pony under the age of four.*

*Geldings aren't found in wild herds. This is a term for stallions who've been "gelded" (had their testicles removed).*

## HOW PONIES SPEND THEIR TIME

Usually, ponies spend about 16 hours a day grazing. Eating small amounts all day like this is called "trickle feeding". Ponies often live in wide open places where the grass is poor, so they need to keep roaming to find enough to eat and to find water, too. Moving all the time means they get plenty of exercise and stay fit.

Ponies need to keep an eye out for danger (see "fight or flight", right), so they only sleep lying down for a total of about three hours each day. Herd members never go to sleep all at the same time. One or two always stay awake to keep guard. However, they can make up for this by dozing while they are standing up.

*These Portuguese ponies are owned by local people, but lead a "wild" life most of the time.*

# PLAYING, ROLLING AND GROOMING

Young ponies play at fighting to learn fighting skills. This is important for colts, who will have to fight other stallions when they are older.

If he feels safe enough to expose his vulnerable belly, a pony will give his skin and coat a good scratch by lying down and rolling on the ground.

Ponies also keep their coats healthy and clean by grooming each other. They nibble each others' coats with their lips and teeth.

*Ponies groom each others' backs and withers. These are areas which they can't reach themselves.*

# FIGHT OR FLIGHT?

Ponies are herbivores, which means they don't eat meat and are not aggressive. They are hunted by meat eaters (predators), such as lions. Many "wild" herds are now owned by people and have few natural enemies, but they still behave cautiously. Because they run faster than most predators, their best defense has always been speed, so they deal with fear and danger by running away. If they can't flee – for example, if they are cornered – they fight as a last resort, by lashing out with kicks and bites.

# HERD BEHAVIOR

Ponies have complex ways of relating to each other. While they all have some characteristics in common, no two ponies are exactly the same. A pony's character makes a big difference to his position in the herd and to how other ponies treat him. It also makes a difference to how he relates to other animals, such as humans.

## NATURAL CHARACTERISTICS

*Nervousness*

A pony always has to be on the lookout for danger, which makes him naturally nervous. If he has a lot of scary experiences, he tends to become even more restless and jumpy.

*Curiosity*

When a pony comes across something new, he doesn't feel safe until he's sure it won't harm him. If it isn't too scary, he approaches it to give it a good sniff.

*Affection*

Ponies know all the members of their own herd, and they like making friends (see right). They have special ways of showing affection, such as touching noses and nickering to each other.

## DECIDING WHO'S BOSS OF THE HERD

Domestic groups of ponies are usually made up of mares and geldings, as most stallions are gelded. However, there is still a dominant pony or "boss" in each group, who can be a mare or a gelding. This pony makes sure that the others follow and obey her (or him).

*The pecking order*

All the other ponies have a position within the herd, too. They submit to ponies above them, but dominate any below. This is called the "pecking order". A pony high in the pecking order gets the best food and water, but one at the bottom, such as a sick or old pony, may be pushed away or bullied.

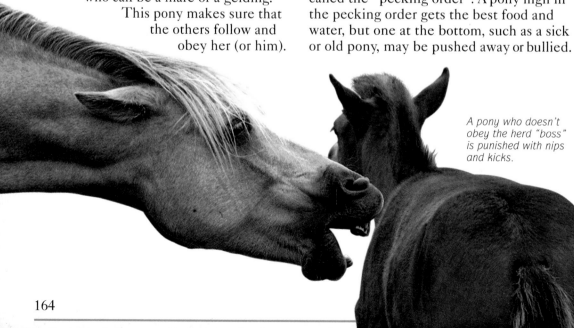

*A pony who doesn't obey the herd "boss" is punished with nips and kicks.*

# FRIENDS AND RIVALS

Ponies make their own special friends within the herd. Often, friends are a pair of ponies of about the same age and height, who hold a similar position in the pecking order. Pony friends graze close together, groom each other, and protect each other if necessary.

New ponies are greeted with squeals, stamps and kicking with the front legs, and they have to be patient and submissive before they find their position in the pecking order.

In the wild, dominant ponies fight to decide who's boss. This usually happens between stallions, and the loser is driven away. If two dominant ponies are kept in a field, though, the loser can't escape. In this case it can take a while for them to sort themselves out.

*Being the same height makes it easier for friends to groom each other.*

## HERD SQUABBLES AND "PERSONAL SPACE"

As long as a herd has established its pecking order, ponies only squabble now and again. While they're grazing, each pony keeps a certain distance away from the others so as not to disturb them. This area around a pony is called "personal space", and he will drive away unwelcome ponies if they get too close (see below). It's useful to remember that ponies don't like humans fussing around them while they eat, either.

# SENSES AND THINKING

Like you, ponies have five senses: hearing, sight, touch, taste and smell. Much of the way they think is based on what they learn from their senses. They have to detect danger before it gets too close, so their sight, hearing and smell are especially good. It's also possible that they have a "sixth" sense, which alerts them to dangers humans aren't aware of.

## HEARING

Ponies have very good hearing partly because they can turn their ears in almost any direction.

They can turn their ears back to hear behind them, or turn just one ear to hear from two directions at once.

If your pony is listening to a noise that you can't hear, you can watch his ears to tell where it's coming from.

## SMELL AND TASTE

A pony's sense of smell is good because wild ponies need to sniff out food and water as well as predators. Ponies tell each other apart by smell, and a stallion can smell a mare who is in season (ready to mate) a long way off. When he meets her, he curls his lip up (see right). This is called "Flehmen's response". A lot of ponies do this when they smell something strange, such as a lemon or garlic, as it helps them to smell it more clearly.

A pony's natural diet is not very varied, but ponies do like some foods more than others. They can also develop a liking for sweets if they are given too many.

## TOUCH

A pony can't see things just in front of him because of his blind spot (see opposite page). For close-up things he relies on touch. The whiskers on his muzzle are very sensitive and tell him all he needs to know.

*A pony's tail helps to swish away irritating flies.*

Ponies also have sensitive skin which is easily irritated by flies, and which is ticklish in some places.

## EYESIGHT

A pony has excellent eyesight, even at dusk. His eyes are on the side of his head, so he can see almost all the way around without moving his head at all. He has just two blind spots, or directions where he can't see anything. One is right in front of him, at the end of his nose, and the other is directly behind him.

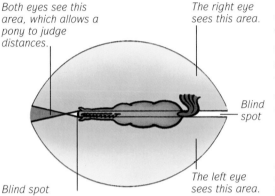

*Both eyes see this area, which allows a pony to judge distances.*

*The right eye sees this area.*

*Blind spot*

*The left eye sees this area.*

*Blind spot*

## THE "SIXTH SENSE"

Ponies do seem to have a strange way of knowing when something exciting or bad is happening. They also seem to know how humans are feeling, and they are especially good at picking up tension and fear.

It's possible that they can do this because their other senses are so good. They may hear things or feel vibrations that we can't sense (for example, the rumble of thunder), and they may smell our sweat when we're afraid.

*This pony has noticed something his rider isn't aware of.*

## HOW DOES YOUR PONY THINK?

A pony's thinking is based partly on his instincts, and partly on his experiences (what his senses tell him). His experience teaches him that some things are "good", and other things are "bad".

It's important to realize, though, that he doesn't figure this out logically. A bad thing is anything that scares or hurts him the first time he comes across it. For example, a plastic bag blowing around may make him afraid of all plastic bags from then on.

However, his strong herd instincts mean he may trust the experience of other ponies and humans, if they are kind. In this way, he may learn to overcome his fear.

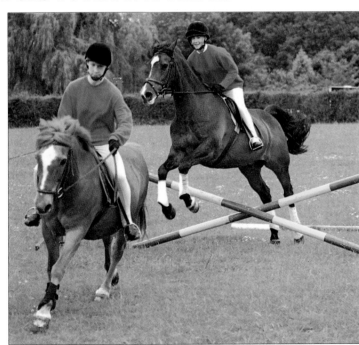

*A young pony can learn from an older one that something such as learning to jump is not as difficult or scary as it looks.*

167

# PONY LANGUAGE

You can tell a lot about how your pony is feeling by watching his expression and the shape of his body (his "body language"), and by listening to the sounds he makes. The more you watch, the more you will see that he looks quite different depending on his mood.

## BODY LANGUAGE

A pony's mood usually shows in his face, especially his ears and eyes. However, he also shows how he is feeling with his whole body. Important clues are given by how he holds his head, neck and tail, and by how tense his muscles are.

### Anger and submission

This picture could be of two ponies galloping playfully, but if you look closer, you can see that one is feeling angry and aggressive, while the other is afraid and submissive.

*This pony is the angry one. His ears are back, and his nostrils are flared. His neck is thrust toward the other pony and his tail swishes out behind him.*

*This pony is submissive. Although he's galloping, his tail is held much lower. His head is tucked in toward his chest, giving his neck a stiff, tense look. His ears are laid back, but out of fear, not anger.*

### Excitement

An excited pony makes a very upright, jaunty shape. Ponies also look like this when they are showing off and flirting with each other.

*His ears are pricked forward and his eyes are alert, bright and interested.*

*His tail is held high, but it's not swishing angrily.*

*His head is held high, his neck is arched and his posture is very alert. He's ready to spring into action.*

### Relaxation

A relaxed pony makes a long, low shape, though he can jump out of it if something catches his attention. If he doesn't, he may be sick (see pages 174-175).

*His ears flick in different directions, and his eyes are half-open, showing that he is almost dozing.*

*His tail is held low, but it's not clamped hard against his body.*

*His head and neck droop slightly, and his mouth looks relaxed.*

*All his muscles look relaxed.*

# SIGNS TO WATCH OUT FOR

● Ears laid back – this is sure to be a bad sign. It is one of the first signs that he is annoyed or unhappy about something.

● Showing the whites of his eyes, flared nostrils – he is feeling afraid or nervous. He is also likely to hold his head high and his neck tense.

● Lifting a back leg, or turning his hind quarters – watch out! He is about to kick, especially if his ears are back as well.

● Pawing and stamping the ground – he may be frustrated, or want to be fed. Sometimes it is a sign of colic (see page 175).

● Tossing head, swishing tail – it may be the flies, but he could be frustrated or annoyed. If he's annoyed, his overall body language will be tense.

● Thrusting his head, snapping and nipping are signs of aggression, though sometimes ponies nip playfully.

● Flicking ears – he is listening to different noises. If they are droopy, he may be relaxed. If they are cold as well, he may not be feeling well.

● Clamped down tail, held low – he is either cold, ill or afraid of something behind him. It is also a sign of submission.

## PONY NOISES

### Neighing

A neigh is a general call between ponies when they are some distance apart. They also neigh when they are upset, for example when they have to leave a friend.

### Snorting

Snorting is usually a sign of nervousness or fear, for example when a pony comes across an unusual object, or sometimes an unusual smell.

### Nickering

Nickering, or snickering, is a low noise of welcome. A mare nickers to her foal, and pony friends nicker to each other. Your pony may nicker to greet you, too.

### Squealing

Ponies squeal when they are excited, for example when they meet another pony for the first time. Stallions also squeal to mares in season.

*Some ponies neigh more than others.*

# YOU AND YOUR PONY

To live happily with humans, a pony needs to feel safe and
secure. In the wild, being with other ponies makes him feel
safe, but if he's domesticated, humans become part of his
"herd", too. So, to relate to him well, you need to build on the
trust and loyalty that herd members have for each other.

## GETTING TO KNOW EACH OTHER

A pony is happiest when he understands his pecking order and knows who's boss. Having a leader makes him feel secure, so he is quite willing to be told what to do. This is why it's your job to be "herd leader". If you're not, he may think he has to make his own decisions, which will lead to a lot of confusion and fighting between you.

Being leader doesn't mean frightening or bullying him. It means being firm, but kind and affectionate, so that he sees you as a friend as well.

To act as leader, keep your commands clear and simple so that he knows exactly what you want. When he behaves well, pat him and praise him in a pleased tone of voice. If he's naughty, scold him in an angry voice. You can slap him on the neck if he bites or kicks, but never hit his head or he will become afraid of having it touched, or "headshy".

You will soon get to know his character and moods. He will come to recognize you and your voice, and he'll learn to understand when you're pleased with him.

## ARE YOU UP TO THE JOB?

A pony knows when he can get the better of someone. If you are not up to being herd leader, you will have constant trouble. For this reason, it is important to have a pony that matches your abilities, and not one that's too much of a handful. You need to be sure that you can give him plenty of

attention, too. Once he has accepted that you are his herd leader, a pony will rely on you for protection, care and affection. If you can't meet these needs (for example, if you don't have enough time) you should think about letting someone else look after him.

*This pony doesn't want to turn and follow his owner, so he pulls away as she pulls him back.*

*She scolds him for pulling and doesn't give way, keeping up the pressure to make him turn.*

*He is still resisting, with his ears laid back. She still won't let him get away with it.*

*The pony realizes she's boss and gives up. He follows and she praises him for being good.*

# GOOD HANDLING

Remember that your pony can't see what's directly behind him. Always approach his shoulder, so he can see you easily.

Talk to him quietly and move calmly so that you don't startle him. Jerky, sudden movements will frighten him.

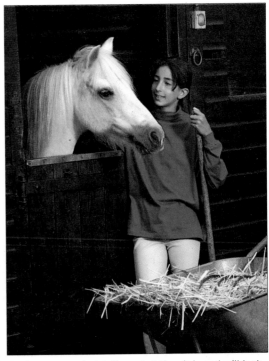

*Ponies are good at telling what time it is and will look forward to your visits.*

Watch him carefully on a daily basis to learn his body language. This will also help you tell if he's acting unusually.

Show him affection, as other ponies would – scratch his back and withers, and talk to him in a soft voice.

A domestic pony doesn't have much freedom, which is stressful for him. It helps if he knows what to expect, though, which is why it's important to keep to a routine. Try to muck out and feed him at the same time each day.

## KEYS TO DEVELOPING TRUST

• Be consistent. Don't scold him for something one day, then ignore it the next. Stick to a daily routine. He'll get upset if you keep changing it.

• Don't spoil him. If you give him tidbits every time he asks and let him get away with things, he will lose respect for you and start misbehaving.

• Spend time with him. If you only see him when you ride, you won't get to know each other. Remember his personal space, though, and don't crowd him too much.

# DAILY LIFE

Ponies that live with humans can't look after themselves in the way they would in the wild. We change their natural lifestyle by riding them, confining them in small spaces, and even deciding what they eat. To keep a pony happy and healthy, it's important to make up for these differences as much as possible.

## STABLED PONIES

Living in a barn is the most unnatural way for a pony to live. A stabled pony isn't free to exercise, he can't graze and can't search for more food if he runs out. He can't mix with other ponies, and living in a small enclosed space is not very good for his health, especially if it's dusty. Bear all these things in mind when you plan his shelter, so that you can meet as many of his needs as possible.

### Exercise
Ponies exercise naturally if they are grazing, but they can get bored and out of shape living in a barn. This can lead to problems (see pages 174-175). To prevent this, turn your pony out as much as possible, and ride him every day if you can.

### Grooming
A stabled pony can't roll to groom himself. He doesn't have pony friends to groom him either, so you need to give him a good grooming every day to keep his skin and muscles healthy.

### Space
The stall should be big enough for him to move around in and at least 4 x 4m (12 x 12ft).

### Bedding
Barns often have hard floors that a pony may hurt himself on when he lies down, so make sure his bedding is deep. Bear in mind that dry, dusty bedding can cause health problems (see page 175).

### Ventilation
Ponies naturally live out in the fresh air, so they need plenty of ventilation. Always leave the top door and any air vents open. If it's cold use a blanket – don't shut the top door.

### Food and water
He should always have plenty of fresh water and hay. Remember that in the wild, grazing would keep him busy nearly all day.

# PASTURED PONIES

Living in a field is more natural than living in a barn, but still not as natural as you might think. A field is much smaller than the open spaces a wild pony can roam, and it usually doesn't have natural sources of water, shade or shelter. It also tends to get soft and muddy in winter, and to grow too much lush grass in spring.

*There should be shelter in the field to protect him from flies, the sun and bad weather.*

*Check his health every day. Lush grass, muddy ground and worms can all cause problems (see pages 174-175).*

*The field must be big enough. Ponies need at least one acre each.*

*Make sure he has a constant supply of fresh water.*

*Don't let him live on one area of land until it gets "horse sick" (some patches eaten bare, the rest weedy and wormy). It helps to divide his field up to give the grass a rest, as shown here.*

# IS YOUR PONY LONELY?

Your pony won't be very happy if he's kept alone, even if you visit him regularly. Ideally, he should be kept with other ponies for company. If he's stabled, he should at least be able to see other ponies.

If you must keep him alone, try to make up for it in other ways. If he lives outside, try giving him other company such as a sheep or cow. If he lives inside, keep visiting him and get other people to visit him too.

## Introductions

When you introduce your pony to strange ponies, you can avoid problems by doing it gradually.

If he is going to share a field with several ponies, it helps to introduce him to just one or two of the friendlier ones first.

If possible, let him meet a new pony over a safe fence or gate, so that they can't kick at each other.

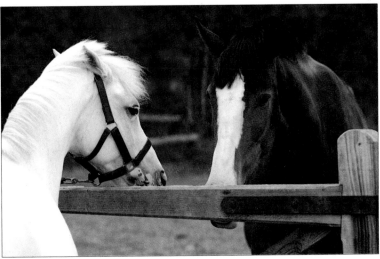

*These two ponies are being introduced over a gate.*

# GOOD HEALTH

Part of knowing your pony well is being able to spot when he's out of sorts. You may even be able to prevent many common problems before they arise. If in doubt, though, always consult a vet rather than try to guess what's wrong.

## DAILY HEALTH CHECK

You should check your pony over every day for signs of pain or poor health. He can't tell you if something's wrong, so you must watch for anything unusual in his appearance or behavior. If you are used to his body language and how he normally looks and behaves, you should be able to tell if he is sick just by looking at him.

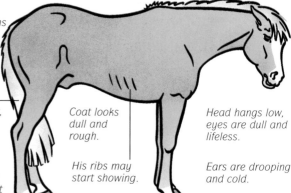

*This pony is showing signs of being sick, or out of condition.*

*Tail is clamped low, next to his body.*

*He's not interested in anything, not even his food.*

*Coat looks dull and rough.*

*His ribs may start showing.*

*Head hangs low, eyes are dull and lifeless.*

*Ears are drooping and cold.*

### Health checklist

• Watch him walk to check for lameness. If a front leg is lame, he will nod his head slightly as he walks.

• Run a hand down each leg to check for any swellings, lumps or cuts, or areas that feel hotter than usual.

• Check that his eyes are bright, with no runny discharge. Gently lift an eyelid to check that the membrane is pink.

• Check his feet for cuts. Make sure his shoes fit him properly, and that his frog is clean and healthy-looking.

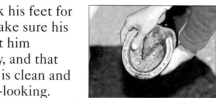

• Check that his nose does not have a runny discharge. If it does, he may have a cold or other infection.

• Watch how he eats. If he dribbles or lets food drop out of his mouth, he may have a problem with his teeth.

• Check his coat for any odd-looking patches or spots, and check for sores on the saddle and girth areas.

• Look at his teeth, especially if he's not eating properly. Look for obvious problems such as jagged edges.

# COMMON HEALTH PROBLEMS

When a pony is stabled, he may develop problems with his breathing and digestion, and his legs may also become stiff from standing in one place. For pasture-kept ponies, laminitis (see below) is a common problem. Your pony will stand a better chance of complete recovery if you can spot these things before they get too serious.

| | Symptoms | Causes | Prevention | Treatment |
|---|---|---|---|---|
| **Colic** | Restless, sweating, tries to roll. Paws ground. Doesn't eat. Looks around at belly and kicks it. | Exercise too soon after feeding, or feeding too soon after exercise. Poor quality feed. Unbalanced routine. Worms. Very rich grass or concentrates. | Keep to routine. Feed plenty of hay, not too many concentrates. Don't feed too soon before or after exercise. Give him plenty of exercise. Worm regularly. | Call the vet. Allow him to lie down in stall with lots of deep bedding. If he tries to roll, keep him standing and walk him around gently. |
| **Coughs** | Coughing. Runny nose. No energy, puffs when exercised. May have a temperature if it's an infection. | If the cough is due to infection, he may have caught it from strange ponies. It's more likely to be an allergy, or because he's out of condition from dusty or poor quality feed, dusty bedding, poor ventilation or confinement. | If infection or chill, keep him warm with a blanket and isolate. Vaccinate against infections. If due to bedding, change to less dusty bedding, such as wood chips or paper. Check ventilation and quality of feed. Soak his hay. | Call the vet. Allow pony plenty of rest to recover before working him hard. Make as many changes as you can to his stall, bedding and feed (see prevention), and turn out as much as possible. |
| **Laminitis** | Pony is lame. One or both front feet are hot. Pony tries to take weight off toes by stretching legs out and standing on heels. | Too much rich spring grass or other rich food. | Don't allow to eat too much spring grass - bring into barn if necessary. Give plenty of exercise. | Call the vet. Bring pony into barn. Give plenty of soft bedding that he can't eat, such as wood chips. Cool feet down in cold water. If very bad, allow to rest, otherwise exercise gently on soft surface. |
| **Mud fever** | Skin around heels is sore, cracked and scabby. Infection may have led to cracks spreading up legs. Heels are hot and swollen. May be lame. | Field too wet and muddy, chapping skin which becomes infected. | Wash legs gently with slightly medicated water and dry carefully. Get correct ointment from vet. Call the vet if it worsens, or if your pony becomes lame. | Don't allow pony to stay out in a very muddy field - change field or bring him in when it's very muddy. Protect legs and heels with barrier cream. |

# LIFESTYLE PROBLEMS

Some ponies find domestic life more stressful than others, so if your pony starts to develop a bad habit, he may be responding to stress. It doesn't make him a "bad" pony. He may have had a bad experience, feel lonely, bored or trapped. Watch out for any warning signs, because once he has a habit, it can be difficult to cure him of it.

## "BAD TEMPERED" PONIES

Biting, kicking, barging and being generally uncooperative in the paddock or barn can become nasty habits if you let them continue. If your pony acts this way with you or other ponies, there may be a number of reasons why.

### With you
• Remember his "flight or fight" instinct. He may be afraid of you, or feeling trapped. You need to reassure him and work on getting him to trust you.
• He may know he can get the better of you. You must be very firm and say "No!" If necessary, give him a slap on his neck.
• He may be spoiled and expects treats all the time. You need to say "No!" and stop spoiling him.
• He may be demanding attention because of being bored or hungry.
• If he's usually good-natured, he may be in pain. Get him checked by a vet.

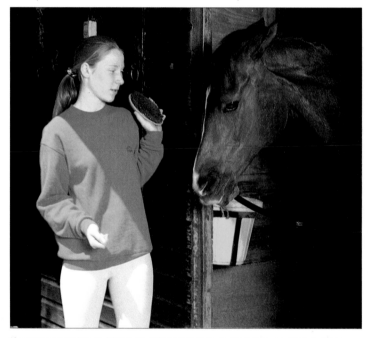

*If your pony tries to bite you, it's natural to jump back, as shown here. However, you must scold him to let him know he can't get away with it.*

### With other ponies
• If he's only aggressive with one other pony, it may be a personality clash. Keep the two ponies apart.

• He may be working out his place in the pecking order. If the ponies have only just met, don't worry, as they will probably sort themselves out. Check him after a few days to make sure that he has found a position in the group.

• There may not be enough food, space or water to go around, leading to fights. In this case, ponies lower in the pecking order won't get a fair share of food or water, so it's important to straighten the problem out.
• He may just be very touchy about his personal space, and snap at ponies who get too close.

# STABLE STRESS AND BOREDOM

If your pony develops a stable "vice", practical, short-term measures can help (see table below). However, you should still treat the cause of the problem by improving his living conditions as much as possible.

● Ride, or exercise him, every day.
● Give him plenty of hay to keep him busy, and don't give him too much rich food unless he gets enough exercise to burn it off.
● Turn him out for as much of the day as possible.

● Keep to a routine.
● Make sure he can see out of the stall.
● Give him some toys to play with, such as a ball that he can kick around.
● Make sure he gets plenty of company (other ponies or humans).

| | Problem | Practical/short-term solution |
|---|---|---|
| *Weaving* | Pony swings his head to and fro constantly. May also rock to and fro on his front legs. If he rocks, the stress on his legs may make him lame. | An anti-weave grille attached to his stall door may stop him from swinging his head. He may just move farther back and continue weaving, in which case you can only try to get to the root of the problem (see above). |
| *Cribbing, windsucking* | When he cribs, a pony holds onto the top of the stall door and chews at it. He may also suck air into his stomach, called windsucking. Cribbing eventually damages teeth, and windsucking makes it harder for him to digest his food, causing indigestion or colic. | To stop the cribbing, you can attach a strip of metal to the top of the stall door so that he cannot chew it, or paint the door with nasty-tasting anti-chew fluid. There are special collars that go around his neck to stop the windsucking. |
| *Stall walking* | The pony walks around and around the stall without stopping. | Check that he is not in pain. If the problem is boredom or stress, try placing objects (for example, tires or bales of straw) in the stall that he has to step around. |
| *Door banging* | He regularly kicks at his door or stall walls, which can damage his legs as well as the door. The noise may upset other ponies too. | Protect his legs by padding the door with something soft, like rubber matting. This doesn't make as much noise, which is partly what he likes, so he may stop. |

# A PONY'S TRAINING

You may not have known your pony when he was young, but if he is well-behaved this is almost certainly because he had good experiences as a foal. If you have problems with him, it may be worth finding out who trained him, and how.

## THE LEARNING PROCESS

The best way to train a pony is to build on his natural process of learning through experience (see page 167). After a new experience, he remembers whether it is good or bad for a long time. His training should therefore be full of positive experiences that he is happy to repeat.

- New things should be introduced gently, with plenty of time for him to get over his fear.
- If he gets scared while learning something, he should be taken back to an earlier stage until he's happy again. He should be allowed to grasp each lesson thoroughly, by repeating it lots of times, before he's moved on to the next.
- If he's good, he should be praised and patted (tidbits will spoil him). If he misbehaves, he must be scolded firmly, but he should never be frightened.

## EARLY EXPERIENCES

Ideally, learning to accept domestic life starts as soon as a pony is born. If he's used to being handled well when he's very young, he learns to trust humans naturally. This makes it much easier for him to accept the later stages of his training.

A foal's first step is to learn that humans won't hurt him, so he should be handled gently, firmly and as soon as possible after birth.

Next, he's taught to walk calmly alongside his trainer when he's being led. When he responds well, his trainer praises him with lots of pats.

Soon, he learns about grooming, and that humans can touch vulnerable places such as his belly and head without hurting him.

## THE FARRIER

If he is used to having his legs and feet touched and groomed, a pony should have no problem learning to stand for a farrier. This does involve strange objects and actions that may frighten him, though, so his trainer should be on hand all the time to calm and reassure him.

## ACCEPTING A BRIDLE

A pony is introduced to a bit and bridle when he's about two. If he's used to wearing a halter, this won't come as a big surprise. It needs to be introduced carefully, though, as he mustn't get the idea that it can hurt him. At first, the bridle shouldn't have a noseband or reins, and should be put on very gently.

*If it's introduced properly, the bit will seem like a toy that he can play with in his mouth.*

## LEARNING TO LOAD

A trailer or van is a dark, spooky place for a pony, and the ramp feels very unstable.

*Let your pony have a good look at the ramp before you try to load him.*

If he learns early on that it's safe, it will save a lot of stress later. He should be given plenty of time to inspect the ramp before he steps onto it, and if possible the front of the trailer should be opened up, so that he can see through it. The idea is to coax him gently onto the ramp, so everyone should stay calm and patient. If necessary, he can be encouraged with some tasty food.

## GOING TO SHOWS

A pony can be taken to shows long before he's ready to be ridden, as being used to all the strange sights and sounds is good experience for when he's older.

He can be entered in an in-hand showing class, (a class for ponies that are led, not ridden) or he can just go along for the experience. If possible, an older pony should be taken to stay near him for the day. This will give him more confidence and help keep him calm.

Going to shows is tiring for a young pony, so he shouldn't be taken too often.

179

# ACCEPTING A RIDER

To an untrained pony, a rider is a scary, heavy object which he can't see properly, and in the wild, the only similar thing he'd come across would be a predator on his back. So, this stage in his training takes very careful preparation.

## GETTING USED TO A SADDLE

Introduction to a saddle or longing pad takes place when the pony is about three. First, he should be given a good look at it.

Next it can be put on his back. The girth should be fastened just enough to stop it from slipping, never tightly or suddenly.

He may try bucking the saddle off, but this is fine. Once he is convinced that it can't harm him, he begins to get used to it.

## LONGING

Longing is a very important part of a pony's training. It helps to develop the muscles, flexibility and balanced posture that he'll need for carrying a rider.

The pony moves in a circle around his trainer, who controls him with a longe line and crop. He is taught to obey the trainer's voice, and the sound of the crop teaches him to move forward on command. In order to make sure that the muscles on both sides of his body are developing properly, he spends time circling in both directions.

After a while, side reins are added. They are attached to his bit and to rings on the saddle. This creates contact with his mouth, preparing him for a rider holding the reins.

## LONG REINING

When a pony has been longed for a while, he is introduced to long reining. Two long lines go from the bit, through the stirrups and back to the trainer, who walks behind. The trainer is positioned slightly to one side of the pony's blind spot. This means he can just see her, but has to go forward independently in response to the aids, as he will have to do when he has a rider.

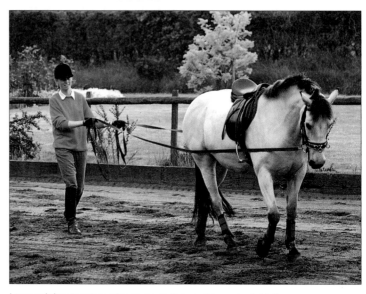

*Long reining teaches him to move forward in a straight line.*

# FIRST MOUNTING

One person holds the pony while someone else is given a leg up, putting pressure on his back.

Next, the rider lies across the pony's back so that the pony can feel her full weight.

The rider now sits astride, but lies flat at first in case the pony is frightened by seeing her there.

Once the pony is used to feeling the rider, she can sit up straight, keeping still in the saddle.

Next, the pony is led around on the longe line. The rider holds the reins, but doesn't take up any contact.

Eventually, the rider begins to put pressure on the pony's sides, and makes gentle contact with his mouth.

## Essentials for training

- As with all training, the trainers should be very knowledgeable and experienced.
- All trainers must wear protective clothing - hats, gloves, and a back protector for the rider.
- Lessons should be kept short, so that the pony doesn't get bored or upset.
- The pony's reactions should be watched carefully. If he reacts badly, he should be taken back to an earlier stage to gain more confidence.
- Every lesson should finish on a positive note.

## THE OUTSIDE WORLD

For a pony to be safe for less experienced riders, he must be used to coping with the outside world. He must be confident enough to trust his rider when something startles or frightens him.

He can be prepared for frightening or unusual objects by being introduced to them at home where he feels safe. When he is first ridden out, it can help if he has a steady, older pony for company.

*By being allowed to investigate this black plastic bag, the pony realizes it won't hurt him.*

# GOOD RIDING

If a pony has been trained to allow mounting properly, you shouldn't have too many problems riding him. It's up to you to ride confidently and well. If you build a good working relationship with him, he shouldn't develop bad habits and will remain a pleasure to ride.

## USING YOUR AIDS

Your pony should have learned to respond to the five natural aids, which are your legs, voice, hands, seat and body. You shouldn't need artificial aids, such as a crop, unless your pony is very lazy or stubborn, and spurs are only needed for advanced riding.

This pony is responding well to his rider's aids.

● Keep your leg commands clear and simple, and keep your weight steady in the saddle. If you keep kicking, moving your legs around and shifting your weight, he won't know what you're trying to tell him.
● Keep steady contact with his mouth, enough for him to feel it but not enough to hurt him. Don't fuss around with the reins.
● Use your voice clearly. Change your tone when you are pleased or angry with him, and give him instructions firmly.

## A BALANCED SEAT

Having a rider on his back upsets a pony's natural balance, but he can regain it if his hocks are under him (called engaging his hocks) and his neck is flexed properly.
A well-balanced seat helps him to do these things, and makes your weight less uncomfortable for him.

*Riding without stirrups helps to develop a firm and well-balanced seat.*

## WATCH YOUR RIDING

If you ride lazily, your pony will probably become lazy too. If you think about your riding and try to improve, you will be less likely to blame your pony for things which are really your fault. Check your legs, hands and seat as you ride, and work out what messages you are giving.

*Doing exercises in the saddle is one way of improving your riding.*

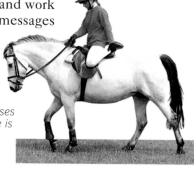

# RESPECTING HIS LIMITS

When you ask your pony to do something new, remember that he learns by experience. This means that he won't understand why you want him to do it.

Instead, he will learn by being encouraged and praised for getting it right, and being corrected when he gets it wrong. This process can take a while, so you must be very patient.

*Working your pony over trotting poles may not seem exciting, but it helps him to develop his skills.*

## Don't overstretch him

If you push your pony too far or too fast, he may lose confidence and so begin to lose trust in you. It's important to understand and respect his limits, and not to ask more of him than you know is possible. He can't read your mind, so being asked to do things he doesn't understand will only confuse him.

## REMEMBER WHO'S BOSS

Even if he has been well trained, a pony will naturally try to get his own way if he can. It's up to you to make sure he stays in the right position in the pecking order, with you at the top. Don't let him get away with lazy habits or with acting up. If he knows you are boss, he will respect and trust you more in the long run.

*Running out at jumps is a favorite trick of naughty ponies, and a sure sign that your pony doesn't have much respect for your riding.*

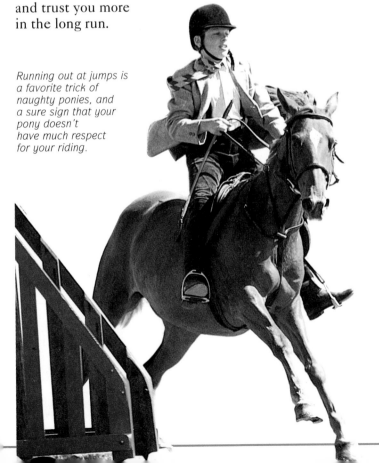

## CONSISTENCY

One of the most important qualities that a rider can have is consistency. This means treating him in the same way every day and in every situation, so that he knows what to expect. If you let him get away with something one day, he will be very upset if you punish him for it the next.

### Keeping him confident

* Ride confidently, so that he knows you are sure about what you want him to do.
* Stop working before he gets tired and stale, and finish work on a positive note.
* Reassure him if he gets confused and tense. Take him back to an earlier stage.
* Always think before you scold him. Was it really his fault – or yours?

# BAD COMMUNICATION

Most ponies misbehave from time to time, especially if they are lively and spirited. However, this is often because of bad riding and communication, not because they're being naughty. If your pony is not doing well, you need to look carefully at your own skills before blaming him. You should also check that he's not in pain (see pages 186-187).

## RIDING PROBLEMS

*This pony is resisting his rider and fighting for his head. His swishing tail shows he's upset. His rider needs to work out why.*

Remember that carrying a rider isn't natural for your pony. When he's ridden badly, he can quickly lose his coordination. He'll start poking his nose out and trailing his legs behind him.

### An undeveloped seat

If your seat is unbalanced, you put a strain on your pony's back, making him tense up. You are more likely to bounce around heavily in the saddle, which can make his back sore. You may also hurt his mouth by balancing yourself with the reins and jabbing him with the bit. It's not really surprising if he becomes unsettled and uncooperative as a result.

### Mixed messages

If your riding skills aren't all they could be, it's very easy to confuse your pony with conflicting aids. You may be telling him one thing with your hands and another with your seat and legs. He will fight because he doesn't know what to do.

This sort of problem can get worse if he is scolded for not doing the right thing. To him, you're just being unfair, and he'll begin to lose his trust in you.

This rider is urging the pony on with her legs, but holding him back with the reins. As a result, his ears are back, his nose is in the air and his back is "hollow".

This pony has just refused. He may be acting up, but refusals are often the rider's fault. Scolding him makes him even more unhappy and confused.

# LACK OF CONFIDENCE

## Yours

Your pony's "sixth sense" means that he can tell if you lack confidence. He relies on your guidance, so if you're nervous, it will worry him and make him nervous too. You're also less likely to ride well if you're all tensed up.

## Your pony's

Inexperienced or young ponies tend to lack confidence. However, poor riding, bad experiences, and having too much demanded of them can make older ponies lose confidence too.

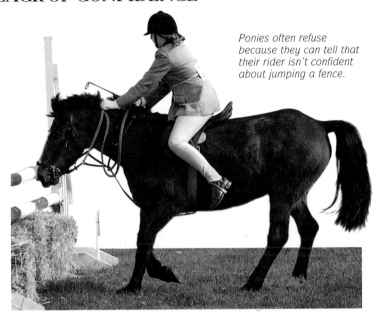

*Ponies often refuse because they can tell that their rider isn't confident about jumping a fence.*

## FINDING A SOLUTION

If your riding needs improvement, ask an instructor to watch you ride. She should be able to spot any problems with your seat or aids. You could go back to being longed for a while to iron out your problems.

If you need to build up your pony's confidence, take him back to a basic stage where he is sure of what he is doing, and build up his work very gradually from there.

### Is he the right pony?

It may be that your pony is too big or too high-spirited for you. If you continue riding him without being able to control him or keep him balanced, he is likely to lose confidence and even develop bad habits. It's a better idea to ride a quiet, experienced pony until your own skills have developed.

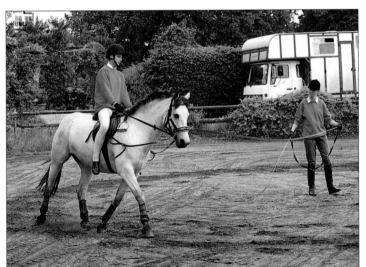

*Riding on a longe again allows you to concentrate on your seat.*

*Many problems arise from riding a pony that's the wrong size for you. Riding one that's too small isn't a good idea as it puts him under strain and leads to lazy riding habits.*

185

# PROBLEM HABITS

Sometimes a minor riding or handling difficulty can develop into a real problem, or even a serious bad habit. Some problems can be managed and cured with understanding, careful handling and retraining, but other habits need expert help.

## IS HE IN PAIN?

Pain is one of the most common reasons for a pony's bad behavior, especially if he's usually good. He can't tell you where he's in pain, or why - he just tries to avoid the problem. Check him for signs of discomfort. If an area is sore, he'll flinch when you run your hand over it. If you can't spot anything, have him checked by an expert.

*Problems with your pony's teeth can be avoided by asking your vet to check his mouth regularly.*

### Common sore spots

*Teeth can get jagged if they're not regularly rasped, and catch on the inside of the pony's mouth.*

*A pony can suffer a lot of discomfort from his girth chafing or pinching.*

*Problems in the legs and feet are fairly easily spotted, as the pony usually goes lame. Call your vet to check what's wrong.*

*A badly fitting saddle can lead to a sore back. Other back and neck problems may be invisible, so consult an expert.*

## WHAT'S HE AFRAID OF?

If you are sure your pony isn't in pain, you need to find out whether he's unhappy or afraid of something.

If he seems afraid of one thing in particular, he may have had a bad experience with it in the past, or more recently if his fear develops suddenly. He may have been trained poorly, or his training may be unfinished. He may even have been treated badly.

He may be unhappy if his home unsettles him, for example if he's being bullied or if his barn is very noisy. He may also become irritable and jumpy if he is fed too much rich food.

*Shying can be a sign of general jumpiness (see right).*

## TREATING PROBLEMS

Remember that one bad experience, which you may quickly forget, can have a big effect on your pony. In addition, problems caused by pain can continue when he's better, as he's learned a new way of behaving.

● Don't underestimate how much an experience may affect your pony. Give him time to get over pain or fear, and retrain him carefully.

● Don't start scolding him for bad behavior until you are sure he is not in pain or afraid - you will only add to his unhappiness.

# PULLING AND PRANCING

If a pony is excited it's natural for him to pull a little. However, if he's always prancing along with his head in the air, there's something wrong. Pain from his teeth, back or tack are common causes, but once you're sure he's fine, you need to look at your riding. If you're tense, you may be pulling, which is making him pull too. He may also have become insensitive to your aids if they're not clear.

## What to do

* Do some basic schooling with an instructor.
* Keep your hands still.
* Don't stop using your legs. Ride him strongly, but try not to get tensed up.
* Feed him fewer concentrates. Ride him often to burn off his energy.

*A prancer may need to be retrained.*

# SHYING

A pony's instincts tell him to shy when he spots something spooky. Occasional shying is fine, but if it's a habit you need to calm him down.

## What to do

* Try to spot a scary object before he does, then turn his head away from it and ride him forward strongly.
* If he's seen it, let him inspect the scary object.
* Give plenty of reassurance.
* Ride out with a calm pony.

# ABOUT BOLTING

When a pony bolts, he's in a panic and is obeying his "flight" instinct, which is to run away. You need to determine what he's running away from, especially if he runs away with you often. He may be trying to escape pain in his teeth, so when you pull on the reins, you make it worse. If you are riding badly, he may be trying to escape from you banging on his back. It's also possible that he's spotted something scary.

## What to do

*Half-halt*

*If your pony bolts, don't panic. He is already frightened, so screaming or clinging on will make him worse.*

*Give*

*Sit up straight and deep into the saddle. Remind him you're there by giving and taking with the reins.*

*Half-halt again*

*Try turning him in a big circle. This may gradually slow him down and get him to take notice of you again.*

# DEALING WITH BALKING

Balking is when you can't make your pony go forward or do what you want. He may try to turn back home or run backward. He may be in pain, afraid, or confused from being given mixed messages. He may feel vulnerable at being asked to do things on his own. It's also possible that he's bored, or thinks he's boss.

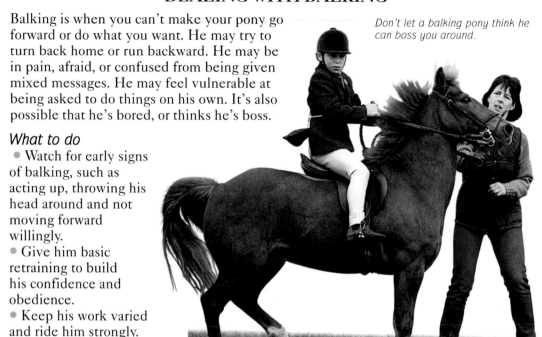

*Don't let a balking pony think he can boss you around.*

## What to do
* Watch for early signs of balking, such as acting up, throwing his head around and not moving forward willingly.
* Give him basic retraining to build his confidence and obedience.
* Keep his work varied and ride him strongly.
* Do some work on your own riding skills.

# TRYING TO BUCK YOU OFF

*This pony has his head down, so it's difficult for the rider to control him.*

Ponies buck occasionally to let off steam, but frequent bucking can be a problem. It's a pony's way of shaking off a predator, so if his back hurts, he may be trying to buck the pain away. If there are no sores under his saddle, have him checked by an expert. If he's a very high-spirited pony, he may just have found that it's a quick way to get rid of his rider.

## What to do
* Cut down on concentrates. Give him plenty of exercise.
* Get back on if he bucks you off, so he knows he can't get rid of you.
* Keep his head up and your legs on if he's about to buck.

# REASONS FOR REARING

A pony may rear because he's in pain, confused or startled by something. You need to find out what's wrong very quickly, as once it's a habit it's very difficult to cure. Don't try to deal with it yourself - always get expert help. A pony that rears is dangerous to ride, because there is the risk of him falling over backward on top of you.

## What to do
● If possible, have him retrained by an expert so that he learns not to rear.
● If he rears while you're riding him, don't balance by pulling on the reins. This may pull him over on top of you.
● Lean forward, then as he comes down again, drive him forward strongly with your legs.

# HANDLING PROBLEMS

| Problem | Cause | Solution |
|---------|-------|----------|
| *Hard to catch* | Not enough time turned out. Not enough time with pony friends. Doesn't trust you or want to be with you. Knows he can get the better of you. | Allow plenty of time turned out with pony friends. Work on your relationship with him. Reward him for being caught with plenty of praise, so he sees it as a pleasant experience. Show you're herd leader by ignoring him when he looks interested in you. Walk away - he may follow. Last resort - leave his halter on so it's easier to catch hold of him. |
| *Hard to load* | Hasn't been trained properly and still sees trailer as dark, unsafe spooky place. Has had bad experience in trailer in the past. He's acting up. | May need retraining - allow him plenty of time to sniff around the trailer and get used to looking into it. Try loading him along with a calm experienced pony - he may follow him in. Tempt him in with tidbits and reward him for each step in the right direction. |
| *Hard to tack up* | Saddle - Pain in back. Associates being ridden with a bad experience. His mounting training wasn't completed properly.<br><br>Bridle - Pain in mouth. May be head-shy through being hit on the head or having head roughly handled. | Have his back and saddle checked. Take him back to a basic level of training until he is comfortable with the saddle and with weight on his back.<br><br>Have his teeth checked. Retrain with gentle handling of head with hand, gradually increasing the amount of contact, until he accepts it without a fuss. |
| *Hard to mount* | He has pain in his back from weight of rider. Associates being ridden with bad experience. He's just acting up. | If he's afraid or in pain, problems are likely to continue during riding. If so, have his back and saddle checked. If he's just acting up, don't let him get away with it. Ask for help in making him stand still. |

# PARTNERSHIP

Getting to know and understand your pony forms the basis for all good riding partnerships, even if you just want to ride for fun. You can also build on your partnership if you want to keep on learning, or enter competitions.

## RIDING FOR FUN

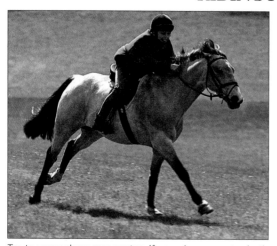

*Try to vary where you canter. If you always canter in the same place he may start setting off before you tell him to.*

Once your pony sees you as his friend and leader, he'll enjoy your company and be loyal, too. However, if you only ride for fun, make sure you don't take him for granted. He still needs a routine and regular exercise. You must also avoid sloppy riding, so that he doesn't develop bad or lazy habits.

### Trail riding tips

● Don't relax your riding skills because you're not in an arena. He still needs clear messages about what you want him to do.
● Don't let him get away with balking. Ride him along different routes so that he can't take control of where he's going.
● Keep him confident. Let him inspect anything scary or new that you come across.

## FURTHER SCHOOLING AND DRESSAGE

To develop your pony's schooling and your own riding skills, you should ride regularly and continue taking lessons. Gradually, you will learn to feel and understand your pony's body and movements, so that you can work on subtle changes.

Once you go on to more advanced work, remember that each pony's ability is different and that some progress faster than others. If he is finding something difficult to learn, you may be asking too much of him, or pushing him too fast.

*Dressage involves moves such as this pirouette in walk.*

Dressage is really another way of saying training, and the work you do on your gaits and transitions around the ring is basic dressage work. The goals of dressage are to help the pony move naturally and gracefully, and for the rider and pony to achieve the greatest harmony possible. The pony can then respond to the lightest of aids.

# COMPETING

A happy, lively pony will want to please you and may well enjoy showing off, too. Entering competitions is a great way of letting him do both. As well as dressage, you could try gymkhanas, show jumping, cross-country or showing. Before you decide which to try, assess your pony's strengths and weaknesses - his size, shape and temperament, and how skillful he is. Think about your own skills, too.

*If he is small and eager, he may make a good gymkhana pony.*

### Tips for competing

● Don't destroy his confidence by entering him for a competition that is too difficult for him.
● Don't ever punish him for losing, especially if he tried his best.
● Shows can be stressful places, so bear in mind that he may get nervous or over-excited. Keep him calm and give him plenty of reassurance.
● Make sure he is well prepared and fit enough, so that he doesn't strain himself on the big day.

## KEEPING ONE STEP AHEAD

However well you and your pony get along, remember that you can never predict exactly how he will behave. It's also important to realize that you can't know everything there is to know, and that you may sometimes need advice from people with more experience. Most important of all, remember that your pony depends on you for nearly all his needs, and he can't tell you when something's wrong. It's up to you to notice and correct it.

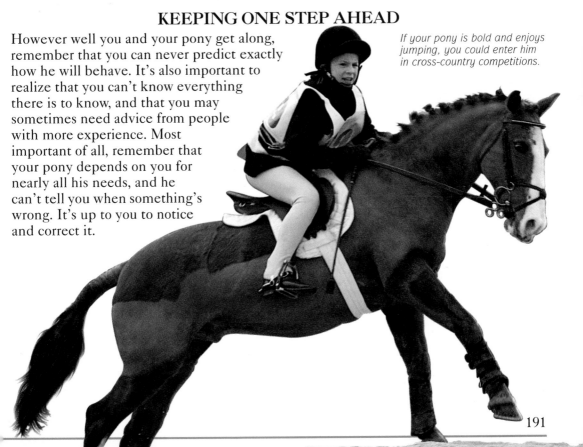

*If your pony is bold and enjoys jumping, you could enter him in cross-country competitions.*

# CROSS COUNTRY

## Contents

# WHAT IS CROSS-COUNTRY ?

Cross-country riding means riding off the roads and outside the schooling ring. It can be across fields, through woods or down country tracks with all kinds of natural obstacles and fences to tackle on the way. Whether your goal is to compete or simply ride for fun, you will need good basic riding and jumping skills.

## CROSS-COUNTRY FOR FUN

### Sponsored or fun rides

These non-competitive events are usually organized in aid of a charity, and are a good introduction to cross-country for you and your pony. They get you used to riding in open country with other ponies, and there are normally a few optional fences. Look for advertisements in local papers, saddlery shops or riding schools.

### Hunting and mock hunting

Hunting is one of the earliest forms of cross-country riding and many of today's events stem from this sport. During a fast chase, riders have to tackle whatever obstacles they meet. These days mock hunting or drag hunting is becoming more popular. Instead of chasing a fox, a scent is laid for the hounds to follow.

# COMPETITIVE CROSS-COUNTRY

## Hunter trials

These events are often organized by local hunts. Originally their purpose was to train riders and horses for hunting, but nowadays they include classes for all ages and standards. The aim is to ride clear around a course of jumps built across several fields, usually within an optimum time limit.

## Eventing

In one-, two-, or three-day events, the cross-country course is one of three parts of the competition. The other two are dressage and show jumping. Eventing is a thorough test of both horse and rider's fitness and stamina.

## Long distance riding

Long distance riding is a competitive sport which involves riding, but not necessarily jumping, across country. Courses are usually from 80 to 120km (50 to 75 miles) long, so you and your pony have to be very fit to take part. Vets are on hand to check the ponies' health at various stages on a long distance ride.

## Team chase

In this event, four riders race around a cross-country course as fast as possible. No points are lost for falls or refusals and it is the times of the first three riders home that count. Team chase is fast and competitive, so it is usually restricted to older, more experienced riders.

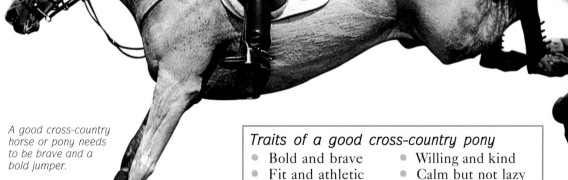

*A good cross-country horse or pony needs to be brave and a bold jumper.*

### Traits of a good cross-country pony

- Bold and brave
- Fit and athletic
- Sound and healthy, with strong legs
- Obedient and well-trained
- Sure-footed
- Willing and kind
- Calm but not lazy
- A good, willing jumper, but also careful
- The right size and strength for you

# RIDING OUTDOORS

Once you leave the relative safety of an indoor ring or enclosed arena, all kinds of factors change. Ground and weather conditions will vary and there are likely to be hills to tackle. Your pony may also be more excitable than usual, so before heading off across country, make sure you can keep control.

## STAYING IN CONTROL

Most people learn to ride in an indoor ring or arena where it is easier to control a pony. Out in the open the pace is usually faster and ponies often become harder to control. If you lose control, your pony could go a long way before deciding to stop.

*This pony is pulling on the reins and could easily get out of control.*

*This rider is in control of her pony and he is listening to her aids.*

### Tips for control
* Try to stay in complete balance with your pony at all times with light contact on his mouth.
* Shorten your reins whenever you pick up speed.
* Sit up well and be firm with your pony.
* If you do get out of control, stay calm. Panicking will make the pony go faster.
* Head toward a large hedge – make sure it is too big for him to jump.
* Head uphill – this will slow your pony down.
* Turn your pony in a circle. Make the circle smaller as he slows down.

## YOUR POSITION

Whenever you go cross-country riding, you need to shorten your stirrups by a couple of holes. This helps you to change your position slightly.

Shorter stirrups allow you to move your weight forward easily. This helps your pony balance at faster speeds and also helps you to keep control.

To steady your pony or urge him on, sit back in the saddle to give the aids. This is the position you will need for the approach to most jumps.

# COPING WITH BAD GROUND CONDITIONS

*In wet weather the takeoff and landing areas of a jump can become very muddy.*

Conditions that make life more difficult for your pony are hard or slippery ground or very soft ground such as deep mud or plowed soil. Hard ground can hurt your pony's legs, causing splint or tendon damage, (see pages 201 and 223) so be careful not to ride too fast or jump too much on it. If you do have to ride on hard ground, let your pony go more slowly and jump smaller fences.

Riding through heavy mud or soft ground is tiring for your pony and will slow him down. It can also cause damage to his legs. Jumping from soft or heavy ground requires a lot more effort.

*Hot, dry weather usually means hard ground. Let your pony go more slowly in these conditions.*

## WEATHER AND MOOD

As well as influencing the ground conditions, weather can alter the mood of your pony. On a hot day he could be sleepy and lazy, while windy conditions may make him excitable and easily spooked.

*On a windy day, a nervous pony will find more things to spook at than usual.*

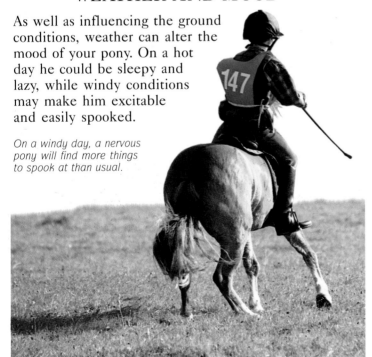

## CROSS-COUNTRY COURTESY

When riding across country, you are usually on someone else's land, so it is important to respect it. You are also likely to be out with other riders, so be considerate to them too.

### Points to remember
* Keep to the trail.
* If there are animals in a field, ride around them.
* Close any gates that you open.
* Approach any other riders calmly.
* If you are having trouble at a jump and someone else is close behind, let the other rider pass ahead.

# HILLS AND SLOPES

Ponies bred in the mountains can be very sure-footed on the steepest of slopes, but other breeds may find hillwork quite difficult. They have to adjust their balance and pace, though you can help by altering your position slightly. Hillwork is good fitness training, but don't overdo it, as too much can put strain on your pony's legs.

## RIDING UPHILL

Going up a hill is easier for your pony than going down or across it. This is because his power is in his hindquarters. It does take extra effort, though, and he will use a shorter stride. To help his balance, fold forward from the hips. This takes your weight off his hindquarters. Move your hands forward so that he can stretch his neck. Your position will depend on the slope. The steeper it is, the farther forward you need to be.

### Warning

Remember to check your girth before riding up and down hills.

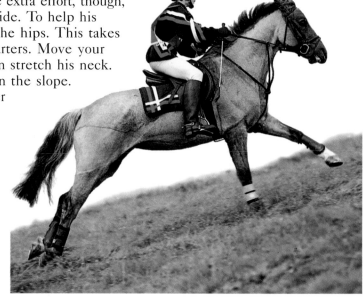

*Attack a steep slope in a bouncy trot or canter so that your pony has plenty of impulsion.*

## RIDING ACROSS A SLOPE

Moving across a hill is very difficult for ponies. They tend to drift downhill. If you have to ride across a gentle slope, aim slightly uphill and keep your lower leg firmly on the girth.

If you need to cross steep ground, ride straight up or down it and look for a flatter route across that will be easier for your pony to tackle.

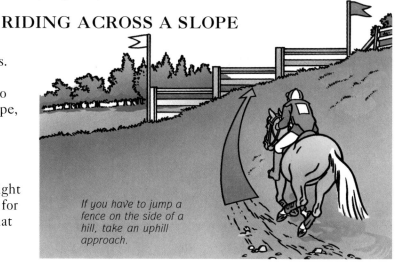

*If you have to jump a fence on the side of a hill, take an uphill approach.*

## RIDING DOWNHILL

It is harder for your pony to balance when going downhill, as his hindquarters are above him. He will tend to take longer strides which makes it easy for him to pick up speed. You need to stay in a safe, upright position. Let your pony stretch his neck out, but don't let him fall forward.

On very steep slopes your pony will take lots of shorter steps. Stay still and straight and make sure he doesn't get out of control.

### Trotting downhill
- Only trot down gentle slopes.
- Avoid trotting downhill if the ground is hard.
- Make sure you are in complete control.
- Keep a rising trot but try not to bump down hard in the saddle.

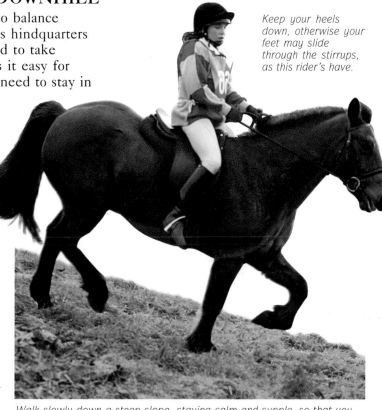

*Keep your heels down, otherwise your feet may slide through the stirrups, as this rider's have.*

*Walk slowly down a steep slope, staying calm and supple, so that you can go with your pony's movement.*

## ADDING STUDS TO YOUR PONY'S SHOES

Studs can be useful on steep terrain or in difficult ground conditions. If you want to use them, you have to ask your farrier to make holes for them in your pony's shoes.

This is usually done on the outside of the shoes. When not using studs, pack the holes with oiled cotton to stop them from filling with dirt. Here's how to put one in:

*Use a farrier's nail.*

*Stud tap*

Remove the cotton from the stud hole and clean it out.

Use a stud tap to clear the thread inside the hole.

Holding your pony's foot firmly, screw in the stud.

Tighten stud, using the tap's other end or a crescent wrench.

# GETTING FIT

Both pony and rider need to be fit for any type of competition, but cross-country in particular will test your stamina to the full. In order to avoid injury, it is important to start training slowly and gradually build up to faster speeds. You will need to build up your pony's food too.

## PLANNING YOUR TRAINING

It takes about eight weeks to get a pony fit for a preliminary cross-country competition. The first four weeks will be slow work at walk and trot. The next four will be longer, faster hacks and schooling work. The table below shows how to build up your work over an eight-week period and the list on the right includes a few other points you need to consider when planning your own program.

### Points to consider

● Before you start, get your pony shod, make sure his vaccinations are up to date and have his teeth checked.

● If your pony has been out of work, allow longer for the early stages.
● If you have already been competing and attending shows or events, you can do less slow work and concentrate on the faster work right away.
● Work your pony six days a week and let him have one day a week off.

● Vary the work as much as possible. From week five try for two long, slow hacks, two schooling sessions and two sessions of faster work each week.
● Follow a day of fast work with a day off or a long, slow hack.

### EIGHT-WEEK PROGRAM

| Week | Hacking | Schooling |
|------|---------|-----------|
| 1 | ½ – 1 hour walk | |
| 2 | 1 – 1½ hour walk | |
| 3 | Add trots | |
| 4 | Add gentle hillwork | |
| 5 | Add canters | From week 5 add basic schooling at walk and trot. |
| 6 | Increase canters | Work at canter Add trotting poles |
| 7 | Longer, steeper hills Add small jumps | Include gridwork |
| 8 | Long, steady canters Short gallops | More gridwork |

# SLOW WORK ON ROADS AND TRACKS

To begin with, simply walk your pony out on firm, flat ground. Quiet roads and tracks are ideal. This helps strengthen the bones, tendons and ligaments in his legs, which will help prevent lameness later on.

Always encourage your pony to walk energetically so that his muscles are toned up too. Introduce trotting and then hillwork a little at a time.

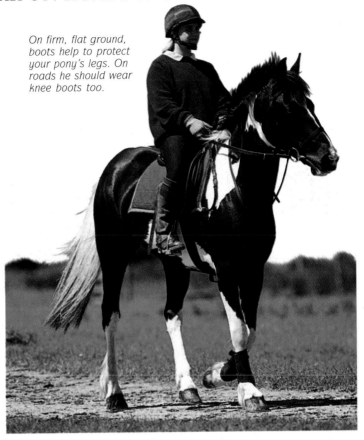

*On firm, flat ground, boots help to protect your pony's legs. On roads he should wear knee boots too.*

## Your pony's legs
Check the ligaments, tendons, and splint bone for heat or swelling after work (see page 223 to find out how to do this).

Splint bone

Tendon

Canon bone

Ligaments

# SCHOOLING FOR RHYTHM AND BALANCE

*Exercises with turns and circles loosen your pony up and make him supple.*

After about four weeks of gentle hacking, start schooling your pony in walk and trot. This will improve his balance and rhythm as well as teaching him to be obedient.

When you are ready to make your pony work a little harder, add some exercises over trotting poles and small cross poles. Start schooling in canter as well as walk and trot.

As your pony's fitness improves, try some gridwork (jumping down a line of small fences). This is excellent jump training and will help make your pony supple.

# BUILDING UP SPEED

A lot of cross-country is ridden at a canter or gallop, so it is important to practice these gaits. Build up to them gradually so as to avoid any unnecessary strains.

*A good gallop is fun for you and your pony, but keep it short and stay in control.*

From week five you can start cantering on your hacks. Start with occasional, short canters and build up to longer, more frequent ones. Make sure your pony stays obedient and that you stay in full control. By the end of the seventh week you should be ready for a short gallop.

When you're out hacking, look out for ditches, hedges or logs that you could use as practice jumps. Always check the takeoff and landing first.

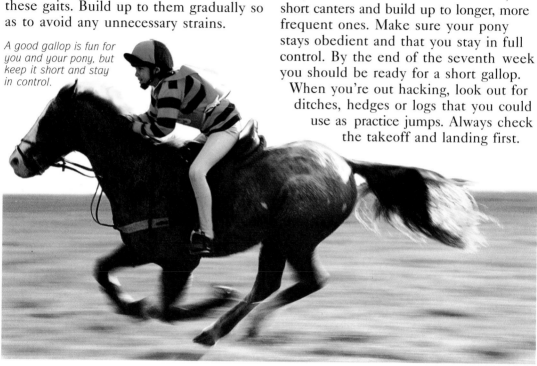

# CHECKING PULSE AND RESPIRATION

As you gradually increase the amount of fast work you do, you need to keep a check on your pony's condition by taking his pulse and respiration after exercise, as shown in the pictures on the right.

After a canter your pony should puff slightly, but not be completely out of breath. After about ten minutes his pulse and respiration should have returned to normal. If they haven't, he is working too hard and you need to build up to fast work more gradually.

## Pulse
A pony's normal pulse rate (the number of times his heart beats each minute) should be 36 to 42. You can feel his pulse under his jaw or just above his eye.

## Respiration
His normal respiration rate (the number of breaths he takes each minute) is 8 to 12. To count them, watch his flanks go in and out, or put your hand near his nose.

# FOOD FOR FITNESS

As you increase your pony's work, you will need to feed him less bulk food and more concentrates. Be careful not to give too much rich food too quickly though, as this can lead to pains in his tummy or cramps. Watch your own pony carefully. Some ponies put on weight very easily. Others lose it fast. A lively pony will be easier to manage if fed more hay, while a lazy one may benefit from more oats.

*Bulk food, such as hay and grass, is what fills a pony up and keeps his digestion working.*

*Concentrates, such as pellets or sweet feed, give a pony extra energy.*

The table below shows how the food of a 14hh pony, eating a total of about 9kg (20lbs) of food a day, may change over an eight-week fitness program.

| Week | Bulk food | Concentrates |
|------|-----------|--------------|
| *1* | 8.6kg (19lbs) | 450g (1lb) |
| *2* | 8.2kg (18lbs) | 900g (2lbs) |
| *3* | 7.7kg (17lbs) | 1.4kg (3lbs) |
| *4* | 7.3kg (16lbs) | 1.8kg (4lbs) |
| *5* | 6.8kg (15lbs) | 2.3kg (5lbs) |
| *6* | 6.4kg (14lbs) | 2.7kg (6lbs) |
| *7* | 5.9kg (13lbs) | 3.2kg (7lbs) |
| *8* | 5.4kg (12lbs) | 3.6kg (8lbs) |

# IMPROVING YOUR FITNESS

*Exercises without stirrups make you work harder and improve your fitness.*

*Push-ups strengthen your upper body, which is useful if you have a strong pony.*

It is just as important for you to be fit as it is for your pony. Cross-country riding can be exhausting and you don't want to be the one to let your pony down. If you ride every day, you will get pretty fit anyway.

If you are unable to ride out every day, plan some other form of exercise. Skipping, jogging, swimming, or even energetic tasks such as sweeping the stables, will improve your fitness.

Add some exercises to help keep you supple, such as touching your toes or doing sit-ups. Ask a gym teacher to show you how to do these exercises correctly, so that you do not damage your muscles.

203

# TACK AND EQUIPMENT

Riding at speed and jumping put more stress on your tack than normal, so it is important to have good quality equipment. Check it regularly and keep it clean and supple. Both you and your pony will need protective clothing too, to guard against knocks and falls.

## YOUR PONY'S TACK

A general purpose saddle is fine for cross-country. Use a comfortable saddle pad, made of natural fibers, under it. Avoid new tack, which can be uncomfortable, but check all used tack for wear and tear. Choose stainless steel bits and stirrups, and rubber reins for a better grip. For additional safety or better control, you may want to use some of the items shown below. However, only use this stronger tack if it is really necessary and always try it out before a competition.

### Nosebands

*Flash*          *Drop*          *Figure eight*

Flash, drop and figure eight nosebands all have straps that fasten behind the chin. This stops your pony from opening his mouth to avoid the pressure of the bit, giving you more control.

### Bits

*Snaffle – a very gentle bit*

*Dr. Bristol – puts more pressure on the tongue*     *Kimblewick – a much stronger type of bit*

A change of bit can help control a strong pony, but the wrong one can do more damage than good. Try several with the advice of your instructor if you feel the need to change.

### Martingales

*A running martingale is the most popular type, but it must be expertly fitted.*

A martingale stops a pony from throwing his head up and causing you to lose control. It also provides you with a neckstrap to grab when your pony takes a particularly sudden or large leap.

### Girths and overgirths

*Overgirth*
*Girths*

One of the worst things that can happen to your tack on cross-country is a girth breaking. This is why top riders use two webbing girths as well as an over-girth, which fastens all the way around the saddle.

### Breastplates

*Breastplate*

A breastplate is sometimes used to help keep the saddle in place and stop it from slipping backward on steep ground. It must be loosely fitted so that it does not restrict your pony's chest as he jumps.

# WHAT YOU SHOULD WEAR

Cross-country dress used to be hunting attire (tweeds and black hat) but since safety vests and hard hats have become obligatory, silks and sweatshirts are more common. You can match them with saddle pads and bandages, but check with your instructor that all of your equipment meets current safety standards.

*Your hard hat must have chin straps and meet safety standards.*

*A bright cover over your hard hat is a colorful addition to your outfit.*

*A firmly-tied stock can give your neck extra support.*

*Shirts or sweaters need long sleeves to protect your arms.*

*Safety vests can be worn over or under sweatshirts but they must meet safety standards.*

*Spurs can be useful for a balking or lazy pony but are not always allowed. Check with the organizers first.*

*String gloves give the best grip. Leather can be slippery when wet.*

*Choose long or short boots with smooth soles, pointed toes and small heels.*

*Breeches or jodhpurs need extra protection and grip inside the knees.*

*A short crop can be useful as an extra aid at difficult fences.*

# PROTECTING YOUR PONY'S LEGS

Your pony's heels and legs can get battered and bruised across country so you need to protect them with boots or bandages. There's a wide range available, but the main areas that need protection are the front and back of the legs and around the fetlock joints. Leather boots are a good choice, as they are easy to put on and don't absorb water. Avoid materials which soak up water.

Tendon boot

Over-reach boot

*Boots should be lightweight, close-fitting and securely fastened. Make sure they do not impede circulation.*

*Bandages must be expertly fitted and sewn in place over quilts, so that there's no risk of them coming undone.*

# CROSS-COUNTRY FENCES

There's a huge variety of cross-country fences. Some of the most common are described on the next few pages. The one feature they all have in common, and which makes them different from show jumps, is that they are nearly always solid so they won't fall over if knocked.

## JUMPING YOUR FIRST SOLID FENCES

Many riders find the thought of a solid fence quite scary. In fact, a solid fence is easier for a pony to see, which means he judges the takeoff better and is likely to make a bolder leap. Your position and technique for cross-country fences is much the same as for schooling fences, though the pace may be a little faster.

When starting out, choose a fence on flat ground, with a good takeoff and landing. Low sleepers, a wide log or small log pile are all solid but easy fences to start over.

For practice jumping on hills or difficult ground, first try a small hedge. It's less dangerous if you do make a mistake. Below are a few general points to remember.

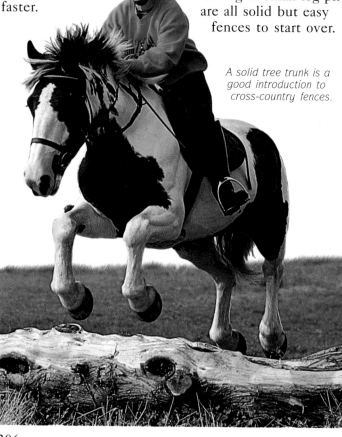

*A solid tree trunk is a good introduction to cross-country fences.*

### Jumping tips

* Keep a straight, controlled approach.
* As you take off, bend forward from the hips not the waist.
* Let your hands move forward with the pony's neck so that you don't pull him in the mouth.
* Keep your lower legs straight. If they swing back, you will tip forward; if they go forward, you will fall back.
* Keep your heels down and your lower legs close to your pony's sides, ready to urge on if he hesitates.
* Look straight ahead, don't lean to one side.
* As soon as you land, get back into position, ready for the next fence.

# SPREAD FENCES

Spreads are wide fences which need to be approached at a stronger pace. Balance is still more important than speed, but encouraging your pony to lengthen his stride will help him to clear a spread fence.

*Tires*

*Tiger trap*

Round or triangular shaped spreads, such as tires, tiger traps or a log pile, are the easiest to jump.

*Table*

*Parallel bars*

Square shapes, such as a table or parallel bars, need a more careful approach in case your pony needs to fit in an extra stride before takeoff.

*Chair*

*Triple bar*

Spreads that start low and get higher, such as a triple bar, or chair, are easier than the squarer shapes, but you will need to take off closer to the fence.

*Spread fences can seem huge, but are often an easier shape for a pony to jump than an upright.*

# UPRIGHT FENCES

Upright fences may look smaller than spreads, but they are often harder for a pony to judge. If he takes off too late he may hit the fence with his front legs. If he takes off too early he may catch it with his hind legs. Approach steadily so that he has time to see the fence and judge the takeoff point.

*Hock*

For an upright fence, your pony's hocks need to be well engaged (tucked in underneath him), so that he has the power to push off and clear the height.

*Post and rails*

*Style*

Narrow uprights, such as a style, need a very straight, controlled approach.

*Stone wall*

*Gate*

*Bullfinch*

*Palisade*

A bullfinch may look higher than other upright fences, but your pony can brush his legs through the top part. Inexperienced ponies may try to jump the full height.

# DITCHES

Ditches of all sizes, shapes and forms are a common cross-country obstacle. You will come across them on their own or as part of another fence. They are not difficult to jump, but many ponies and riders find them scary. Practicing over plenty of small, simple ditches will help both of you to build up confidence.

## NATURAL DITCHES

Most ponies find natural ditches less scary than man-made ones, so practicing back and forth over a small natural ditch is a good way to build up confidence. Always check the takeoff and landing. If it is slippery or muddy, approach with extra caution.

Bear in mind that your pony won't see a ditch until he gets quite close, so approach slowly enough for him to realize what he has to jump, but fast enough for him to clear the ditch easily. The wider the ditch, the longer his stride needs to be.

A pony can jump a small ditch from a standstill, so if your pony stops, try urging him on rather than turning around to approach again. Be ready for a large leap.

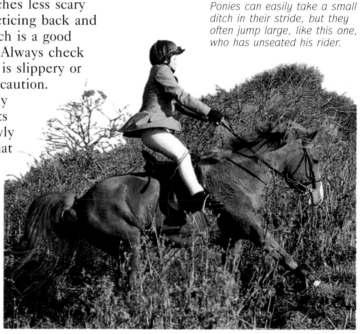

*Ponies can easily take a small ditch in their stride, but they often jump large, like this one, who has unseated his rider.*

## TACKLING A COFFIN

A coffin is a difficult three-part combination fence. It includes a fence in, a ditch (often with a slope down into it) and a fence out.

To jump it successfully, you need to approach at a steady pace and keep impulsion all the way through.

*Approach at a steady, bouncy canter.*

*If you jump the first part too fast, your pony might land too close to, or even in the ditch.*

*Be ready to urge your pony on in case he spooks at the ditch.*

# FENCES WITH A DITCH

## Ditch away

When there is a ditch behind a fence (a ditch away), your pony will not know it is there. Approach at a strong pace so that your pony jumps out boldly and clears the ditch.

## Open ditch

A ditch in front of a fence is called an open ditch. It can be quite helpful as it gives a guideline for takeoff, which encourages your pony to make a bold leap.

## Trakhener

*If the rail of a trakhener is at an angle, aim for the middle.*

A ditch with a rail over it is called a trakhener. The rail makes your pony jump higher and wider.

Approach at a steady pace and be ready to urge your pony on if he suddenly sees the ditch and spooks.

*Never look down into a ditch. Your pony will be able to sense your fear.*

*Sit back in the saddle as soon as you land, in order to keep a safe position and maintain impulsion.*

*There is usually room for one, or sometimes two strides between each part of the fence.*

*Keeping a good, straight line all the way through the coffin will help ensure that you have an accurate approach at the last fence.*

# WATER

Most ponies are naturally frightened of water, and yet, with training, many come to love it. Cross-country events usually include some kind of water obstacle, so it is worth getting your pony used to water if you want to compete.

## WATER TRAINING

Whenever you are out hacking, look for opportunities to introduce your pony to water. On a rainy day there will be lots of puddles which are perfect to splash through.

Shallow streams are good, but make sure the bottom is firm. If your pony starts sinking into mud or tripping on rocks, he will be even more nervous.

Remember that your pony does not know how deep the water is. He has to trust you. A very nervous pony will often be happier following another pony. Let them stand in the water together and splash around so that they get the feel of it.

Once your pony is confident about walking and paddling in water, try

trotting him through. Then you are ready to try a jump in or out of water (see opposite).

Take your pony through as many different water obstacles as possible, so that he is confident with all water, not just familiar spots. Remember that most ponies find man-made water obstacles more spooky than natural ones.

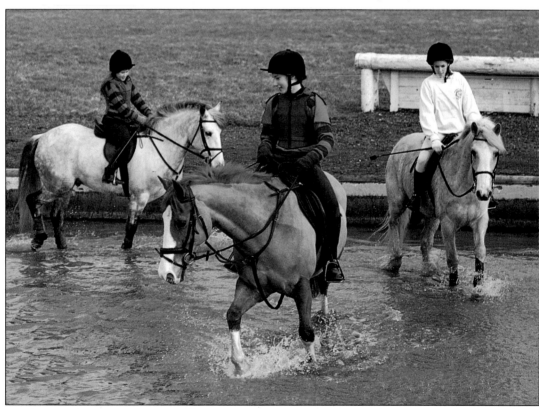

*Allowing ponies to splash around together teaches them that water can be fun, not frightening. Once they have overcome their fear, they will begin to enjoy trotting and jumping in water.*

# JUMPING OUT OF WATER

Once your pony will trot through water confidently, try a small jump on the way out. At first, position the jump a stride away from the water, so that your pony can take off from dry land.

*Start with the jump a stride away from the water.*

Then move the jump closer so that he has to take off from the water. Approach at a strong trot and keep urging him on so that he has enough impulsion to jump. The drag of the water will slow him down.

*Then move the jump so that you take off from the water.*

## JUMPING INTO WATER

As with the jump out, start with the fence a stride away from the water, so that your pony can land on dry ground. Keep it small so that if your pony stops, you can encourage him to step over it rather than turning away. Once confident over this, try a small drop directly into water. (For more about drop fences see page 213.)

For larger drops or fences you will need to approach in a trot or gentle canter, but keep it slow and steady so that your pony can drop gently into the water.

*Landing in water will slow your pony down suddenly, so if you approach too fast you might both be caught unprepared.*

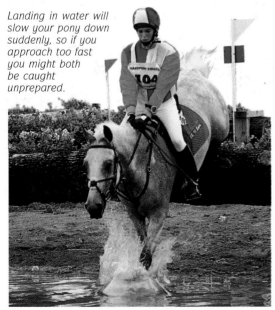

## TACKLING A FENCE IN WATER

Water slows your pony right down, so jumping a fence in water requires a lot of effort. It is also hard for your pony to judge how high to jump, so you need to be ready to urge him on strongly. This means it is essential for you to get your balance back, after a jump into water.

211

# STEPS, BANKS AND DROPS

Fences set on hills or slopes are a test of your pony's energy and balance. The problems they present are similar to those of riding up and downhill (see pages 198 and 199), but because they involve jumping, they demand even greater effort and control.

## STEPS UP OR DOWN

Approach steps in the same way as normal upright fences – not too fast, but with plenty of impulsion. Let your pony jump up a single small step at first so he gets used to landing on higher ground. The more steps there are, the more impulsion you need. Urge him on all the way up.

Jumping down a step is more difficult for your pony, but he needs very little impulsion. Start over one small step, and if he is nervous, let him stand at the top and look down. Never turn away or he will learn to refuse. If necessary, take a lead from another pony. Be ready for a huge leap when he does go, and have a neckstrap to hold onto, or grab a piece of mane so you don't pull his mouth. As he gains confidence he will jump smaller.

*Once your pony jumps confidently down a single step, try him over a series. Always approach slowly.*

## BANKS

Banks are tackled in a similar way to steps. Sit slightly forward for the jump up, but then adopt an upright seat on top of the bank, ready for the jump down.

*A bank is a step up... followed by a step down.*

## SUNKEN ROAD

A sunken road is like an upside-down bank. Approach in a steady, bouncy canter and concentrate on keeping good balance all the way through.

*A sunken road is a step down... followed by a step up.*

# DROP FENCES

A drop fence is one where the landing is lower than takeoff. Your pony may not know this when he takes off, so you must keep good balance and not interfere. The landing is the hard part. Sit slightly back and keep your lower leg forward to help you balance. Above all, be ready to slip your reins (see bottom of this page) so that you do not jab your pony in the mouth. Keep a controlled approach, but increase the stride, so that your pony jumps out over the drop rather than landing in it.

*Sit upright, or slightly back for landing.*

*If your approach is fast and the stride long, your pony will land a long way from the fence.*

*If your approach is slow and the stride short, your pony will land too close to the fence.*

*A steady approach with a medium-length stride will result in a more comfortable landing.*

*This rider has slipped her reins to let her pony have his head. Her lower legs are well forward and her heels down, giving her a secure position for landing.*

## SLIPPING YOUR REINS

Your pony uses his head and neck for balance, so when jumping downhill he must be able to stretch his neck out. But because you need to sit up or even slightly back in order to keep your balance, the only way to let him have his neck, is to allow the reins to slip through your hands. You recover them like this:

As your pony stretches his neck, open your fingers to let the reins slip through your hands.

To pick up contact, put both reins into your right hand and slide your left hand down the left rein.

Then hold both reins in your left hand and slide your right hand down the right rein.

Your reins should now be the correct length to take back control and continue your ride.

213

# COMBINATION FENCES

A combination fence is one where you have to tackle two or more jumps in a row. Most cross-country courses include a few. They vary from a simple jump in and out, to a more complex system of fences where you must choose your own route through. Before tackling any combination, you need to figure out how many strides your pony will take between each jump.

## JUDGING YOUR PONY'S STRIDE

Set up schooling fences at home to figure out how many of your strides are equal to one of your pony's. Three short strides are often about equal to one pony stride, but it is best to work it out for yourself as it will depend on the size of both you and your pony. You need to include a couple of your strides for your pony's takeoff and landing strides too (see the diagrams below). When you come across a combination, pace out the distance between the fences. If you manage only nine strides between the fences, try to steady your pony so that he can put in two shorter strides. If you manage eight, urge him on to take one longer stride.

*Here, ten rider's strides equal two pony strides.*

*Include a couple of strides for the pony's takeoff and landing.*

Pony's stride – about 3m (9ft)    Rider's stride – about 1m (3ft)

1  2  3  4  5  6  7  8  9  10

*Here, seven rider's strides equal one pony stride.*

Pony's stride    Rider's stride

1  2  3  4  5  6  7

## A SIMPLE IN AND OUT

Before tackling two jumps in a row, figure out how many strides you think your pony will take between them (see above). There may be room for several, but the fewer there are, the more accurate you must be in figuring out the number of strides. Steady your pony on the approach, so that he has time to see the jump, and keep him straight, so that he cannot run out at the second one.

*This in and out allows room for two short strides, so the rider has been careful to approach steadily.*

*She concentrates on keeping her pony straight through the middle, steadying him slightly...*

*...and then urges him on to make sure they clear the second part of the in and out easily.*

# BOUNCE FENCES

In a bounce fence, the two parts of the combination are so close that your pony has to jump in and "bounce" straight back out again, without taking a stride. It is best to approach this type of a fence in a short, bouncy canter. Steady your pony several strides away so that he knows to expect something tricky, then urge him on, keeping lots of impulsion.

*Practice bounce fences at home first, over show jumps that will fall down when knocked.*

# CHOOSING YOUR ROUTE

When you are given a choice of routes through a combination, there is usually a slower, easier one and a faster, more difficult one. As long as you remember to keep the red flag on the right and the white flag on the left, you can choose the route that suits you best.

*The diagrams below show some examples of the types of combination fences you might encounter in a cross-country competition.*

*Tight turns*
Some combination fences involve jumping in one way, and then turning and jumping out in a different direction. This involves good control and a much slower approach.

This shows the
fastest, hardest route.

This shows the
slowest, easiest route.

This shows an
intermediate route.

# CORNERS AND ARROWHEADS

Corners and arrowheads require very accurate riding, and, because of this, they are often part of the fast but difficult option in a combination fence. It's a good idea to practice these jumps at home first, using blocks and poles that will fall down if things go wrong.

## CORNERS

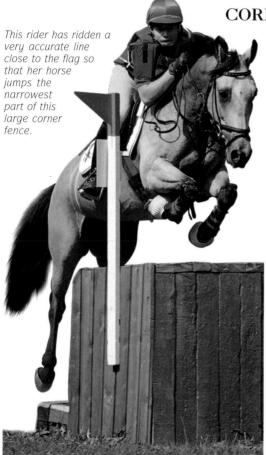

*This rider has ridden a very accurate line close to the flag so that her horse jumps the narrowest part of this large corner fence.*

On cross-country courses, a corner is usually part of an angled rails fence which offers several possible routes. If your pony is jumping well, and you can ride accurately, it's a good option to take.

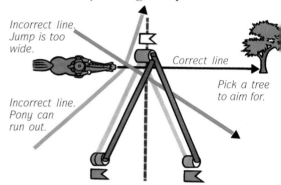

*Incorrect line. Jump is too wide.*

*Correct line*

*Pick a tree to aim for.*

*Incorrect line. Pony can run out.*

It's important to get the angle of your approach right. If you aim straight at the front rail, the jump becomes very wide. If you aim straight at the back one, your pony may run out. Imagine a line cutting the corner in two (like the dotted one in the diagram above) and ride straight at that. Pick a landmark in the distance to help you aim straight. See opposite for more tips on riding a straight line.

## PRACTICING CORNERS

*A wing will help stop your pony from running out at first.*

*Remove the wing when your pony is used to the jump.*

*Practice from both directions.*

Use blocks and poles to build a narrow corner at first. If necessary, add a wing to help guide your pony into the fence. Once your pony is used to the jump, take the wing away. Then gradually widen the angle of the corner. Practice jumping the corner from both directions so that your pony doesn't become one-sided.

# TACKLING ARROWHEADS

An arrowhead is a difficult fence and therefore often the hardest option in a combination fence. You could be expected to jump either into the arrow or against the point (see the diagram below).

*Jumping into the arrow*

*Jumping against the point*

*This rider has made a good straight approach right against the point of the arrowhead and as a result is making a very successful jump.*

With either approach, the arrowhead requires accurate riding and a very straight approach. Most ponies will try and jump to one side, which can be disastrous with a solid fence, so you should practice this at home first.

## Tips for keeping straight

- Look straight ahead.
- Keep both legs firmly against your pony's sides.
- Keep an even contact with the reins.
- Approach slowly in a short, bouncy canter so that you have plenty of control to direct your pony to the center of the jump.

# PRACTICING ARROWHEADS

*Leave a gap.*

Begin by leaning two poles on a single rail, as shown here. Keep your pony very straight and aim right for the middle.

Then move the poles together so that they narrow to a point. Be very strict about making your pony jump the point.

Take the horizontal pole away and balance the other two on a block or straw bale. You can gradually make the V narrower.

Once your pony jumps this well, try approaching from the other side. This is harder because the poles no longer act as wings.

# OTHER OBSTACLES

Cross-country courses vary from area to area and each has its own unique jumps, so you'll often have to tackle something completely new. These pages deal with some other common obstacles, such as riding through wooded areas and opening and closing gates. Last, but not least, is the ordeal of the starting gate for competition riders.

## RIDING THROUGH WOODS

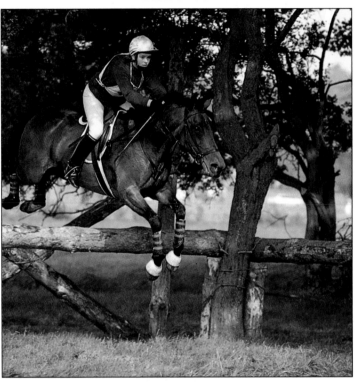

*Riding through wooded areas brings new obstacles, such as overhanging branches or changing light conditions (see below).*

Unless you live in an area of very open countryside, you are likely to be riding through woods at some point. This usually means following rugged tracks or narrow paths, and dealing with tight turns and overhanging branches.

Ground conditions in woods are often rougher than in the open, and you will need to keep an eye open for tree roots and other hazards.

At events you need good control and accurate riding in order to be able to tackle these areas at a sensible speed.

Watch out for turns off a main track onto a smaller path as this is a real test of control, particularly just before or after a jump.

## CHANGING LIGHT CONDITIONS

Wooded areas also mean changes in the light. This can make a simple fence into or out of the woods look far harder to your pony than it actually is.

Approach this type of fence with lots of impulsion, but not too fast, so that your pony's eyes have time to adjust. Be ready to urge him on if he hesitates.

Fences in partial shade, such as those on the edge of the woods, can also cause problems. A pony may shy away from the darkness, and therefore run out.

# HOW TO OPEN AND CLOSE A GATE

Opening and closing a gate while mounted can be tricky, but it is an essential skill for all types of cross-country riding, so it is worth practicing. An obedient pony makes it much easier. A gate is sometimes included as part of a hunter trial course too, where you might be judged on style or speed.

1. Ride alongside the gate and bring your pony to a halt when his head is just past the catch.

2. Put the reins and crop in your outside hand, so that you can use the other one to undo the catch.

3. Push the gate open and walk your pony through. Keep hold of the gate, if possible, while you do this.

4. Turn your pony around, keeping close to the outside of the gate, so that it doesn't swing wide open.

5. Put the reins and the crop into your other hand, push the gate closed, and then fasten the catch.

# COPING WITH THE START IN COMPETITIONS

At the start of most competitions you wait in a small, fenced-off area called the start box. The starter counts you down and as soon as he or she says "Go!" you must head toward the first fence.

Some ponies get nervous and excited while waiting; others are reluctant to set off and leave "home". Make sure your pony is warmed up before you go to the start and then keep him walking around calmly until you are called into the start box.

Avoid going into the box too early if your pony is excited, and when you do go in, face the back. A calm pony can go in earlier and face the start. If he is reluctant to set off, give him a tap with the crop.

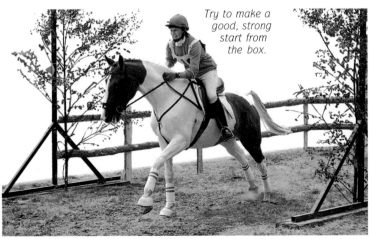

*Try to make a good, strong start from the box.*

# ENTERING AN EVENT

One of the best chances you will get to ride over a course of cross-country fences is by taking part in a local event, such as hunter trials. These are usually organized by the local hunt or Pony Club. You can find out about them from saddlers, riding schools, Pony Clubs and local newspapers.

## HOW TO ENTER AN EVENT

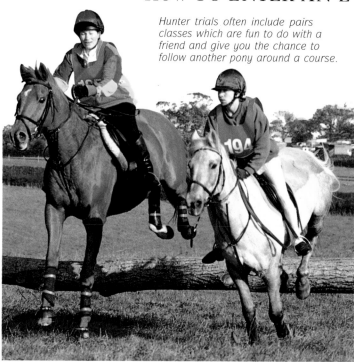

*Hunter trials often include pairs classes which are fun to do with a friend and give you the chance to follow another pony around a course.*

Send off for a schedule and check the conditions of each class. They are usually divided according to the experience of the rider and pony or height of the jumps. Only enter one or two classes, making sure they are the most suitable.

*Checklist*
- Send off for schedule.
- Choose class or classes, checking rules carefully.
- Send back entry form and fee by closing date (with a stamped addressed envelope, if requested).
- Find out if you are to be given a start time before the day. If so, make a note of when to call for it.

## WHAT TO DO ON THE BIG DAY

If you plan to walk the course the same day, you will need to arrive at least two hours before the start. Try to park on flat ground so that your pony is as comfortable as possible while he is waiting.

Visit the secretary's tent first to collect your number and the course map. Check whether things are running on time and find out whether you need to put your name down for the start or whether you have already been given a starting time.

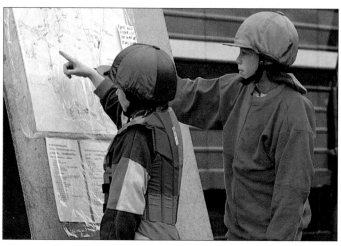

*Study the course map and check the details of your class carefully.*

# WALKING THE COURSE

Walking the course is the one chance you get to study the jumps up close and learn the route you are going to take. The course may be open the day before. Don't forget to wear comfortable shoes or rubber boots if there's water to wade through.

*Pick up a course map, or study the one at the secretary's tent before you start walking.*

## Course checklist

- Study each takeoff and landing. Muddy ones are likely to get worse during the day, so plan an alternative approach.
- Check fence numbers. Each class uses a different color, so ensure you know which is for your class.

- Look out for turning flags – two red and white ones you have to go through; a single red you must keep to your right.
- Look at any fence with options. Plan your best route plus a second in case the first goes wrong.
- At each fence, choose a line that will bring you in straight. Try to find a landmark to help.
- Walk the exact route you plan to ride.
- Look for any things that your pony might find spooky, such as hidden officials.

- Jot down notes on your map as you go. You can read through them just before you set off.
- If time, go back to the course to watch other competitors ride it.
- Check where the finish flags are and make sure you ride through them.

# WARMING UP

Your pony needs a gentle 15-20 minute warm-up before setting off on the course. Pop over the practice jump a couple of times – no more, or your pony may get bored before he starts. If you have to wait at the start, walk around at a brisk pace. Have a short trot and canter just before you set off to ensure your pony is alert.

# AFTER AN EVENT

Riding a cross-country course is exhausting work for your pony as well as for you. It is very important that you take good care of him immediately after finishing the course and over the next few days in order to prevent him from becoming stiff, cold or even lame.

## WHEN YOU FINISH THE COURSE

1. When you finish the course your pony is likely to be hot and breathing quite fast. Pull up slowly, so that he doesn't stumble.

2. Come back to a steady walk and then halt and dismount. Now you can loosen the girth and run up the stirrups.

3. Walk him around until he has cooled off and caught his breath. It should take about ten minutes (see page 202).

4. Once back at the trailer, remove his saddle and check him over carefully, paying particular attention to his legs (see opposite).

5. On a warm day, sponge his neck and saddle patch with cold water. Otherwise just use a sweat scraper to remove the sweat.

*Offer several small drinks rather than one long one.*

6. Put on a sweat sheet and continue walking him around until he is cool. When he has stopped puffing, offer him a drink.

7. Remove bandages, boots or studs. Rub his legs with a towel to dry them and get the circulation going. If it is warm, wash them.

8. If it is a cold day, add an extra blanket on top of the sweat sheet. Now you can give him a little hay and leave him to rest.

9. When you have taken care of your pony, you can get some food for yourself and return your number to the secretary's tent.

# GETTING HOME

*Make sure your pony is blanketed and warm for the journey home from the competition. Put shipping bandages on to protect his legs.*

As soon as you get home after an event, walk your pony around again to prevent him from getting stiff before putting him in the stall. Check his legs again, put on his night blankets and give him a small feeding. Make sure he has plenty of fresh water.

If he lives at pasture and it's cold, add a turn-out blanket. Check him once more before you go to bed.

# THE NEXT DAY

Check again for signs of injury. Pick out his feet and check his shoes. Then turn him out in the field for an hour or two. When you bring him in, groom him, making sure to remove any dry sweat. Let him have a day off and two easier working days before you jump him again. Watch for signs of poor health and feed less concentrates and more bulk when he's not working.

## Health checklist
* Is he behaving normally?
* Are his eyes bright?
* Does his coat look shiny?
* Does he seem cheerful and lively?
* Is he eating well?
* Do his droppings look the same as usual and are they as frequent?

# CHECKING AND CARING FOR THE LEGS

Your pony's legs can easily get injured across country. After work, run your hand down each leg carefully, checking for any cuts, heat or swelling.

## Treating cuts
Wash cuts gently and hose them with cold water. If they are minor, apply a little antiseptic cream or spray. If more serious, just hose them and call the vet in case your pony needs stitches, antibiotics or a tetanus booster.

*Stand near the girth area when you hose your pony's legs, in case he kicks out.*

*Holding a stream of cold water over your pony's legs is the best way to treat any cuts, bruises or swelling.*

## Heat and swelling
Heat and swelling may just mean some bruising or it could be a symptom of something more severe, such as a strained tendon. To treat heat and swelling, hose the affected area with cold water for about 20 minutes three or four times a day. H'ding an ice pack on th helps (a bag ( peas is excel' swelling per pony is lam should cal'

# DRESSAGE

## Contents

# WHAT IS DRESSAGE?

Dressage is a method of training your horse and improving your riding skills so that you and your horse work well together and understand each other clearly. With practice, dressage should make your horse supple so that his movements remain flowing when you ride him. It should also help to make him more confident and eager to please you.

## STARTING DRESSAGE

*When horses are out in the field, they move with light, easy steps. The goal of dressage is to maintain these flowing movements.*

You can start to learn dressage at any time. It doesn't matter how long you've been riding, or how experienced you are. In fact, you learn some basic skills of dressage, such as how to sit in the saddle correctly, when you first start to ride.

Dressage movements are designed to make your horse strong, supple and balanced. As you continue dressage training, the movements gradually become more challenging for you and your horse.

Although dressage does not involve jumping or riding at high speed, it improves your accuracy and control, which will help with all your other riding activities.

## THE HISTORY OF DRESSAGE

The art of teaching horses to obey their riders willingly was first practiced by the ancient Greeks over two thousand years ago. In the 16th century, riding schools in Europe trained noblemen in the art of horsemanship. Cavalry horses were taught difficult movements which would frighten enemies in battle. Displays of these impressive skills became popular.

In 1735, the Spanish Riding School opened in Vienna, Austria. Modern dressage developed from the teachings of this famous school. The Spanish Riding School is still based in Vienna and its riders and horses continue to perform all over the world.

*This horse and rider from the Spanish Riding School are performing a movement called the capriole which was originally used in battle.*

226

# DRESSAGE SHOWS

Taking part in a dressage show is a great way to see how well you and your horse are progressing. It also gives you the chance to watch other horses and riders of different levels. Dressage is becoming a popular sport, and there are plenty of competitions and levels to choose from.

*Advanced horses and riders make complicated dressage movements look easy, but it takes years of training to reach such a high standard.*

# POINTS OF A HORSE

The different parts of a horse's body are called the "points." These terms are often used in dressage, so it's important to know what they mean.

Poll  Neck  Withers  Girth  Croup

Shoulder

Hindquarters (quarters)

Forehand (front legs)

Hindlegs (back legs)

Near foreleg

Hock

Near hindleg

Knee

Off foreleg

Off hindleg

Fetlock

Pastern

# YOUR POSITION

Developing your riding position is an important part of becoming a dressage rider. A good position will help your horse keep his balance and make it easier for him to move naturally. Although there's a lot to think about when you work on your position, try to stay relaxed.

## ACHIEVING A GOOD POSITION

It takes practice to achieve a good riding position. Even experienced dressage riders continue to work on this part of their riding. Try to sit tall and balanced in the saddle. If you are sitting crookedly, your horse will find it hard to keep his body straight. Ask someone to watch you while you ride. They can then pinpoint any problems you may not be aware of. This rider has a good position.

*Her head is up and she is looking straight ahead.*

*Her shoulders are level.*

*Her back is straight but not stiff.*

*Her elbows are bent and flexible.*

*She is sitting in the center of the saddle, with her weight evenly spread between her seat bones.*

*Her knees are resting gently against the saddle flaps.*

*Her feet are pointing forward. The balls of her feet are resting on the stirrup bars.*

*Her upper legs or thighs are relaxed.*

*Her lower legs are in contact with the horse, next to the girth.*

*Her heels are lower than her toes.*

## RIDING WITH LONGER STIRRUPS

Dressage riders lengthen their stirrups so that they can ride with longer legs. Riding with longer legs means more of your leg is in contact with your horse's sides. This helps you to give lighter, clearer leg aids (see page 230). You'll need to have good balance before you start to ride with longer stirrups.

*Your stirrups should be two holes longer than normal. There should be a vertical straight line from your hip to your heel.*

*In contrast, short stirrups are used for jumping. They help you to lean forward, so your weight is off your horse's back.*

# IMPROVING YOUR POSITION

One of the best ways to improve your riding position is to have some longe-line lessons. The instructor controls your horse with a longe-line, while you concentrate on keeping a good position. You can also practice riding without reins or without stirrups in longe-line lessons. Riding without stirrups is good practice for dressage, as it helps you to prepare for lengthened stirrups.

*Try to relax the small of your back and allow your seat to move with your horse.*

*Cross your stirrups over in front of the saddle so they don't bump against your horse.*

*Try not to use the reins to balance.*

*Working without stirrups will improve your balance so that you don't have to depend on reins or stirrups to help keep your position.*

## EXERCISES ON THE LONGE-LINE

There are lots of exercises you can do on the longe-line. The ones described here will loosen your muscles and joints so that you don't become stiff. They will also help to make you more supple, so that you can absorb your horse's cantering and trotting motion through your seat, hips and back. Working on the longe-line can be tiring at first, so make sure that you and your horse take frequent breaks.

Put your arms out to the sides and swing around to face each side. Try to keep your legs still. Then do the exercise at a trot, with your hands on your hips.

Keep your feet in the stirrups. Hold the pommel with one hand. Lift your other arm in the air. Swing it backward in a circle. Repeat with the other arm.

Take your feet out of the stirrups. Bend one leg until you can hold your foot with your hand. Stretch your thigh so your knee points down, then straighten.

# USING THE AIDS

You can give signals to your horse which tell him what you want him to do. These signals are called aids, and you give them by using your hands, legs, seat and voice. You can also use artificial aids such as whips and spurs. In dressage, your aids must be as clear and light as you can make them, so that your horse can understand you quickly and easily.

## USING YOUR LEGS

To give leg aids, your legs should be relaxed, with your lower legs in contact with your horse's sides. You use leg aids to ask your horse to move ahead, to keep him working energetically and to tell him where to go. The message you give him depends on where you put your legs and how firmly you use them. To move straight forward, use both legs near the girth. To bend, keep your inside leg at the girth, and your outside leg behind it.

*This rider's aids tell her horse to bend to the right. Her legs are well positioned, but her left shoulder and arm should be further forward.*

Outside leg | Inside leg

*Your outside leg is the one nearest the outside of the arena or circle. You use it to control your horse's hindquarters.*

*Your inside leg is the one nearest to the middle of the arena or circle. You use it to ask your horse to bend toward the inside and move with energy.*

## HAND AIDS

You can use your hands to send signals to your horse along the reins to his mouth. Always try to keep the feeling with his mouth soft and light. Squeeze your fingers on the reins to slow him down. If you pull hard on your horse's mouth he may start to ignore or resist your hand aids.

*Use the inside rein to ask for a bend toward the inside.*

*Use the outside rein to control your horse's bend and speed.*

### Tips for giving aids
※ To give clear aids you must have good balance, and be in a correct position.
※ If your horse does not respond, check that you are giving the correct aids.
※ Try to keep your hands, legs and seat still when you are not using them.
※ Try to use your aids as sensitively as possible, so that your horse remains responsive to you.
※ Try not to give your horse conflicting aids such as pulling on the reins when you are using your legs to ask him to move forward.

## SEAT AIDS

Your seat and body can be used to slow your horse down. On a correctly trained horse, they can also be used to create more energy and to ask your horse to bring his hindlegs farther underneath him. Your seat and body should be in balance with your horse, so don't tip forward or backward.

## USING YOUR VOICE

You're not allowed to use your voice in dressage tests, but you can use it to reinforce other aids while you're training. Your horse understands the way you say words, rather than the words themselves. Quick, high-pitched commands will keep him moving, while slow, low-pitched commands will slow him down.

*To slow your horse down, sit tall, with your weight down into your heels.*

*Try to sit still. If you move around, your horse may become confused.*

## DRESSAGE WHIPS

If your horse ignores your leg aids, you can use a whip to emphasize what you mean. Give your horse the correct leg aid first. If he doesn't respond, tap him with the whip just behind your leg. If you're using a standard crop, put the reins in one hand, so you can use the other hand to apply the whip without pulling on the reins.

*Standard crop*

*Dressage whip*

*Dressage whips are longer than standard crops, so you can use them without taking your hands off the reins.*

*Hold your whip in your inside hand.*

## SPURS

Spurs are worn by experienced dressage riders to give light leg aids. Riders only start to use spurs when they have developed a good leg position and are able to keep their legs still, so that the spurs never touch the horse by mistake.

*The shank of the spur should be no longer than 3cm (1in).*

*Only blunt spurs can be worn in US Pony Club dressage tests.*

# THE GAITS

Your horse can walk, trot, canter and gallop. These different steps are called his gaits. In dressage tests, you will be asked to show how well your horse moves in each gait, except gallop. Before you can begin to improve your horse's gaits you will need to understand how he moves in each one.

## MOVEMENTS IN WALK

Your horse walks by moving his legs one at a time. On a hard surface, you should be able to hear four separate sounds, called beats, as each hoof hits the ground. His back hooves should step into the marks left by his front hooves. This is called "tracking up." With training, his hindlegs should "over-track" and step over the hoof prints from his forelegs. If a horse moves two legs at the same time, he is gaiting rather than walking. This is a serious fault. A horse may gait if he wasn't trained properly when he was young, or if his rider keeps the reins too short.

*Beat one*          *Beat two*          *Beat three*          *Beat four*

*Off (right) hindleg hits the ground.*      *Off foreleg*      *Near (left) hindleg*      *Near foreleg*

## MOVEMENTS IN TROT

When your horse trots, he moves his legs in diagonal pairs. As he springs from one pair of legs to the other, there is a moment when all his legs are off the ground. This is called "the moment of suspension." Your horse's trot should have a regular rhythm and his hindlegs should track up into the hoof prints of his forelegs. The speed of your horse's trot is important. If he trots too fast, he won't have time for the moment of suspension. If he's too slow, he will start to drag his feet.

*Beat one*                              *Beat two*

*Off hindleg   Near foreleg*                    *Near hindleg   Off foreleg*

*The horse's off hindleg and near foreleg hit the ground at the same time.*    *All the horse's legs are in the air for the moment of suspension.*    *His near hindleg and off foreleg then hit the ground at the same time.*    *Another moment of suspension follows, then the sequence continues.*

# CANTER

There should be three quick beats to your horse's canter, followed by a moment of suspension when all his feet are off the ground. Your horse should canter with even strides. Most of his weight should be on his haunches, and he should step well under his body. A lazy horse may lose the moment of suspension or move his inside hindleg and outside foreleg separately instead of together.

*Beat one*

*Beat two*

*Beat three*

*Near hindleg*

*Off hindleg*   *Near foreleg*

*Off foreleg*

*This horse is cantering on the right leg. He pushes off with his near hindleg.*

*His off hindleg and near foreleg hit the ground at the same time.*

*Then his off foreleg steps forward and hits the ground.*

*All his legs leave the ground for the moment of suspension.*

# DIFFERENT TYPES OF WALK, TROT AND CANTER

Dressage horses can vary the length of their steps in each gait without changing their speed. It's hard work for horses to shorten or lengthen their strides and it takes careful training. The ultimate shortened and lengthened gaits are called "collected" and "extended." You can learn about them on pages 240 and 241.

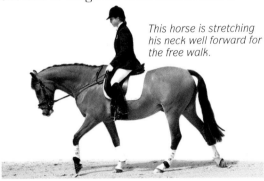
*This horse is stretching his neck well forward for the free walk.*

*In medium trot, the horse stretches out his body to take longer steps.*

## Walks

Your horse's normal walk is called "medium walk." In lower level dressage tests you may also be asked to show "free walk." For free walk, give your horse a long, but not completely loose, rein so he can stretch out his back and neck and take longer steps. He should move forward actively, without slowing down.

## Trots and canters

Your horse's normal trot and canter are called his "working" trot and canter. In lower level dressage tests you will have to show that your horse can take slightly longer steps than in his working gaits. This is the first stage toward "medium" trot and canter, in which your horse lengthens his stride.

# WAY OF GOING

A horse's "way of going" describes the way he moves. If your horse is moving along and working correctly he will be feeling relaxed and happy. You will also find him comfortable to ride. Here are some important points which will affect your horse's way of going.

## KEEPING YOUR HORSE STRAIGHT

Your horse should be able to keep straight in all his gaits. This means that his hindlegs should follow in the tracks of his forelegs and not swing out to the sides. His body should be straight from the tip of his nose to his tail, or gently curved if you are riding a circle. If your horse isn't straight, it may be because you are riding crookedly, or because you have stronger contact on one rein.

*This horse has started to shift his body to the right because his rider is sitting crookedly.*

It could also be because your horse is not responding to your aids properly. Longeing exercises (see page 229) will help you to sit straight, while transitions (see page 236) will help to make your horse "listen" to your aids. Practice riding straight lines across the arena so that your horse doesn't start to rely on the rail or fence of the arena to keep himself straight.

## STAYING CORRECTLY BALANCED

To be correctly balanced, your horse must be moving forward actively (with lively steps) in response to your aids. He must be working with plenty of impulsion (see next page) from his hindquarters. If he starts to rush, he may lose his rhythm and put more weight on his forehand. He may lean against the reins to balance, and he'll be more likely to trip. A horse who is well balanced is said to be in "self carriage."

### Rhythm and tempo

● Rhythm is the regularity of your horse's hoof beats. When his rhythm is steady, his balance will be good.

● Tempo is the speed of your horse's rhythm. In dressage, your horse's tempo should stay constant.

*Hillwork when you're out on the trail is an excellent way to improve your horse's balance.*

# CREATING IMPULSION

Impulsion is the energy your horse uses to move forward. When you use your aids to control this energy, your horse will take lighter, springier steps. His hocks will engage, which means he'll put more of his weight onto his hindquarters and use his hindlegs to push himself along. His hindlegs will step further underneath his body.

*The horse in front is moving with impulsion. His hindlegs are underneath him and his hocks are engaged.*

*The hocks of the horse behind are not engaged.*

# ACCEPTING THE BIT

When your horse accepts the bit, he will move forward until he can feel a light but steady pressure, called contact, between the reins and the bit. You will be able to feel this contact too. There should be no resistance to the bit felt in his mouth, neck or back. His frame (the shape his body makes) should become rounder. A horse won't accept the bit until he is straight, balanced and moving with impulsion.

*This horse has accepted the bit and his outline is well rounded. His back and loins are supple and relaxed.*

*The horse's neck is gently curved from the withers to the poll and his jaw is relaxed.*

*This horse is not accepting the bit. His outline is "hollow" and his ears are back as a sign of resistance.*

*His tail is soft and swinging.*

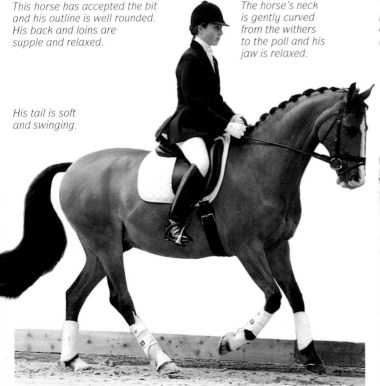

## Helping your horse to accept the bit

- Use your legs to push your horse firmly forward.
- Keep your hands still.
- Don't try to create contact by pulling on the reins.
- As soon as your horse accepts the bit, relax your aids slightly to reward him.

# TRANSITIONS

A transition is a change of gait, such as from walk to trot, or from working trot to medium trot. Transitions teach your horse to pay attention to your aids and help to improve his balance and impulsion. They are included in all levels of dressage, from Introductory to Grand Prix.

## UPWARD TRANSITIONS

Upward transitions increase the pace, for example, from walk to trot. Before you ask for an upward transition, make sure your horse is attentive and moving energetically.

Sit lightly in the saddle. Close your legs on your horse's sides by the girth. Follow his head movements with your hands but don't lose contact with his mouth.

*Walk*

*Let your body move forward with your horse. This will help you to balance in the next gait.*

*Trot*

## UPWARD TRANSITION TO CANTER

Your horse should canter with his inside leg leading. Go into sitting trot before you ask for canter. Use your inside leg on the girth and your outside leg behind the girth. This tells your horse to start, or "strike off," with his outside hindleg, so that his inside foreleg leads the canter (see page 233). Asking for canter as you go around a corner will encourage your horse to start with the correct leg.

## DOWNWARD TRANSITIONS

*Don't pull on the reins to slow your horse down. It's uncomfortable for him.*

*This horse is cantering with the correct, inside leg leading.*

Downward transitions slow the pace. To ask for one, sit taller in the saddle, with your weight down in your heels. Keep your legs lightly on your horse's sides. Close your fingers around the reins and squeeze, as if you were squeezing a sponge.

# DOWNWARD TRANSITION TO HALT

When your horse halts, he should stand straight and square. This means that he has equal weight on each leg, and that his front and back legs are in line. He should be able to keep still, without fidgeting or shuffling around. Keep a light rein contact during the halt, so that he stays alert, waiting for your next command.

### Stepping back

If your horse steps back, it may be because your hand aids are too strong. Loosen your rein contact as soon as he stops, but don't let the reins go loose.

### Crooked halt

If your horse's halt is crooked, make sure your left and right aids are even. Try placing two poles on the ground and halting between them.

### Resisting

*Don't try to force your horse to stop by pulling the reins.*

If your horse resists the halt, it may be because your aids were unclear, or because your horse was not moving well before the halt. Try to use clear aids.

## USING THE HALF-HALT

*In dressage tests you will be asked to change gait at specific markers. Giving a half-halt is a good way to prepare your horse for transitions.*

*This rider should have a little more weight in her heels.*

A half-halt is a set of aids which alert your horse that you're about to ask him to do something different, such as change gait. It also tells him to engage his hindquarters and hocks. Half-halts can be used in all gaits, but practice in trot first. Sit tall in the saddle and put your weight into the stirrups. Close your legs around your horse's sides (telling him to go forward) and close your fingers on the reins so that they restrain him.

# CIRCLES AND TURNS

Dressage tests consist of a series of circles, turns and transitions. These movements are designed to show off your horse's ability and training. More advanced dressage tests involve smaller circles and tighter turns. With regular practice, your horse's suppleness and balance will improve so that you can start to ride smaller, more precise shapes.

## HOW A DRESSAGE HORSE BENDS

When a horse bends correctly, he curves his whole body, from his tail to his poll (the top of his head). His outside hindleg steps into the same track as his outside foreleg, while his inside hindleg steps well underneath his body. He is well balanced, his rhythm and tempo stay the same and his body has a rounded outline. He looks in the direction he's going and doesn't bend his neck towards the outside.

*This horse is bending correctly. His whole body is bending along the curve of the circle.*

*This horse is bending incorrectly. His shoulders are "falling-out" from the curve of the circle.*

## AIDS FOR BENDING

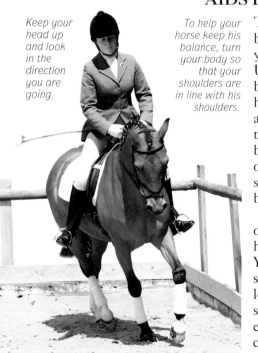

*Keep your head up and look in the direction you are going.*

*To help your horse keep his balance, turn your body so that your shoulders are in line with his shoulders.*

To encourage your horse to bend his whole body, use your inside leg on the girth. Use your outside leg behind the girth to control his hindquarters. Squeeze and release the inside rein to make sure your horse bends his neck. Use your outside hand to control his speed and stop his neck bending too much.

Your horse may be stiff on one side and find it harder to bend that way. You will need to work this stiff side a little harder to loosen it. Start your training sessions with circles on his easier side before you change to his stiffer side.

### Bending terms

*A change of direction is called a change of rein.*

*A circle or bend to the right (in a clockwise direction) is called a circle or bend on the right rein.*

*A circle or bend to the left (in a counter-clockwise direction) is called a circle or bend on the left rein.*

# RIDING CIRCLES IN THE ARENA

The picture below shows how a small dressage arena is laid out. Letters are placed at specific points around the outside. Because they are in the centre, the letters D, G and X are not marked in the arena. When you ride a test, you will be asked to begin each circle at a particular letter. You may be asked to ride a 20m (66ft) circle, a 15m (49ft) circle, or a 10m (33ft) circle, which is the most advanced.

Your horse will have to bend more when you ride smaller circles.

Look at the four points of the circle and ride smoothly between them.

Point one

Point two

10m (33ft) circle at M

15m (49ft) circle at C

20m (66ft) circle at A

Point three

Point four

This smaller arena is 20m (66ft) x 40m (131ft). A standard arena is 20m (66ft) x 60m (197ft).

## Other dressage shapes

Shallow loops involve a slight bend.  Figures-of-eight change your direction.  Serpentines are a series of loops.

# TURNS IN THE ARENA

In dressage, a bend from one straight line to another is called a turn. You will need to plan ahead in order to ride accurately. The most difficult turn is onto the centerline. Practice riding it from both directions.

It takes practice to turn smoothly onto the centerline.

## Centerline turns

● Look down the centreline before you start to turn onto it.

● Ride the turn with an even bend, then straighten up by using equal rein and leg contact on your horse's sides.

● Look ahead and sit in the center of the saddle.

● If your horse drifts left, use your left leg to push him back to the center.

239

# COLLECTING AND EXTENDING

Dressage horses can take longer or shorter steps in each gait, while keeping the same rhythm and tempo. This is called extending and collecting. You can start to collect and extend when, as a result of transition and circle work, your horse has become supple, balanced and responsive. Walk is the hardest pace to collect or extend, so begin training in trot and canter.

## COLLECTED GAITS

In collected gaits, the horse takes shorter, higher steps. He covers less ground with each step, so that in trot and canter, the moment of suspension is more pronounced. The movement of the gait has an upward, rather than a forward, feel. The rider stays in sitting trot.

*This horse is in a good collected trot. The rider is well positioned and is sitting lightly in the saddle.*

*The horse's head is almost vertical.*

*His neck is raised and arched.*

*Most of the horse's weight is on his hindquarters, so that his forelegs are "light."*

*His hocks are well engaged and his outline is rounded.*

*He is bending his legs well to make his steps higher.*

## WORKING TOWARDS COLLECTION

Your horse will be expected to show the first stages of collection in lower level dressage tests. At each test above First Level, a greater degree of collection will be required.

It's difficult for your horse to collect his gaits. Ask him to shorten his steps for a few strides at first, then push him into his working gait.

### The aids for collection
- Close your legs around your horse's sides so that he moves forward with impulsion.
- At the same time, close your fingers on the reins to contain your horse's forward movement.
- Listen to your horse's rhythm and tempo. They should stay the same.

*Small circles are good training for collection.*

# EXTENDED GAITS

In extended walk, trot and canter the horse takes long strides. In extended walk and trot, his hind feet over-track. In order to extend, the horse has to stretch out his body, which gives him a longer outline, or frame. His tempo and rhythm should stay the same.

*This horse is in a good extended trot. He is moving with impulsion and his frame is long and rounded.*

*His hindquarters are well engaged and he is light on his feet.*

## LEARNING TO EXTEND

Try extending in trot first. Use posting trot at first, as this will encourage your horse to take longer steps. Collect your horse's trot on the short side of the arena then use the extending aids (see below) as you go up the long side. Only ask for four or five lengthened strides at first, so he doesn't lose his balance, or start to take faster, shorter steps.

*This horse is not extending well. His outline is "hollow." His hindquarters are not well engaged.*

### The aids to extend

● Use your legs to make your horse move with more impulsion.
● Let your hands follow the movement of his head and neck, so that he can lengthen his frame.
● Don't let the reins go loose, or he'll go faster.

● Make sure his rhythm and tempo stay the same in the extended gait.
● Only ask for a few extended steps at first.
● Work toward medium trot (see page 233) before you ask your horse to fully extend his trot.

## COUNTING STRIDES

You can check whether your horse is extending and collecting by counting his strides. Count the number of strides he takes between two markers in working trot and canter. Ride between the markers again, asking your horse for collection or extension. Count his strides in each gait.

*Horses should take more strides when they collect and fewer strides when they extend.*

*Your horse's rhythm and tempo should stay the same.*

241

# LATERAL WORK

In lateral work, a dressage horse moves his body sideways, so that his hindfeet do not follow in the tracks of his forefeet. There are several different lateral movements, some of which are included in dressage tests. Others are not included in tests, but are useful training exercises for you and your horse.

## TURN ON THE FOREHAND

To do a turn on the forehand, a horse moves his hindlegs around to the side, while his forelegs stay in the same place. He should keep the same sequence of footfalls as in walk (see page 232), so that his forelegs mark time on the spot. His hindlegs should cross over each other as he moves them. Turn on the forehand is not asked for in tests, but it's a good introduction to lateral work.

*Start with a quarter (90°) turn. Build up to a half (180°) turn, as shown here.*

### Aids for turn on the forehand
* Turn into the middle of the arena and establish a good halt.
* Use your inside leg firmly at the girth to ask your horse to move his hindquarters to the side.
* Keep your outside leg lightly behind the girth.
* Use your inside rein to encourage your horse to look towards the inside.
* Use your outside rein at the same time as your inside leg, to stop your horse from moving forward.

*Outside leg*

*Inside leg*

*Your horse should move away from your inside leg into the contact of your outside rein.*

## POSSIBLE PROBLEMS

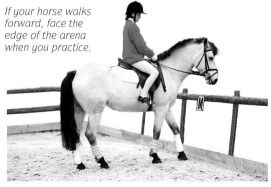

*If your horse walks forward, face the edge of the arena when you practice.*

If your horse resists your aids, he may need more practice at circles and turns, or your aids may be unclear. If he starts to step back, use firmer leg aids, and lighten your hand aids.

If he walks forward, you may be asking for too many steps too early, or your aids may be incorrect. If he bends his neck too much, lighten the inside rein and use the outside rein to control the amount of bend.

# TURN ON THE HAUNCHES

To do a turn on the haunches, a horse moves his forelegs in a half circle around his hindlegs. He begins from a collected walk and puts his weight on his hindquarters to move his forelegs. Turn on the haunches is harder for a horse than turn on the forehand.

Give your horse a half-halt before you give him the aids for turn on the haunches. Ask for a quarter turn at first. It's better if your horse makes a small half circle with his hindlegs rather than stepping back, which is a serious fault.

*Turn on the haunches are included in Second Level tests and above.*

*Your horse's body should bend slightly in the direction he's going.*

*When you have completed the movement, always walk your horse forwards.*

## Aids for turn on the haunches

* Half-halt to collect your horse's walk.
* Use your inside leg at the girth to maintain inside bend and impulsion.
* Use your outside leg behind the girth to control your horse's hindquarters.
* Use the inside rein to ask your horse to bend toward the inside.
* Use the outside rein to control his speed and stop him from moving forward.
* Use the outside rein close to your horse's neck and the inside rein away from it to encourage him to move his forehand around.

*Inside leg*

*Practice quarter turns first, then build up to half turns.*

## COMMON FAULTS

*If your horse's quarters swing out to the side, use your outside leg more firmly to control them.*

*Outside leg*

If your horse stops moving his inside hindleg or loses the correct sequence of footfalls, use your inside leg to increase his impulsion. Don't ask for too many steps at first, and walk him forward when you finish the movement.

If he steps back, you may be using too much outside rein. If he doesn't bend his body, ask for more bend in preparation, and use more inside leg and inside rein.

# LEARNING TO LEG-YIELD

In leg-yield, a horse moves forward and diagonally sideways at the same time. His body should be straight, apart from his head, which should bend slightly away from the direction he's travelling in.

The leg-yield is used in First Level tests and it's a useful exercise because it teaches your horse obedience and balance. It also helps you to co-ordinate your aids and use them sensitively.

### Aids for leg-yielding

- Use your inside leg firmly at the girth to move your horse sideways.
- Use your outside leg gently behind the girth to move him forward and stop his hindquarters from swinging out to the side.
- Use the inside rein gently to ask your horse for a slight inside bend at his poll.
- Use the outside rein firmly to steady your horse.
- Keep your weight in the center of the saddle. Try to stay in a balanced position.

Turn onto the 5m (16ft) line. Ride straight for a few steps, then use the aids described to leg-yield onto the outside track.

Leg-yield in walk at first, then trot.

Edge of arena

Try decreasing the size of a circle from 20m (66ft) to10m (33ft), then leg-yield back onto the 20m (66ft) circle.

## SOLVING LEG-YIELDING PROBLEMS

If your horse leads with his quarters, he probably lacks impulsion. Ensure you are riding straight before you ask for leg-yield, and ride him firmly forward.

If your pony trails his quarters and leads with his shoulders, use more outside rein. Use your inside leg further back to push his quarters over.

If he bends his neck too much, ease the contact with the inside rein. Ride him forward with plenty of impulsion to keep him straight in the leg-yield.

# WHAT IS SHOULDER-IN?

When riding shoulder-in, a horse moves forward, with his body bent away from the direction he's travelling in. You'll be asked to ride shoulder-in in Second Level dressage tests and above. Shoulder-in will encourage your horse to engage his inside hindleg, making it easier for him to learn collection (see page 240).

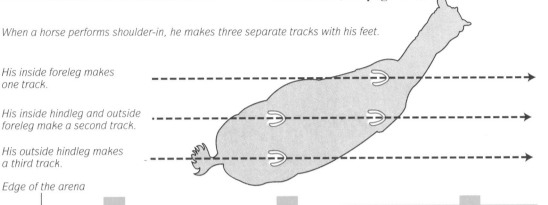

*When a horse performs shoulder-in, he makes three separate tracks with his feet.*

*His inside foreleg makes one track.*

*His inside hindleg and outside foreleg make a second track.*

*His outside hindleg makes a third track.*

*Edge of the arena*

*For true shoulder-in, your horse should be angled 30° from the track. Concentrate on your leg aids and your outside rein.*

*Edge of the arena*

*30°*

## Riding shoulder-in

Ride a 10m (33ft) circle at the letter M, in walk. Then ride on as if you were going to begin another circle. As you leave the outside track, give the aids for shoulder-in. Riding a circle before you ask for shoulder-in will ensure your horse has the correct body position. At first, keep your horse's angle from the track very slight.

## Aids for shoulder-in

- Use your inside leg at the girth to ask your horse to turn his body toward the inside.
- Use your outside leg behind the girth to prevent his quarters from swinging outwards.
- Use the inside rein very gently to reinforce the amount of bend.
- Use the outside rein to control the amount of bend and the speed.

## Common problems with shoulder-in

- If your horse lacks impulsion, use your inside leg more firmly and check that he has not bent inward too much.
- If your horse varies the amount he bends, check you have the right balance between your inside leg and outside rein.
- If he is bending his neck too much, use more outside rein and less inside rein.
- If his quarters fall out, use your outside leg more firmly to control them.

# EXERCISES IN CANTER

In lower level dressage, your horse should canter with his inside foreleg leading. This is known as "true canter" or being "on the correct leg." If you change the rein (see page 238), you must ask your horse to change his leading leg, so that he stays in true canter. Your horse's true canter should be well balanced on both reins.

## WALK TO CANTER, CANTER TO WALK

*This horse and rider are practising walk to canter and canter to walk transitions.*

*Transitions are good preparation for simple changes of leg (see below).*

For walk to canter, make sure your horse has plenty of impulsion. Ride a 10m (33ft) circle as preparation. This will help your horse to engage his inside hindleg and help you to place your aids correctly. Use clear, firm canter aids when you are ready for the transition.

For canter to walk, ride a couple of steps of trot before you walk. This is called a progressive transition. Collect the canter first and keep your lower legs on your horse's sides to maintain the collection and impulsion. Use light hand aids when you ask for the transition.

## SIMPLE CHANGE OF LEAD

*Change of lead*

*Try simple changes of lead across the diagonal, or on the E to B line.*

*Change of lead*

A "simple change of lead" is when a horse changes his leading leg in canter by trotting (or when more advanced, walking) for a few steps, then cantering again with his other leg leading. To ride a simple change of lead, use the canter aids (see page 236) to canter. To change your horse's lead, ask him to trot for three or four strides. Then use the canter aids again, but with your other leg behind the girth.

### Possible problems

● If your horse resists your aids, he may not be ready for simple changes. Practice general transition work.
● If your horse pulls on the bit or trots faster, try simple changes on the E to B line so he has less room to speed up.
● If your horse canters with one leg leading in front and the opposite behind he is "disunited." Go back to walk or trot.

# BEGINNING COUNTER CANTER

Counter canter is the opposite of true canter. The horse uses his outside leg to lead, with his body slightly bent towards the leading leg. He needs to be obedient, so he resists his natural impulse to lead with the inside leg. Counter canter will improve a horse's suppleness and balance, because he'll have to use different muscle combinations. Try the exercises below to introduce him to this difficult movement.

*Counter canter*

*Counter canter*

Begin by cantering with the inside leg leading. As you reach the long side of the arena, ride a shallow loop. When your horse turns back into the outside track he will be counter cantering for a few strides.

As his balance improves, canter a 15m (49ft) half circle at the end of the arena. Turn back onto the track, so that your horse is in counter canter. Maintain counter canter to the quarter marker.

*This dressage rider is performing a balanced, steady counter canter.*

### Keeping balanced
If your horse breaks into a trot or changes his leading leg, he may have lost his balance. Here's how to prevent this.
- Introduce your horse to counter canter gradually.
- Ride shallow loops smoothly.
- Try not to move suddenly in the saddle.
- As you turn back towards the outside track, keep your aids the same.

# SADDLERY AND DRESS

When you enter a dressage test, read the rule book carefully to find out what you and your horse should wear. On the day, groom your horse thoroughly, and check that your clothes are clean and tidy. Knowing that you both look your best will boost your confidence when you enter the arena.

## WHAT TO WEAR FOR DRESSAGE TESTS

*This saddlery and dress should be suitable for most Pony Club and Lower Level tests, but always double-check in the relevant rule book.*

Plain, leather snaffle bridle

Cavesson, flash or drop noseband. Figure-8 nosebands are only permitted in eventing (page 251)

English or dressage saddle

White, cream, or black saddle pad

Girth to match horse's color

Helmet that meets current safety standards

Hair net if your hair is long

White shirt and plain stock (see below)

Hunt coat or black dressage jacket

Gloves

Dressage whip (not compulsory)

White, cream or beige breeches or jodhpurs

Black or brown riding or jodhpur boots

## HOW TO TIE A STOCK

This bit of the stock goes at the front of your neck

Pull the loose ends into a knot.

Stock pin

Put the middle of the stock on the front of your neck. Wrap the ends around your neck. If there is a loop on the stock, feed one end through it at the back.

Pass the right end over and under the left. Pull tight. Form a loop with the left end as shown. Pass the right end over and through the loop. Pull into a knot.

Arrange one end of the stock neatly over the other, so the knot is hidden. Secure the ends together with a plain stock pin, fastened horizontally.

# BRAIDING YOUR HORSE'S MANE

Braiding your horse's mane for a dressage test makes him look smart. It also helps the judge to see the shape of his neck. Sew the braids and use white plastic tape, as shown below. You will also need some small rubber bands, a needle and thread, and a mane comb. You needn't braid your horse's tail, just make sure it's clean.

*Divide the mane into one-inch wide sections.*

*The braids should be even and smooth.*

*Make sure the tape is in the same position on each braid.*

Split the mane into sections three-quarters of the width of your comb. Comb each section and fasten with a rubber band.

Take the rubber band off the first section. Split into three parts. Braid them together. Sew the end of the braid to secure it.

Fold the braid under twice. Sew it into place. Wrap white plastic tape around the end of the braid. Make one braid from the forelock.

# ADVANCED DRESSAGE

In upper-level dressage, riders use dressage saddles and double bridles. Dressage saddles have long, straight saddle flaps. The girth tabs are also long, while the girth is short, so that the buckles do not sit under the saddle flaps. This helps the rider to keep his or her legs close to the horse's sides.

Double bridles have two bits, and two sets of reins. They give the rider more control over the horse's action.

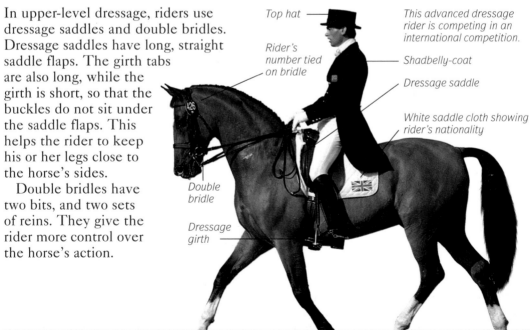

*Top hat*

*Rider's number tied on bridle*

*Double bridle*

*Dressage girth*

*This advanced dressage rider is competing in an international competition.*

*Shadbelly-coat*

*Dressage saddle*

*White saddle cloth showing rider's nationality*

# DRESSAGE COMPETITIONS

As well as being exciting and challenging, dressage competitions are a good way of seeing how your training is progressing. In a competition, you will have to perform a four to five minute dressage test, consisting of various different movements. The best way to find out about competitions in your area is from your local riding school or Pony Club branch.

## WHICH TEST TO ENTER

| TEST | | | DIRECTIVE IDEAS | POINTS | COEFFICIENT | TOTAL | REMARKS |
|---|---|---|---|---|---|---|---|
| 1. | A | Enter working trot rising. | Straightness on center line. | | | | |
| | X | Develop medium walk continue to C. | Smoothnes of transition. Steadiness of tempo in trot. Quality of walk with relaxation. | | | | |
| 2. | C | Turn right in medium walk. | Balance of turn. | | | | |
| | H-X-K | Walk. Develop free walk. | Quality of walk with relaxation. | | | | |
| | K | Develop medium walk. | Straightness of diagonal line. Smoothness of transitions. | | | | |
| 3. | A | Working trot rising Continue down long side to C. | Quality and steadiness of tempo in trot, straightness on long side. | | | | |
| 4. | C | Circle left 20m. | Steadiness of tempo in trot. Quality of trot. Roundness of circle. | | | | |
| 5. | H-X-F | Change rein, working trot rising. | Steadiness of tempo in trot. Quality of trot. Straightness of diagonal line. | | | | |
| 6. | A | Circle right 20m. | Steadiness of tempo in trot. Quality of trot. Roundness of circle. | | | | |
| 7. | A-K-E | Working trot rising. | Steadiness of tempo in trot. | | | | |
| | E | Turn right. | Quality of trot. Quality and smoothness of turn. | | | | |
| 8. | B | Turn right, continue to A. | Balance of turn. Steadiness of tempo in trot. Quality of trot. | | | | |
| 9. | A | Down center line. | Quality and smoothness of turn. | | | | |
| | X | Halt through medium walk. Salute. | Straightness on center line. Smoothness of transition. Immobility of halt. | | | | |

Leave arena in free walk on long rein. Exit at A.

Dressage tests are divided into seven levels: Introductory, Training, First, Second, Third, Fourth, and FEI or International Level dressage. There will be several different tests to choose from in your level. Copies of the tests are available through your pony club chapter or directly through the United States Dressage Federation. Send off to the show chairperson for the class schedule and read it carefully before you decide which to enter. Choose a test that has dressage movements you know you and your horse can do well.

### Test sheets
Test sheets tell you:
● The order in which you should ride the movements.
● The marker at which you should start each movement.
● What each movement should be.
● The gait in which you should perform each movement.
● The maximum number of points the judge can give you for each movement.

## LEARNING THE TEST

Once you've decided on a test, try to learn it by heart. Some competitions let you have a "reader" who calls out what comes next, but it's better to rely on memory. To help you, draw the test out on paper. Go through the movements in your head too. Imagine how you could avoid possible problems. Practice the movements on your horse, but not always in the same order. If he learns the test, he may try to start the next movement before you reach the correct marker.

*Try marking out a mini arena on the ground so you can learn the test by walking it.*

## ARRIVING AT THE SHOWGROUNDS

Make sure you arrive at the showgrounds in plenty of time, as there is a lot to do before you compete. Settle your horse out of the wind, in the shade if it is hot. Leave someone experienced in charge, while you go and check in with the secretary. Find out which arena you will be competing in and confirm your number and start time. Also find out where you can warm up (see page 252).

*It's a good idea to watch some of the other competitors in your class, as you may pick up some useful tips.*

## EVENTING COMPETITIONS

*Eventing competitions give you a chance to practise your jumping skills.*

You could also enter an eventing competition, which includes cross-country and show jumping as well as dressage. Eventing requires all-around skills and stamina from riders and their horses. Your dressage test is marked normally (see page 253), then converted into penalty points (so the lower your score the better). Your show jumping and cross-country scores are added to your dressage score. The rider with the lowest overall score wins.

# RIDING A TEST

When you ride a test, your performance will be watched closely by the judge. He or she will usually sit behind the C marker. The arena will be marked out by low white boards, and it may have tubs of flowers around the outside. Make sure your horse is familiar with these things before you take a test so that he doesn't "spook."

## WARMING UP

Before the test begins, you must warm up or school your horse. This makes sure that his muscles are supple and that he is concentrating properly. The amount of schooling he will need depends on his temperament. An easygoing, placid horse will need about twenty minutes, while a lively, excitable horse may need much more. Bear in mind the weather too. You'll have to warm him up for longer on a cold, windy day. Begin your warm-up session by walking him on a long rein before you move on to any trotting or cantering work.

Leg wraps can be worn during warm-up, but not for the test.

### Rules for the warm-up ring

* Let other people know you're about to enter the warm-up area by calling out "I'm coming in."
* Walk your horse on the inside track. The outside track is for faster paces.
* Don't halt your horse on the outside track.
* Pass other riders left shoulder to left shoulder.
* Give way to riders doing lateral work.
* If you need to adjust your tack, go outside the warm-up area.

## FINAL PREPARATIONS

Aim to finish your warm-up about ten minutes before your test starts. This will give you time to take off any leg wraps or protective boots your horse has been wearing and check his girth. Check your appearance too, then relax for a few moments and collect your thoughts.

# RIDING THE TEST

When the rider before you finishes his or her test, start to ride around the outside of the competition arena. When the judge is ready for you to start, he or she will ring a bell or sound a whistle. Tests start at the A marker and finish with a salute to the judge. When you've finished the test, walk your horse back to the A marker, where you should leave the arena.

## Tips for the test

* Concentrate hard on what you are doing.
* If a movement goes badly, don't panic, just move calmly onto the next one.
* Don't rush the test.
* Enjoy the movements you do well.
* Make a fuss of your horse after the test.

*This rider is saluting correctly. Ideally, her horse should be in a square halt (see page 237).*

## Saluting

* Halt at the correct marker.
* Look towards the judge.
* Put your reins and whip (if you have one) in one hand (usually the left).
* Drop your other hand down with the back of your hand facing inwards.
* Nod your head down and up again.
* Count to three before you move off.

# HOW TESTS ARE SCORED

The judge gives each movement a mark from 0 (movement not carried out) to 10 (excellent). The rider with the highest number of marks wins the competition (unless it is an event - see page 251). At the end of the competition, you will be given a scoresheet which shows your marks and the judge's comments. The judge will also give you a set of collective marks. These refer to your horse's way of going and your riding skills throughout the test.

*In advanced competitions there are normally several judges. They sit inside a judging box.*

# ADVANCED DRESSAGE

You can learn a lot from advanced riders, whether you go to see them at a show, or watch them on the television. Advanced dressage horses have a high degree of collection (see page 240), enabling them to perform the most difficult dressage movements, some of which are described below.

## PIAFFE

Piaffe is an extremely advanced dressage movement. The horse trots in place with light, springy steps. His hindlegs should be well underneath his body, taking most of his weight.

The horse should keep his legs moving in a regular trotting rhythm, with a clear moment of suspension between each step.

*The Piaffe is considered the highest level of obedience and collection, because the horse must trot in place.*

*The toe of the foreleg should be above the fetlock joint of the other foreleg.*

## PASSAGE

Passage is a very dramatic movement to watch. The horse springs forward in a slow, dancing trot. The moment of suspension between each stride is long and the

horse's steps are high. Passage should be a smooth movement showing the horse's contained energy. Any jerkiness is considered a serious fault.

*Horses who can perform passage will have reached the highest level of obedience and collection.*

# FLYING CHANGES

A flying change involves the horse changing his leading leg in canter, during the moment of suspension (see page 233), rather than through walk or trot. Flying changes are a real challenge to both the horse and the rider because they require split second timing. The rider must give clear, firm aids at exactly the right moment, while the horse must understand instantly what he is being asked to do.

*This horse and rider are beginning to work on flying changes. They need to keep the same rhythm and speed.*

# CANTER PIROUETTE

In canter pirouette, the horse canters around his hindlegs in a half or full circle, without moving forward. The horse should take high, collected steps, and his hindquarters should be visibly lower than his haunches. Canter pirouettes are extremely hard work for a horse, so he needs to have well developed muscles and excellent balance. The horse should keep the correct sequence of footfalls and a steady rhythm as he carries out the canter pirouette.

*This horse and rider are performing a canter pirouette in the World Equestrian Games.*

*A full canter pirouette should be completed in five to seven steps.*

# INDEX

With thanks to riders Holly Acuta, Chloe Albert, Nayla Ammar, Victoria Barnes, Flossy Castle, Rose Castle, Sally Crisp, Clare Davies, Aimee Felus, Claire Foreman, Ciara Gourley, Linda Green, Heidi Jane Hagger, Kylie Holland, Ria Holland, Tarn Holland, Sophie Hyde, Nicola Leese, Robert Leese, Margaret Mackie, Keely Martin, Kerry Mason, Tania Mizzi, Charlotte O'Neill, Hannah O'Neill, Joe Parker, Hannah Paul, Charlotte Read, Philippa Reed, Stephanie Sarno, Glenn Whitbread, Katherine Woolmer, and to their ponies, Ben, Bobby, Cnapaton Rosewood, Comberton Classic, Dorian, Fionnula, Ginger, Harry, Harry Houdini, Inca, Jigtime, Kes, Lady, MacTarn Flite of Fancy, Moonlight Trickster, Pepe, Polly, Princess Leya, Solly, Speedy, Tiggy, Top Gun, Whinberry Quality Way and Yogi. Thanks also to Robin Dumas, Didi and Michael Kingscote, all the staff and ponies at Trent Park Equestrian Centre, Coleman Croft Master Saddlers and the Horse Unit at Writtle Agricultural College.